"A fast-paced, politically savvy potboiler, Deadly Cold is a quick and engaging read."

"Any action fan will find Deadly Cold a good way to spend a couple of hours. It's a quick, enjoyable, refreshing romp through a well-realized natural and political apocalypse. Similarities to both Tom Clancy and Clive Cussler are strong enough that Deadly Cold is a good read-alike for both authors."

– Foreword Clarion Review

"Memorable characters and an intriguing storyline make this a page-turner that will appeal to a wide range of readers. Apocalyptic fiction, suspense/thriller, and mystery fans alike should find this a highly entertaining read."

– BlueInk Review

"A lot happens in just 400 pages . . . A fascinating, epic tale in compact form."

– Kirkus Reviews

DEADLY COLD

Jed O'Dea

authorHOUSE®

AuthorHouse™
1663 Liberty Drive
Bloomington, IN 47403
www.authorhouse.com
Phone: 1-800-839-8640

Published by AuthorHouse   03/09/2015

ISBN: 978-1-4969-3731-5 (sc)
ISBN: 978-1-4969-3730-8 (e)

Print information available on the last page.

This book is printed on acid-free paper.

Dedicated to the life of
Carol Ann Wetterling

PRELUDE

WANAKA, NEW ZEALAND - NOVEMBER 27TH: She could smell the sour body odor of the intruder. She guessed that the total absence of light forced her other senses to sharpen. Maya Cherokee was torn between the paralysis she felt in this temporary blind condition and the advantage she would have in the dark over what might be a potential killer. The wine cellar was at least familiar territory to her. The intruder must have intentionally flipped the circuit breaker to the wine cellar, so he could operate in this pitch blackness. Maya thought to herself, "Why would the intruder do that unless he had night vision goggles or some other tactical advantage?"

She knew that she was close to an emergency pull cord tied to a battery which would sound an alarm. She reached out into the darkness in an attempt to locate the cord.

Something passed over the top of her bare feet. Chills ran up her spine and made her shudder involuntarily. Maya reached out and ran her hand along the dry wall to get her physical bearing; nothing helped her orient herself. "Where is the damn pull cord?" she thought to herself, frustrated and anxious.

The sound of a single footfall reminded her of the danger she was in. The slow transfer of weight from one foot to the other was accompanied with sounds of muscles tightening and tendons stretching inside clothing. A red dot moved around the cellar looking for a target. As his odor intensified, she could triangulate and determine his relative location. She wondered if her perfume helped him identify her location.

Maya continued her search for the elusive emergency pull cord only to find her hand wrapped around a smooth, leathery, dry, cold and silky one-inch diameter living thing -- a snake. Though she knew that if she screamed it would give her position away, she couldn't help herself. With her eyes shut tight, she screamed.

When she opened her eyes she was staring at a pair of wide aqua-colored eyes with long, thick eyelashes. Maya Li Cherokee had awakened from her nightmare, peering into her five year old daughter's piercing eyes. Star Cherokee asked, "Mommy, who is the smartest person in the world?"

Maya, a 5-foot, 9-inch tall athletic blue-eyed beauty, was still trembling from her nightmare but managed to regain her composure in the presence of happy-faced smiling Star who was stroking Maya's long shiny and satiny black hair.

Maya said a little breathlessly, "Well, the smartest person in the world may not be the most intelligent. I think it's your father. He was smart enough to marry me."

Star maintained the perpetual smile on her face that was surrounded by long curly auburn hair and said, "Daddy says it's you. Because when I asked him how the sun works, he told me to ask the smartest person in the world, Mommy!"

Maya, with a PhD in Physics from the University of Chicago, had specialized in particle physics. She met Tucker at the Department of Energy's Fermi Labs outside of Chicago where basic science research was conducted. She was better qualified to answer Star's questions than daddy Tucker, whose science-based knowledge was broad, but not as deep as Maya's in solar science.

"Well, sweetheart, the sun burns hydrogen in a process called fusion. The sun is really hot; in fact, the sun is 93 million miles away but you still can't look straight at it without damaging your eyes, and if you stay outside too long without skin protection, it can burn you. Isn't that amazing?" answered Maya.

"Will it always stay the same?" asked a continuously inquisitive Star.

"It's been working pretty well for the past 4.5 billion years. It doesn't always stay the same; it changes a little bit. It gets spots on it and sometimes flares up."

"What happens when it changes?"

"Well, sometimes it makes the earth a little bit hotter or sometimes it makes the earth a little bit colder."

Out of the blue, "Mommy, what passed over your bare feet?"

"What? How could you........."

Before a flabbergasted Maya could respond to the shocking question, a siren blasted in the compound's study -- an intrusion detector that was wired to a warning alarm system activated. Maya grabbed Star and rolled to the area rug in the center of the room that covered an escape hatch. She broke the grasp of the rug's Velcro strips, opened the hatch and placed Star on the slide which guided her down to a secure basement play room where her best friend and protector, Ram, a 95 pound well-trained German Shepherd, resided. Star was calm through it all, because they had practiced this emergency many times.

In the side of the hatch opening was a pocket which contained a 9mm Beretta with 13 rounds in the magazine.

As the doors of the study flew open and two armed men wearing ski masks raised their automatic weapons towards her, Maya got off four accurate shots to the chests of the attackers. The two attackers went down, but continued their rapid fire; they must have been wearing bullet-proof vests. One of the wounded intruders spraying the room with his automatic fire put one round into Maya's chest.

The shot stung her, but it wasn't as painful as she would have expected. She fell backwards onto the floor. She laid there for a couple of seconds before she rolled onto her left side. There was a lot of blood on the floor and on her blouse. "Wait a minute," thought Maya; "the blood was the wrong color, too light; something was not right."

It was paint; the attackers had used automatic paint guns. The two wounded men pulled off their ski masks and said in unison, "Job well done, Maya! You shot both of us squarely in the chest, but you need to learn to take head shots."

A very angry Maya said, "You sons of bitches. You freaking assholes. Enough is enough. I'm trained already. Don't ever do this again. You *White Knight* guys are overtraining me. I know that it's your job to train Tucker and me to protect ourselves from would-be assassins and kidnappers, but after almost six years in this remote secure compound of a safe house, after six years of close-quarters combat and weapons training, after six years of constant state-of-the-art upgrades in electronic security, I don't believe we need these 'exercises' anymore!

"And you, Tucker; I'm amazed and shocked that you would go along with this test. Why would you do this to me? We've had this discussion. And when did you put blanks in the Beretta? Oh, and by the way, your daughter did it again and this time I wasn't even awake."

Tucker didn't smile. He didn't react to Maya's outburst and castigation. His eyes didn't even blink.

Maya said, "Oh no. What don't I know?"

Tucker calmly and compassionately said, "We have a new enemy." After a few seconds of silence he asked, "You weren't even awake?"

CHAPTER 1

DUST IN THE WIND
(DAY ZERO)

YOGYAKARTA, INDONESIA – APRIL 19th, SIX MONTHS EARLIER: Thousands of White-Handed Gibbons began noisily squawking, acting unusually anxious, as if forecasting impending doom. They ascended and descended trees rapidly and repeatedly in the dense tropical forest, frequently pulling aggressively on each other's thick reddish-brown fur. Their hairless black faces showed stress; the sounds they made resembled crying children. Island Thrushes took flight in panic. Other species joined in the cacophony of frightening noises. It was like the entire animal kingdom was screaming for mercy.

Another small tremor ensued. The sounds of the rainforest immediately stopped; the deafening silence took on an eerie edge.

In nearby Yogyakarta, Java chickens were immobile, apparently fearful of whatever might come next. The oppressive heat and humidity exacerbated the feeling of dread, but Melatie Lestari shook it off and felt compelled to quiet her French Mastiff, Louie, before the humorless dog-hating police officer across the street applied his own method for quieting him. Louie often growled at neighbors and delivery people, and occasionally barked -- but never howled like this, along with the other neighborhood dogs. Melatie had lived in her hometown of Yogyakarta all her life, in a rare part of town which accepted dogs as pets, but she had never experienced the chilling moans and howls which she was hearing today. It was making her feel melancholy, but she did not know exactly why.

Melatie was a pretty 35-year-old nurse at the Yogyakarta Hospital and sometimes worked multiple shifts. The doctors at the hospital loved working in Melatie's space. They occasionally -- and accidentally, of course -- rubbed up against her voluptuous figure. At least one doctor a year proposed to her, but until recently, none of them had flipped her switch. Just now, though, she was seriously considering a proposal from a very gentle and kind surgeon. She just mused, though, that he could be more physically attractive. A smile crossed her face when it occurred to her that maybe she should try him out by letting him have his way with her; maybe his skills as a lover could generate an excitement that she had not felt before. Maybe his approach to her tentative "come hither" could show her how special they could be together.

She had just finished a ten-hour shift; she was exhausted but was thinking about "her" surgeon. Melatie felt a little dizzy and disoriented but attributed her dizziness to fatigue. Then, her dizziness was accompanied by a framed family picture falling off the living room wall.

It was another tremor, a minor earthquake.

She instinctively looked through the kitchen window in the direction of Mount Merapi. "Surely not," she thought to herself. Mount Merapi is one of many known active volcanoes in Indonesia, a nation with more active volcanos than any other country. Mount Merapi had not erupted since the year 1548!

She felt it before she heard it.

The blast was like nothing ever experienced by mankind, **the most powerful volcanic eruption in 300,000 years**. When the pressure of many decades of accumulating gas finally overcame the magma, the Mount Merapi eruption was twenty-five times more powerful than the Mount Pinatubo eruption in the Philippines which spewed many millions of tons of sulfur dioxide, and a cubic mile of ash and debris, into the atmosphere.

This eruption caused the average temperature world-wide to drop a whole degree Fahrenheit!

The Mount Merapi volcanic eruption was accompanied with a Richter 9.2 earthquake. Melatie was instantly driven against the edge of the kitchen counter, knocking the wind out of her and depositing her onto the floor. Louie was by her side and nuzzled against her, before the ceiling collapsed. The pain Melatie experienced was greater than anything she had ever previously experienced. She was mashed by a ceiling beam, blinded by flying glass, painfully deafened by the blast, and nauseated by the disgusting smell of sulfur, yet she thought about getting out from under the weight of the building debris so that she could get to the hospital and help others. But she couldn't move. Louie was silent -- this was not a good thing.

The propagated noise was painful and indescribable; the blast was rumored to have been heard 3,000 miles away in Perth, Australia. Mercifully, death was quick for Melatie Lestari -- and all the residents of Yogyakarta. In a few short minutes, the city was covered with a rain of 900 degree Fahrenheit smoldering ash to a depth of seven feet with a pressure wave that traveled at 675 miles per hour. There were no survivors, people or animals, within a radius of 23 miles from Mount Merapi. The volcanic vents, in concert with the earthquake, created tsunamis -- one was over 140 feet high -- destroying homes and drowning tens of thousands of people on the islands of Java and Sumatra.

The volcanic eruption column punched through the troposphere into the stratosphere to a height of 55 km -- 34 miles. The ash and debris in the atmosphere partially blocked the sun's ability to heat the earth. Within 35 hours, visibility was impaired between latitudes from as far north as Chicago, Illinois and as far south as Buenos Aries, Argentina -- and the planet's surface temperature began to drop. By the third day after the eruption, air quality was unhealthy and unmanageable, affecting every nation on earth. Commercial air transportation was prohibited by responsible governments when the amount of volcanic ash and suspended dust particles exceeded the safe upper limit for flying. Satellite communications became erratic and unreliable. The lava flow continued for weeks, completely and permanently changing the geography of the region. For hundreds of miles, fires were ignited by far-flung molten debris. Toxic gas and molten lava left communities outside the death radius at risk of lung damage and other health problems. Water supplies were contaminated and millions lost electric power. Ocean shipments were interrupted, leaving country after country wanting for food and fuel.

The Australian government was the first to reach the disaster areas with humanitarian aid and assistance, followed by the governments of the United States and Japan. Medical personnel from USARPAC's 18th Medical Command (Deployment Support) were deployed to the disaster scene. U.S. and Australian teams conducted joint assessments on the remaining critical infrastructure and drinking water systems. The Red Cross contributed tarpaulins, blankets, clothes, water containers and face masks. The People's Republic of China air-dropped emergency tools and evacuation equipment in difficult-to-access locations.

At the end of the first month after the eruption, the airborne ash and particulates reached equilibrium so that the concentration of ash in the air was the same everywhere -- whether in Finland, Burma, Egypt, or Cuba. What was particularly disturbing to volcanologists and environmentalists alike was the fact that the ash was not precipitating or falling to the ground at a rate anticipated or experienced after prior historical eruptions. This eruption was different; the force of energy released changed the post-volcanic paradigm. There was 25 times the ash and debris in the atmosphere than had ever been released in recorded history, and it appeared that the ash and debris would stay airborne much longer than from any of the thousands of volcanic eruptions recorded by mankind.

The average temperature around the world dropped by 9 degrees Fahrenheit within 45 days as a result of the Mt. Merapi eruption. Unfortunately, there were more natural disasters to come. Deadly cold weather would eventually envelop the world, smother optimism, and stimulate the survival instincts of the desperate. And worse, intentionally-created well-planned man-made deadly disasters, created to exacerbate and take advantage of the crisis were tragically forthcoming.

CHAPTER 2

PENTAGON
(ZERO + 61 DAYS)

ARLINGTON, VIRGINIA – JUNE 19TH, TWO MONTHS AFTER THE ERUPTION OF MOUNT MERAPI: It didn't feel like June; it felt more like April, with the high temperature for the cloudless but sunless day predicted to be around 59 degrees Fahrenheit with a slight seven mile per hour breeze from the west. Brigadier General Ray LaSalle was wearing a painter's mask over his nose and mouth to keep from breathing the gray airborne haze as he was walking back to the Pentagon from a rare out-of-the-office luncheon engagement. As he was double-timing it back, he couldn't help but notice that Arlington restaurants which were normally packed with anxious customers waiting impatiently for the next available table were, at best, 30 to 40 percent full. People were staying home, not wanting to get out into the depressing soup made of volcanic ash and dirt. Ray wished that he had worn different shoes, as it was impossible to keep a spit-shine while trudging through an eighth of an inch of ash everywhere he stepped. LaSalle felt his cell phone vibrate, then viewed the smart phone's window to see that it was his assistant, and asked "Yes, Lieutenant; what is it?"

The Lieutenant, his assistant, said, "W3 called; you've been summoned to stand before the Joint Chiefs of Staff." W3 was the nickname given to the Chairman of the Joint Chiefs of Staff's secretary, the "Wicked Witch of the West." Ray had been expecting the summons. Ray ran the Pentagon's contingency planning operations. His team of analysts was the best in the world at forecasting the consequences of any scenario or event. Their accuracy at predicting the impact or consequence of any given event was uncanny. LaSalle had developed some sort of an algorithm or something that Wall Street would kill for. Ray, a 26 year Air Force veteran, was obsessive-compulsive, and took his job seriously; too seriously. He was humorless and constantly anxious. He dressed meticulously, shaved twice a day, washed his hands every hour, and rarely ate food outside his sterile home. He had but one inconsistency in his otherwise obsessive compulsive habits: he was a dog-lover and loved to be with his best friends. General LaSalle instructed his assistant to collect the DVD which he had prepared for what he anticipated was the reason for his summons.

At 5'11" tall, 170 pounds, Caucasian, blue eyes and bald, the 50 year old General walked unnoticed in the

Pentagon, as just one of 23,000 other people in the largest office building in the world -- with its 17.5 miles of corridors. Though it would be easy to feel like just another ant on the ant hill, he always felt honored to be there. Adjacent to the Potomac River with a view of the Washington Monument, the Capitol, the Smithsonian Institute and the Jefferson Memorial, there was a sense of pride to be a part of the worlds' most powerful, yet philanthropic, nation. The building possessed an air of importance that could not be ignored.

As General LaSalle was making his way to the Chairman's office, he was recounting the fact that he had started analyzing possible geopolitical scenarios, performing threat assessments and considering military risks the day after Mount Merapi erupted. His team was further energized after other natural events occurred that contributed further to the drop in average world temperature. He was surprised that it had taken 33 days after the second volcanic eruption for the Joint Chiefs to call on him. He suspected that the White House and the Secretary of Defense (SecDef) must have prompted this threat assessment and analysis.

LaSalle had a Power Point Presentation prepared and thought, "They are not going to like what I have to say." But LaSalle's reputation protected him from **not** being taken seriously. Before entering the Chairman's office, he stopped at a rest room to brush ash off his uniform and use a paper towel to remove the dust from his shoes. He was reluctantly escorted by humorless and hateful-looking W3 into the private conference room of the Chairman of the Joint Chiefs of Staff. This was odd, but he asked no questions. There were much larger and better-equipped meeting rooms than the Chairman's private conference room, for a meeting with the Joint Chiefs.

Once inside, he understood. Not only was the full complement of the Joint Chiefs in attendance, but the SecDef, Jane Bolton, and President Winston Allen were present. This caught LaSalle by surprise, and he felt an anxiety attack coming on; he started to hyperventilate. A perceptive president calmed him down with a warm and embarrassing litany of compliments from the president's knowledge of LaSalle's past accuracy and successes.

Winston Allen was an iconoclastic man -- his appearance defied what popular opinion and pundits believed one must look like to be president. Winston Allen was short, overweight, bald, and with dark eyes -- and he always looked like he needed a shave. But when he spoke, you felt compelled to listen. He didn't mix words and he never said something he didn't mean. There was not an ounce of bullshit in his rhetoric.

President Allen said, "I have half an hour, General LaSalle, so let's get right to the point. What is your assessment of the consequences of the sudden and painful drop in world temperature on the United States, and on international stability?"

"Sir," began Ray LaSalle, "In anticipation of this question, I have prepared a presentation that I would like your permission to present." Allen merely shook his head affirmatively. LaSalle inserted the prepared DVD into the conference room computer wired to an overhead projector.

"Slide one -- This is the most recent photograph of earth from the Space Station. Sad, isn't it? The 'blue planet' is no longer 'blue' from space; earth is now a 'gray' planet as our atmosphere is drowning in volcanic ash and debris." Though everyone in the room had seen the photo before today, the photo was still shocking and depressing; it was like viewing a tragedy from the holocaust.

"Slide two -- The United States will be one of the **least** impacted nations in the world by the severe weather change. We are blessed, madam and sirs, with abundant energy sources which allow us to protect the majority of our population from the threats that accompany unusually cold weather. However, the minority of the

U.S. population who are at risk include the consistently poor, the weak, the elderly, and children of the poor. As you no doubt know, oil prices are at an all-time high of $233/barrel with some experts forecasting $400/barrel by the end of this year. This means, of course, that heating fuels including oil, propane, diesel fuel, kerosene, natural gas and carbon-based electricity become out-of-reach for many. When people can't keep their children or elderly parents from freezing to death, we should expect repercussions in the form of riots, looting, and class warfare. U.S. citizens will likely demand energy as a right, much like the citizens of Detroit demanded water as a right when they couldn't afford to pay for it." LaSalle paused for effect, and saw mostly deadpan faces. This audience was experienced in crisis management and took bad news with a grain of salt. He continued.

"Slide three -- The energy-poor and densely populated nations of the world will reach a potential state of anarchy long before the U.S. unless, of course, the governments of these nations are successfully proactive instead of just reactive. After the eruption of Mount Merapi, you can understand if some governments didn't react to or assess the potential consequences of events." President Allen looked a little uncomfortable after this statement, but General LaSalle continued. "After the announcement by

NASA and world science academies that the sun is going through a cooling cycle, it was prudent that governments would begin to assess the impact to their respective nations to a potential drop in world temperature. Finally, when on May 16th Mount Nyiragongo erupted in the Virunga Mountains of the Democratic Republic of the Congo, spewing additional volcanic ash and particulates into the atmosphere and exacerbating an already severe set of natural disasters, well, energy-poor countries undoubtedly had to do some survival planning.

"Slide four -- My team of brilliant and dedicated soldiers, sailors and airmen prepared a computer program based on a sophisticated algorithm. The output from the computer program is a matrix where energy-poor nations in the highest northern latitudes or lowest southern latitudes are compared against the countries with the greatest potential for military aggression." General LaSalle hesitated, cleared his throat and looked the president in the eye. "The matrix uncovered or highlighted a watch list of nations which are likely to become desperate for energy and who have military prowess. The watch list includes North Korea, Japan, South Africa, Great Britain, Israel, and Argentina."

"Stop right there," blurted President Allen, "Why do you believe that our friends in Japan and Great

Britain are in the same category as North Korea as it relates to potential for military aggression? That seems counter-intuitive."

"Ah," responded Ray LaSalle, "The key word here is 'potential.' Military aggression, sir, does not necessarily mean aggression against the United States. Desperate people do desperate things. I merely point out that Great Britain and Japan are going to, if they have not already, become desperate for energy. As an example, compared with energy-rich countries like Saudi Arabia, Great Britain has a powerful military. The potential exists for Great Britain to use that military to save its people from deadly cold weather."

The Chairman of the Joint Chiefs of Staff, Admiral Maxx Longstaff, spoke for the first time, "General LaSalle, I know that you know that Japan has little discernable military, in keeping with long-standing post-WWII treaties and agreements. Why is Japan on this list?"

"The Japanese have honored all treaties and agreements to the best of our knowledge, including the San Francisco Treaty and the Security Treaty. Honor is culturally important, but when their rice patties begin to freeze and their elderly people begin to die off because there is too little energy available to keep them from freezing to death, then the very resourceful third largest economy in the world will do something to protect its people. It is my estimate that it will take Japan about 10 minutes to go nuclear. After all, for some reason, the U.S. stores 300 kg of weapons grade plutonium in Japan. The nuclear power industry in Japan took a big hit with the Fukushima Daiichi disaster, but the expertise is there to manufacture nuclear weapons despite its long-standing aversion to them. They have weapons-grade materials as a result of their recently completed fuel reprocessing plant at Rokkasho-Mura. The prime minister of Japan has been openly supportive of increasing Japan's military independence due to the unreliability of the United States in honoring its commitments to other allied nations.

"Ah, sir," General LaSalle said to the president, "I'm speaking about prior administrations.

"Japan has a space program and the ability to launch nuclear weapons if they were to build them. Our analysis is that Japan is, in fact, a potential military threat to weaker energy-rich nations." Heads shook in disagreement and disbelief. Jane Bolton, the Secretary of Defense, was noticeably agitated with LaSalle's analysis.

"May I continue?" Heads nodded.

"Slide five -- This slide presents a list of energy rich nations with comparatively weak defense capabilities. The list includes Saudi Arabia, Kuwait, Qatar, United Arab Emirates, Venezuela, Nigeria, Angola, Algeria, Australia, Norway and Iraq. I left Canada off this list because of the small chance that an aggressive nation would attack our neighbor. That would be suicide. Militarily, I think that Australia can defend itself -- but maybe not against a nuclear-armed North Korea or Japan."

Secretary of Defense, Jane Bolton, asked, "Do you have probability estimates for each of the scenarios?"

"Yes, Madam Secretary. If you allow me one more slide, the probability analysis will have a better context." SecDef nodded as did the others in the room.

"Slide six -- This shows the reduction in food supply based on a two-year period of sustained cold weather. You see here that the breadbasket of the United States is predicted to have a 20% loss of agricultural productivity at the end of the first year and a 35% loss at the end of the second year. There is a similar, though somewhat larger, impact to our Canadian friends. The Ukraine is the hardest hit at 38% the first year. This is serious, as the Ukraine represents the largest source of sustenance to Russia. China is also going to experience a loss of food supply at a rate similar to the United States. Japan will lose 28% the first year and 41% by the second year. North Korea's pathetic food supply will be even further diminished.

"To answer your question, Secretary Bolton, we estimate that there is an 87.5% probability that in the short term (within two years) war will break out somewhere as a result of the continuation of this extremely cold weather."

The room was silent. The prediction was shocking; none there wanted to admit that LaSalle's conclusions could be true, and most of the powerful people in the room hesitated to accept the results of the LaSalle analysis.

"I have five minutes left before I am supposed to meet with my National Security Advisor," announced an irritated President Allen. "Do you have a slide that provides recommendations?"

"Yes, sir; let me jump to Slides 11 and 12. First, deploy the National Guard to protect our most important energy assets like the Strategic Petroleum Reserve, the Alaska Pipeline, Palo Verde Nuclear Plant, the Hoover Dam power plant, LNG plants, etc. If the situation reaches a state of anarchy, irrational rioters tend to take their anger out on symbols of the source of their anger.

"Second, help Charleston Energy Holdings -- CEH -- to increase the production rate of NEUREMs -- Neutrino Electricity Using Rare Earth Metals -- or what CEH renamed MEGs -- Magnetic Electric Generators -- to offset the demand for grid based electricity. At this time, only about 10% of the country has access to this electricity generation without fuel technology, also called Tucker's *Discovery*. CEH has a production backlog that extends for years. The U.S. Government has worsened the problem by acquiring a large fraction of the units manufactured to date. The Pentagon, here, has 13 units alone. Expect a black market for stolen Government-purchased MEGs.

"Third, redirect the Department of Energy's basic research capabilities at Government Laboratories like Argonne, Los Alamos, Sandia, Oak Ridge and others away from "Global Warming" research and in the direction of "Global Cooling" research. The smartest people in the country need to be working on this issue."

"Fourth, waive all the recently promulgated Environmental Protection Agency rules against coal. We need the energy as do other nations that want to buy our coal and frankly, a little additional greenhouse gas in the atmosphere at this point is a good thing."

"Fifth, protect military aircraft by either replacing or in-situ coating existing turbine and propeller blades with an electrostatically applied nano-carbide coating which can protect against the erosion caused by the very abrasive volcanic ash in the atmosphere. Sign an executive order compelling airlines to do the same. Otherwise, we will have to ground all aircraft or witness numerous airline crashes.

"Sixth, you have seen that our visual wavelength satellite imagery and satellite phone systems have been compromised due to the high content of ash in the atmosphere. Our GPS technology is now practically unusable. Fortunately, most of our more recent satellites have been equipped with other methodologies and technologies that are unique to military applications. I'd suggest sharing that technology with our 'friends.'

"Seventh, anticipate a recession. With fuel prices going through the roof, productivity dropping due to people unwilling or unable to work in this unpleasant environment, retailers closing their doors, unemployment increasing exponentially, the labor participation rate falling, and food prices quadrupling, I see no way for the world to avoid a serious financial crisis. There will be enormous political pressure on the U.S. to get us to help those nations less prepared, and this will also take its toll.

"I saved this last recommendation as a lame attempt at humor, something I recognize I'm not known for. Open the southern border -- everyone will want to go south."

As a grim president rose to leave, he said without cracking a smile, "What does your algorithm conclude about the economy -- should I buy or sell?"

"Sir, it would be illegal for me to use government-funded insider research results for personal gain," answered General LaSalle with signs of perspiration emerging on his forehead for the first time.

LaSalle missed the wink the president gave the Chairman and said, "Someone needs to investigate General LaSalle's net worth here and his off-shore accounts. Alert the Internal Revenue Service." Jerking LaSalle's chain was the last time the president would enjoy himself for a long time.

CHAPTER 3

PLANNING FOR THE COLD
(ZERO+90 DAYS)

WANAKA, NEW ZEALAND- JULY 18TH: Winter was more brutal than normal this year on the South Island of New Zealand; spring seemed light-years away. The gray grit from volcanic ash turned an otherwise gorgeous estate into a dreary home. Tucker Cherokee was pensive, deep in thought and contemplating the fact that he was tired of being imprisoned under FBI witness protection in the "Gray Compound" thousands of miles from his home in Virginia. Though it was great to be filthy rich, justly rewarded for his and Maya's part in discovering a world changing technology -- the Neutrino Electricity Using Rare Earth Magnets (NEUREM) generator that made electricity without fuel -- he longed to return to America and the simpler times.

Tucker, Maya and Star had a beautiful home with a formerly spectacular view of Lake Wanaka. They were well known locally by their witness protection surname, the Grays, and were respected as philanthropists in the community. The Grays contributed significantly to the

New Zealand-sponsored charity to help the volcano, earthquake, and tsunami victims in Indonesia. The Grays were also revered in local restaurants as big spenders and tippers -- though the entourage of personal protection always seemed overdone to the restaurant staff.

Tucker actually enjoyed his first year under witness protection; he spent the majority of his time receiving personal training from his mentor, Powers, and his best friend, Tank. At 6 feet, 1 inch tall, and now 195 pounds, he was fit and muscled with lightning fast hands. His green eyes, inherited from his mother's side of the family, on his decisively Native American looking face, made him look a bit unusual. His nose was aquiline; he had a cleft in his chin, and almost no facial hair. His green eyes were graduated with the outside of his irises a darker green than the inside. His grandfather was a member of the Cherokee Nation and a direct descendent of Wilma Mankiller. Living with the surname Mankiller added an additional burden to life, so his father changed their last name to "Cherokee" before Tucker was born.

Tucker had jet black hair that he had allowed to grow shoulder-length. His hands looked like they belonged to a concert pianist -- long, slender, perfectly and naturally manicured. Anyone would rue the day, however, that they underestimated him either physically or intellectually.

During the beginning of their second year in witness protection and after Star was born, Tucker received a call from Stephen Sanders, CEO of his former employer ENTROPY Entrepreneurs, LLC.

"Good to hear from you, boss," answered Tucker; "how is your knee and how did you get this number?" Sanders had been shot in the kneecap by an intruder, an international intellectual property thief and assassin after a secret formula.

"I will never walk without a cane but at least I'm alive. I got your number from one of the two or three people who know where you are. *I* still don't know where you are -- just a number which I understand intentionally provides disinformation. According to my phone, you are in El Salvador."

"Damn," Tucker said, "the secret is out." About that time, sensing his anxiety, Ram moved closer to Tucker as if sensing a threat.

"The reason I called is that I wanted to know if you and Maya would like to get back to work; you have to be bored to death hiding away somewhere. It's a tragic waste of brainpower for you two to be sitting around."

"What kind of work?"

"DARPA -- the Defense Advanced Research Project Agency -- has hired ENTROPY to develop a method of improving our warfighters' ability to sustain combat readiness in high temperature environments like those our soldiers were exposed to in Iraq and Libya."

Tucker said, "You must have bid on that job to win it; what was your original concept which apparently isn't working out?"

Sanders laughed out loud and said, "That's what I love about you Tucker, your speed at grasping complex issues! Anyway, that's irrelevant. What do you say -- you interested?"

Tucker looked down into Ram's eyes and suddenly understood Ram's concern. His eyes said, "You better not do it without Maya's buy in!"

"Sounds interesting, Stephen, but let me talk it over with Maya and call you back. Will you help us with any laboratory equipment we need?"

"Sure, I'll bring it down to El Salvador myself."

Later that same day, Sanders received a call from what appeared to be from Bangkok, Thailand. "Yes," Sanders answered.

"This is Tucker. Maya and I have discussed your proposal and determined that it would be good for us to reengage our scientific interests and stimulate our dormant synapses. We're in."

During the following 18 months, Tucker and Maya came up with a lotion, much like suntan lotion or UV protection lotion, which could be applied to the body of a warfighter (much like war paint) to allow soldiers to endure high temperature environments better than opponents without the war paint. This invention was a godsend for the warfighter and, no doubt, saved many NATO lives.

Today, **three years later**, it was July 18th. Tucker received a follow-up call from Stephen Sanders at ENTROPY. Sanders said, "I see that you have relocated to Cape Hope in South Africa. I love your phone disinformation feedback system."

"It's always good to hear from you, Stephen."

"This request is not from me. This request is from the President of the United States, Winston Allen."

"OK. You've adequately piqued my interest. Wow."

"Is the formula for the high temperature war paint reversible?"

"What are you talking about?"

"Can you modify the formula to keep war fighters from freezing to death?"

"Ah," said Tucker; "good fucking question."

CHAPTER 4

THE BAG LADY
(ZERO+182 DAYS)

**VANCOUVER, BRTISH COLUMBIA –
OCTOBER 16th:** Sean Christianson was complaining to himself -- the incredibly cold weather was great for business, but exposure to the frigid cold sure was unpleasant. The demand for Alberta tar sand oil had skyrocketed over the past few months. A cold and desperate Japan was paying a premium for an oil supply guarantee. Japan just happened to be Sean's account, wrestled from an incompetent sales manager and negotiated prior to the recent onslaught of what appeared to be a mini ice age. Timing was everything. At 27 years old, he was proud of his success. He was on his way up the ladder to bigger and better things. With success came money. With money, he could become the stud he always wanted to be. Money is the great equalizer, especially if you looked like a cross between a nerd and a troll.

Normally, Vancouver had a temperate climate by Canadian standards, with average lows in the winter around 1 degree Celsius (33 Fahrenheit) and average highs in the summer months of around 22 degrees Celsius (72 Fahrenheit). "Not bad for Canada," Sean mused. On this fall day, the temperature was 14 degrees C below normal for this time of year with a wind chill factor pushing past historical boundaries. It's a biting cold -- ***cold to the bone***. There were precious few people out and about; Vancouver didn't appear to be as vibrant as it once was. As Sean approached the Port of Vancouver where supertankers which held millions of gallons of oil destined for Yokohama were docked, he noticed a homeless old lady pushing a shopping cart filled with junk and covered with tattered blankets in the direction of an enclosed pumping station. "She must be seeking shelter," he mumbled to himself. "This cruel weather must be taking its toll on the homeless."

Sean had overheard conversations on the radio about shelters having been set up around the city by the Red Cross for the homeless. Inspired to perform a random act of kindness, unusual for him with his self-absorbed persona, Sean decided to stop, help the hunched-over old lady out of the biting cold and escort her to a homeless shelter.

Sean drove another block before he could make a U-turn. By the time he returned to the location where he last saw the old lady, she was gone. He thought to himself, "She's probably inside the pump house to escape the wind chill." Sean parked the car illegally alongside the road, got out, and hurriedly approached the pump house. Because he was freezing and caught up in his own sense of goodwill, and because the likely occupant of the pump house was just an old lady, he never considered that there might be repercussions from invading the pathetic homeless lady's space. Sean opened the pump house door and stepped in. Too late, he wondered why the pump house was unlocked.

Sean was greeted with a warm and endearing smile, sparkling gray eyes that betrayed her age, and a six-inch hunting knife. Gracefully and without hesitation, she slit Sean's throat.

As Sean dropped to the floor with a bewildered expression on his face, she said, "Thank you, young man, for your attempt to save me." Sean gurgled, lost consciousness and bled out quickly. It's funny how one's mind works as the end nears. His final thoughts were about how surprisingly little pain he was in, how cold he felt, and how he regretted not having a will.

The old lady took a stick of dynamite from the shopping cart, attached an electronic detonator, and placed it atop Sean's still-warm corpse. She removed more sticks of dynamite from the cart and strategically positioned them under the pump. Over the next two and a half hours, she set explosives with detonators on two additional targets. Earlier in the week, she had placed explosives on five pre-selected targets. All explosives were set to detonate three hours from now at 5:00 pm Pacific time. This gave the old lady time to leave the area; she didn't want to be caught in the unpleasant aftermath of her tasks.

On schedule, eight explosions occurred simultaneously. One was detonated on the bridge of the supertanker, *Eliza*, fully loaded with oil from the Athabaska Oil Sands in Alberta, docked at the port of Vancouver's largest terminal. It was scheduled to embark to Japan in two hours. It was actually going nowhere, soon. The old homeless lady was not so old or homeless when she entered the captain's quarters as a cleaning person and managed to drop a sleeping cocktail into his drinking water bottle. Six hours later, the cleaning person was able to find the Captain's keys to the bridge and plant explosives and a detonator under the main control panel. The explosion eliminated the ability to start and navigate the *Eliza*. It would take weeks to repair the damage. But the impact to Japan was more egregious. The oil headed for Yokohama was moored in Vancouver. No other dock in Vancouver could handle a supertanker. *Eliza* was immovable so no other supertanker could move oil to Japan from Canada. The people of Japan would suffer unless the Government of Japan could find another source of fuel for heat in this very competitive market; a result of the drop in temperatures.

The second and third explosions occurred at the Vancouver-Hayden Island railroad bridge. The explosions, the largest two of the eight, didn't bring the bridge down, but were large enough to prevent oil transport by rail for months. The old homeless woman and the *Eliza* cleaning person -- who were one and the same -- had no constraints when placing explosives with detonators on either side of the bridge. The extremely large amount of TNT placed adjacent to the main structural girders deformed them beyond repair. Structural engineers would have to assess the damage. No coal, fuel oil, natural gas or refined products would be transported across the bridge during the assessment and analysis of the structural integrity of the bridge. The ultimate completion of repairs would take even longer.

The fourth explosion occurred at the main transformer yard which fed 60% of Vancouver's power grid. 35% of the residents of the greater Vancouver metropolis depended on electricity for heat, either using space heaters, heat pumps, direct electric heating, or for pumps and controls to supply kerosene, diesel fuel, propane, or natural gas from their storage tanks to their heaters or generators. The fence around the transformers was defenseless against bolt cutters. A closed-circuit TV caught the perpetrator. When utility investigators reviewed the digital recording days after the explosion, they witnessed the Michelin Man entering the hole in the fence with what appeared to be a portable drill. The heavy ski jacket, ski mask, gloves, scarves, headgear, and large reflective sun glasses made it impossible to identify the criminal. The investigative team could not agree on gender, age, or ethnicity. They did conclude that the perp was short, somewhere between 5 feet 6 inches and 5 feet 9 inches in height.

The fifth explosion disintegrated Sean Christenson. Trace DNA evidence ultimately identified his remains. The sixth explosion took out the pump house and pump that moved the oil from railroad tank cars to the supertankers.

The seventh explosion took out the Vancouver Island natural gas pipeline. The pipeline itself was not well guarded. The transfer stations were fenced, locked, and had intrusion detection alarms. But the transfer stations were unguarded. It was a piece of cake for the terrorist to bypass the alarm system and destroy the continuity of the pipeline. Natural gas provided heat to 40% of the residents of the greater Vancouver metropolitan area.

The eighth explosion occurred on the Kinder Morgan Trans Mountain Pipeline on its route to the west coast ports in Barnaby and the Westbridge Marine Terminal within Port Vancouver. The oil pipeline from Edmonton, Alberta carried crude oil and refinery products to the port. The bomb was located under a huge pump, 60 miles northeast of Vancouver.

The impact to the people of Vancouver was devastating. During Vancouver's coldest winter in recorded history, the means to stay warm was eliminated for 75% of the residents. At the Dorchester Senior Living Home in nearby Coquitlam, the temperature dropped fast. Within four hours, the average inside temperature was 1 degree Celsius. The Dorchester General Manager contacted every bus transport company in the area without success, in an attempt to move the weak and elderly to heated shelters in the region.

Emergency response, as well as search and rescue teams -- from Seattle and Portland -- were dispatched with fuel, generators, blankets, and warm clothing. However, within five days, the death rate by freezing plateaued at 325 a day in the greater Vancouver metropolitan area -- with no end in sight to the deadly cold weather.

CHAPTER 5

WHITE KNIGHT
(ZERO+183 DAYS)

KYOTO, JAPAN- OCTOBER 17TH: The tall, handsome, gray-haired Prime Minister of New Zealand, Samuel Snyder, had agreed to attend a symposium on Global Climate Change in Kyoto over a year ago. With the current cold weather crisis in full bloom, Prime Minister Snyder thought the meeting of world leaders on the subject would be entertaining, if not informative. He had never before taken his lovely first lady to Japan and thought this symposium would be a great opportunity.

New Zealand didn't have a Secret Service equivalent to the U.S. So the Government of New Zealand hired one of the most famous personal protection companies in the world, *White Knight Personnel Security, LLC,* owned and operated by Tank Alvarez, an American resident of Wanaka, New Zealand. It was not a coincidence that *White Knight* had moved its headquarters to Wanaka after Tucker and Maya Cherokee were relocated there under witness protection. The FBI hired *White Knight* to provide witness protection for the Cherokees (or the Grays, as they were known to the locals). Even President Snyder did not know who the Grays really were. What President Snyder did know was that the Grays were extremely wealthy Americans and their contributions to the nation of New Zealand had been more than generous.

The truth was that Tank Alvarez and Tucker Cherokee had been life-long best friends. In their youth, Tucker saved the lives of Tank and his sister and, therefore, Tank felt forever indebted to Tucker. Tank was a good person to have as a friend, because you sure wouldn't want him as an enemy. Tank grew from his high school football tackle size of 6 feet 4-1/2 inches tall and 310 pounds to 6 feet 7 inches tall and 295 pounds of broad shoulders and muscle. Despite his size and tree trunk thighs, his quickness, speed, endurance and close combat skills were frightening. In following his lineage, it was difficult to understand where his size came from. He was just an anomaly. The love of his life, Jolene, called Tank her Hispanic Howie Long. His face had a serious look; he didn't smile often in public, and he showed a constant state of intimidating alertness.

As owner and CEO of *White Knight*, he didn't have to actually guard anyone himself. He had an elite staff of former seals and rangers to call on to protect *White Knight* clients. But for the most important customers, like President Snyder, Tank felt obligated to take on the challenge personally.

There was no reason to believe that the President of New Zealand was at risk in Japan. President Snyder had not done anything in office that would energize political extremists.

Kyoto was a beautiful city, the imperial capital of Japan for over a thousand years. Heads of States from around the world arrived with both anticipation and intrigue about how the leaders who were previously committed to preventing global warming would handle the current cold weather crisis. *White Knight* did a lot of preparation and investigated organizations which might want to protest or cause mischief at the Kyoto gathering. A lot of wind was taken out of the sails of the anti-greenhouse gas bunch and it was too cold to expect much in the way of protests. Nonetheless, Tank's team thoroughly investigated all attendees and the manifests of most airline flights into Narita. No alarms went off -- nothing looked suspicious.

Tank and Jolene Landrieu, a retired marine, stayed alert and vigilant even while enjoying the beauty and architecture of the Kyoto Palace from inside the warm and comfortable limousine. Jolene was driving, with Tank on the passenger side; President and Mrs. Snyder were in the back seat, safe and warm. Suddenly, Tank said firmly, "Stop!" Jolene applied the brakes to achieve a sudden stop. Tank opened the passenger door, ran around the back of the limousine and began chasing a pedestrian. Jolene drove the vehicle in the opposite direction, away from whatever danger Tank had identified. She would take the Snyders to their hotel and guard their room until Tank contacted her.

The pedestrian didn't know that Tank was after him until it was too late. Tank tackled the man at full speed -- a rhinoceros couldn't have withstood the attack.

When Melvin woke up, his first thought was that he was extremely cold. When he tried to move, he realized that every part of his body hurt. He had no memory of what had just happened. He turned his head to observe the largest human he had ever seen. Tank, when fully dressed in his Eskimo suit, Cossack hat, ski mask, and arctic gloves, looked even larger than he really was. And he looked warm and comfortable.

Melvin, on the other hand, was virtually undressed, in only his skivvies, as they sat next to the ice-fringed Kyoto River. Tank said, "Melvin, my old acquaintance, what is a scum bag like you doing in Kyoto? Is it just a coincidence that you are here at a time when there is a special event with high ranking, high profile dignitaries here?" Melvin hung his head; he recognized the voice -- how unlucky could he be to run into Tank on this assignment.

Melvin said, "I'm cold; can you get me my clothes or a blanket? I'll talk afterwards."

"Melvin, you know how this works. You talk first. If you think you're cold now, wait until I throw you into the river. Take all the time you want; I'm perfectly comfortable. It is never a coincidence when criminal mercenaries show up at a location where heads of states gather. How many of you are there? What is your mission?"

"Tank, you know the protocols. If I spill my guts, well, they'll be lying on the ground in a week or less."

"Maybe. Probably. On the other hand, you'll die here now, if you don't spill your guts. Hey, look at the bright side; you'll have an extra week to live!"

"You won't kill me; that is not your style. You don't even have your pooch with you."

Tank picked up Melvin and threw him into the semi-frozen river.

Tank picked up some rope he'd secured while Melvin was unconscious and began casually walking downstream, along the boardwalk. Melvin's head came out of the water, gasping. Tank said, "My pooch is on assignment. You have two minutes before your heart stops, less before your arms and legs quit functioning. What's it going to be, Melvin?" All Melvin could do was mouth an "OK".

Tank threw one end of rope in Melvin's direction and said, "Grab the rope while you still can." Tank pulled the mercenary out of the river but didn't give him anything to dry himself off with. The wind was slight but brutal on Melvin's wet, bare skin.

"Please, I'm freezing to death. Give me your coat."

"You know, Melvin, the first things to freeze are appendages like toes, fingers, and your Johnson. You don't need that anymore if you just have a week to live, right?"

"There are five of us. Our assignment is to use an IED to take out the President of India at his hotel. We are being paid by a Pakistani militant group."

"What hotel? And when is the mission scheduled to be complete?"

"The Kyoto Brighton Hotel. Tomorrow morning, 0430."

Tank took off his coat and handed it to Melvin while he simultaneously called Jolene.

Jolene answered the phone on the first ring.

"Change of plans. Move the Snyders out of the Brighton ASAP and take them to the Hyatt Regency. While you're mobilizing them, get me the name of the head of Kyoto Brighton's security."

Tank took out handcuffs and placed them around Melvin's wrists, behind his back. "You're coming with me, just in case you are lying to me." Tank dragged Melvin to a taxi stand, threw him into the back seat of a taxi, and asked the driver to take them both to the nearest police station. The English-speaking driver, paralyzed with fear, did as he was told.

Tank showed his credentials to the Kyoto police and told them that he had uncovered a potential act of terrorism. They agreed to hold Melvin until Tank's return. Though their English was poor and Tank's Japanese was zero, the message was completely understood.

Tank didn't just want to stop the mission; he wanted to capture all the mercenary terrorists without endangering people in the hotel. He called Jolene.

"Are you with guests?"

"Yes."

"Do you have a name?"

"Tomoyoshi Yamaguchi."

"You were in Iraq during the ugly days of IEDs. What should we be looking for?"

"Look for a vehicle with seemingly low tire pressure, overweight and close to the ground. I'd look for a food catering service vehicle; they're common for hotels. Be looking for terrorist body size and language that is not indigenous to Japan."

"Who would you call to get frequency jammers immediately?"

"Tank …?"

"Of course; I'll call immediately.

"Jolene."

"Yes."

"Pull the fire alarm on your way out of the hotel."

"Roger that."

Tank called Powers. Powers was retired Special Forces. He trained Tank and Jolene. Powers turned Tank into practically a one-man army. The United States had the most capable special operations forces in the world, and Powers was known to be at the head of the class. As a Green Beret, he led a 12-man A-team multiple times in Black Operations. He later became famous within the Special Forces community by training candidates in hand-to-hand combat, close quarters combat, martial arts, hand weapons, and tactical weapons. Powers was now the *White Knight* trainer and head of security for the Tucker Cherokee compound. Powers answered the phone.

"So how's the sushi and sake?"

"We need frequency jammers in Kyoto now. Can you make that happen?"

"Now, no. In short order, yes. Where?"

"Kyoto Brighton Hotel."

Three hours later, two Blackhawk helicopters with Japanese insignia landed 10 kilometers away, triangulated from both the hotel and the Kyoto Palace. Ten Japanese Special Forces soldiers with five bomb sniffing dogs emerged. Each of the soldiers had a frequency jammer. They got into vans which were waiting for them. The vans drove the 10 km and parked close to the Kyoto Brighton.

Tank met with Tomoyoshi Yamaguchi and briefed him on the plan. The Brighton security manager looked like a former Sumo wrestler -- though not as tall, he was bigger than Tank. And he was angry. An angry Sumo wrestler was not a pretty sight. Fortunately, his anger was directed at the mercenary-terrorists. He wanted to deal with them personally. Sounded like a good idea to Tank.

At 0200 all the jammers were turned on and remained on until the mission was complete. Of course, no one's cell phones worked but communications were worked out with direct connections. At 0415, a laundry service vehicle rounded the corner as if it was going into the back of the hotel's service entrance. It was heavy and the tires were almost to the rim. Two bomb sniffing German Shepherds were released and went crazy as they tried to tear into the van. All four tires were shot out. The jammers kept jamming. The mercenaries had no intention to sacrifice themselves for the mission; they were not the suicide type.

They ran -- three of them -- right into the Japanese Special Forces soldiers. There were no warning shots. There was no mercy. Though Tank would have liked to have interviewed them, he was comfortable with their silent fate at the ends of bayonets.

One terrorist was still missing -- four out of five ain't bad, but it would have been good to close the case. He was probably the guy responsible for detonating the bomb. He had to be close by. He might even have detonated the bomb with the three compatriots in it. But all the frequencies were jammed. He could be anywhere.

The bomb squad arrived and disarmed the IED that contained enough TNT to eliminate a square block. The Japanese Special Forces soldiers canvassed four square blocks but did not find the fifth mercenary.

Tank told Tomoyoshi Yamaguchi that one of the perpetrators was at the police station, awaiting his arrival, to be interviewed.

Poor Melvin. The former Sumo wrestler had tried some new moves on Melvin, and quite a few old moves. Yamaguchi outweighed Melvin by about 300 pounds, and simply overwhelmed him. Melvin never actually lived the extra week which Tank had promised.

Though a few world leaders left Japan in the aftermath of the apparent terrorist attack in Kyoto, the majority stayed for the symposium. Prime Minister Snyder was one of the brave who was not going to give in to terrorists. Tank and Jolene escorted the Prime Minister and his wife to the plenary session of the symposium where the keynote speaker was the author of the United Nations' Intergovernmental Report on Global Warming.

The scientist, a distinguished looking, self-confident Englishman strolled up to the podium and looked out at an audience of world leaders, media, corporate executives, and lawmakers. He maintained a deadpan serious expression on his face and said, "It is extremely cold out. It is cold everywhere. It is so cold that even the lobbyists on 'K' Street in Washington, D.C. and the lawyers in Piccadilly Circus in London have their hands in their own pockets."

It broke the ice and allowed him to discuss the dichotomy between the current frigid weather and the global warming model. "The world is a dynamic place with an infinite number of influences. Some of these influences are beyond man's control; for example, we can't do a thing about the sun. If it acts up, burns out, creates sun spots, flares, expands, contracts, cools off, releases magnetic bursts or has a sudden burst of neutrinos, we can't do a thing about it -- we just deal with it the best we can.

"The same is true if the earth's magnetic poles shift or the earth changes its tilt relative to the sun. Mankind can't do a thing about it.

"The global warming models we put together did not incorporate the influence of the sun or solar changes in the earth's rotation or orbit; why would we -- we couldn't do anything about it. What we did include in our model are those influences on the earth's weather pattern which we might be able to alter. We stand by those models. Sometime in the near future, literally after the dust settles, after the average temperatures return to normal, and the current natural disaster is only read in history books, we'll be right back to where we have to be concerned with greenhouse gasses and man's deleterious conduct which ultimately creates a condition of global warming.

"Thank you very much. I hope to see you again at the next Global Warming Symposium in five years or so. Are there any questions?"

A distinguished man strolled up to a microphone set up in the floor aisle with a very large man standing behind him. "My name is Samuel Snyder, Prime Minister of New Zealand. Our islands extend to the very low latitudes. Our citizens are cold today. We would like to see that the current funds which you enjoy from all the members of the United Nations be redirected in the short term to methods of reducing the impact of the record cold weather on the citizens of the world. Would you share your plan with us today?"

"At this time, the United Nations has no plan to study options for dealing with historically cold weather."

Prime Minister Snyder looked around the audience of world leaders and Global Climate change scientists and asked, "Would anyone in the audience currently working on a solution for dealing with 'global cooling' please stand up, come to the microphone and share with us what you are doing?"

No one stood up.

Prime Minister Snyder turned and walked out of the Symposium without looking back, but with Tank in full protective mode.

CHAPTER 6

POWERLESS
(ZERO+183 DAYS)

WASHINGTON, DC – OCTOBER 17TH**:** Former Governor of Wisconsin and now President of the United States Winston Allen called his advisors into the White House Situation Room. The president was agitated, angry, and hyper-intense. As his advisors entered the room, he was uncharacteristically cold to each -- with ash in their hair, still removing their dust masks. He instructed his staff to set up a tele-video-conference with the Prime Minister of Canada in Ottawa. The mood in the situation room was dour. The Prime Minister's sad, disheveled and depressed face filled the wide-screen, his eyes swollen, his hair uncombed and his usually pleasant smile and disposition gone.

President Allen expressed the willingness of Canada's southern neighbor to help in any way possible to provide humanitarian aid to the citizens of Vancouver. All the resources of the emergency response capabilities in Seattle would be available to support the city of Vancouver.

President Allen asked, "Is there anything that we can do for you and your country in this time of need?"

The Prime Minister of Canada, Michel Merlot, said, "I received a phone call on my personal home land line in Ottawa. This is not an easy number to get; it's very privately held. The call was allegedly from an organization called the *Society for Environmental Justice*; they were claiming responsibility for the Vancouver acts of terrorism. The message was "Stop Exporting Oil or there will be more death and destruction." We could use some help from you to determine the origin of the cowardly acts. Frankly, I have doubts about the legitimacy of the claim. Further, the president of the *Society for Environmental Justice* was contacted by the press for comment, but the organization denied any responsibility for the terrorist acts in Vancouver."

President Allen asked Prime Minister Merlot what he speculated might be the motive behind the attacks. Merlot was in his early 70s, white hair, 50 pounds overweight, with a red bulbous nose. President Allen was concerned; he had never seen the Prime Minister look so awful. "Interestingly," answered Prime Minister Merlot, "the eight explosions resulted in very significant capital loss but only one direct casualty. Yet, the impact of the attack on energy platforms is likely to result in hundreds if not thousands more casualties -- of the weak from exposure to the extremely cold weather."

"So," added President Allen, "these terrorists made some sort of statement about energy sources? They attacked almost all methods of providing heat -- oil, natural gas, coal and electricity. It's interesting that they didn't attack wood burning methods, ethanol, the new neutrino-based technology or any renewable energy method. Can we conclude that the terrorists are environmental wackos?"

The National Security Advisor, Dawn Carson, one of the advisors in the Situation Room, spoke up and said, "Mr. President, Mr. Prime Minister, I caution you against jumping to any conclusions about the terrorists' motives. Our observation is that the nation most impacted by the attack outside of Canada is Japan. This may be an attempt to aggravate Japan's already precarious situation. Japan has no coal. Japan has no oil. Japan has no natural gas. Their nuclear program to make electricity has been greatly compromised by the Fukushima Daiichi disaster and their curtailing of the nuclear industry afterwards. Without coal, oil, and natural gas from Canada, Japan is in a vulnerable position."

"What are you saying?" asked Prime Minister Merlot. "That the terrorists hate Japan?"

"No" said the National Security Advisor, "that the terrorists are trying to push Japan into war over energy."

"OK," said President Allen, "What do others here in the Situation Room have to say?"

"Mr. President, Mr. Prime Minister," stated Director of the Central Intelligence Agency, Richard Watts, "we cannot discount the motives of the People's Republic of China. As you are both aware, China has abundant energy resources in Manchuria and has been sold the technology for the neutrino-based energy source. They would love to force Japan to buy Chinese energy."

Prime Minister Merlot said, "Director Watts, if you have any evidence of this claim, you need to share that information with us. What you are suggesting would be an act of war against Canada."

The Secretary of State, Arlington Goodyear, spoke up and said, "The Chinese, over the last five years at least, have upheld their end of the bargain after the last conflict the U.S. had with them. I'd be surprised if the Chinese were behind the Vancouver attack.

"The organization responsible for this attack, though, must have resources. Instead of looking at state sponsored terrorism, maybe we should look at corporate sponsored terrorism. Who gains financially from the Vancouver attack? Who is going to replace the energy sources trapped in Vancouver? The Bakken oil reserves in North Dakota, the tar sand oil in Alberta, the fracking based natural gas deposits in western Canada and the United States, and the production companies of all those sources stand to gain financially. As they say, 'follow the money.'"

President Allen said, "In normal times, I'd consider your scenario possible, but today, all energy companies have a buyer for their product; in fact there is a shortage all around the world because of this brutally cold weather. Corporations don't need to do anything drastic to find buyers.

"We need our intelligence agencies to present some ideas about the organizations which would benefit from the Vancouver acts of terrorism. Let's adjourn for now. I expect to see all of you at 0700 tomorrow with a status report.

"Mr. Prime Minister, I'll keep you informed of any progress we make. Please, advise me as soon as you learn anything, and together we'll bring the terrorists to justice. In the meantime, we'll help you find transportation for Vancouver area victims, to areas with energy to keep your citizens warm."

"Mr. President," asked Prime Minister Merlot with an edge to his tone of voice, "What is the United States' plan for dealing with this extremely cold weather if it continues? I know the leader of the free world has a plan. Please, share your plan with us as soon as you can."

There was no response from President Allen. The video-conference call was disconnected. President Allen looked around the room at his advisors and cabinet members and asked, "What the hell *is* our plan?"

CHAPTER 7

BRAINSTORMING
(ZERO+183 DAYS)

WANAKA, NEW ZEALAND – OCTOBER 17TH:
Playful and energetic white mice were running around the cage, showing no signs of abnormal behavior -- as if nothing in the world were different. The cage was in a cryogenically controlled Plexiglas test unit. Maya asked Tucker, "So what is the temperature down to?"

Tucker answered, "33 degrees Fahrenheit. Even at this temperature the mice have normal appetites and show no signs of intelligence modifications or cognitive deterioration."

"How much of the nano-chemical did you spray on them?"

"Only 2 mils per mouse or 0.5 milligrams by weight was applied to each specimen."

"How long are you planning to keep them at that temperature?"

"Another 2 hours; then I'll drop it another degree."

Maya walked over to another set of mice in another test cage and asked, "What happened here? This is obviously a failed test."

"The spray apparently turned the mice into uncontrolled nymphomaniacs. They had too much sex; they overdid it. Can't you tell by the smiles on their faces?" Maya smiled and patiently waited.

"I used a different formula on that pair; apparently, I used too much alcohol in that formula."

"You know, Tucker, we're not going to be able to release this spray or lotion for human testing until ENTROPY gets U.S. Food and Drug Administration -- FDA -- approval. How are we going to get approval in time to be of value to the millions of people who need it today to keep from freezing? By the time the FDA approves the spray, the freezing weather crisis may well be over. It could be years!"

Tucker smiled.

"OK, my devious husband, what do you have up your sleeve?"

"Have you ever heard of an executive order?"

"There is no way President Allen will issue an executive order to fast-track the spray; there is way too much political risk and liability. What if there are horrible side-effects? He'd get lots of criticism for rushing this to market."

"He'll get criticism if he ***doesn't*** make it available to his freezing constituents. If he knows the spray was developed and he didn't make it available to a freezing public, just think how much criticism he would receive. However, that's irrelevant. I'm talking about getting Prime Minister Snyder of New Zealand to issue an executive order. We'll make this a New Zealand patent by Catherine and Brinton Gray under ENTROPY New Zealand, LLC."

Catherine Gray (Maya's name in witness protection) moved over and leaned her sleek body against Tucker, shook her head so that her lustrous waist-long black hair fell across his shoulder and said "Star's asleep." This was code for "I'm in the mood for romance." Brinton Gray (Tucker's name in witness protection) translated the message into: "Oh, boy; a night of whoopee!"

Lovemaking in the Cherokee household was the antithesis of what would be expected from two scientists who spent their entire lives being methodical, deliberate, analytical, and structured. Tucker and Maya threw all their idiosyncrasies and inhibitions out the window and engaged in impromptu no-holds-barred experiments. Fortunately for all in the compound, their bedroom was designed and constructed with soundproof wheat straw insulation. Sound didn't leave; only the sound they wanted got in, electronically.

EIGHT DAYS LATER, OCTOBER 25TH (ZERO+191): Maya was holding Star in her arms while reviewing the test results with Tucker. Tucker said, "And these two have survived 3 days now at 5 degrees Fahrenheit with no change in behavior. However, these two mice over here have been stiff for two days. The only difference is that the ones I sprayed are still alive; the ones I didn't are not.

Star said, "I'm sad, Daddy."

"Don't be sweetheart, because these experiments may save the wildlife in Yellowstone from freezing to death."

Maya asked, "So what's your next step, superman? Is New Zealand's Prime Minister Snyder giving you approval to try this on humans -- on his own citizens?"

Star giggled. Then she relaxed into a full contagious laugh. Tucker rolled his eyes up to the heavens.

Maya asked, "What is so funny?"

Star, still giggling from reading Tucker's thoughts said, "Daddy has already tested it on himself."

Tucker cleared his throat and said, "I knew that you would object. To avoid an argument with you, I just went ahead and sprayed it on myself two days ago."

Maya's face turned bright red, a telltale sign that he'd messed up; "Any side effects?"

"I think that I overheated at first, but I drank a lot of water to compensate. The dosage needs to be refined, but it damn well keeps heat in the body and prevents its escape."

Maya was speechless.

"I have permission from Prime Minister Snyder to have some of it air-dropped into the Antarctic research center which is partially funded by New Zealand. Scientists are stuck in Antarctica and can't get out. They are desperate and willing to be guinea pigs and test the spray or lotion.

Someone from the New Zealand research center is on their way here to pick up a test batch.'

Maya remained silent.

Tucker was experiencing an entirely different kind of cold -- a frigid Maya Cherokee.

CHAPTER 8

BLACKOUT
(ZERO+183 DAYS)

CARIBOU, MAINE – OCTOBER 17TH: Ken Partridge sometimes wondered why he stayed in Caribou; so did his loving wife, Denise. They enjoyed their cabin on the river just downstream from the Caribou dam where the fishing was the best in the county. They were simple people and still in love after 31 years of marriage. The childless Partridges did not like crowds or the noises that accompanied an urban environment; they much preferred a country setting. In the spring, summer and fall they rode mountain bikes, walked trails, camped, fished, observed animal wildlife, and bird-watched. But the winters were brutal and sometimes overwhelming. During the past winter, Ken and Denise endured 133 inches of snow and were exposed to temperatures as low as 21 degrees Fahrenheit below zero. Forecasts predicted that this winter would be significantly colder than the prior frigid winter. It was only October, and they were already experiencing weather similar to the middle of last winter!

The deteriorating weather conditions made Ken's life a little tough. With the weather, the new air quality problem and higher winds than normal, an indoor desk job began to sound appealing to him. He decided this was his last year in Caribou; he was going to miss the moose, but he was getting too old for this shit.

Ken liked his job as an inspector for Integrys Energy Services (IES); it kept him out of the office, out of company politics, and off his ass. Though Partridge was a civil engineer by education from the University of Maine, and a registered professional engineer in the State of Maine, he also performed electrical and mechanical inspection for IES.

Today, he was going to inspect the Caribou dam and hydro facility on the Aroostock River that only produced 900 kilowatts of power. As he entered the Caribou dam's small powerhouse, he used his LED flashlight and UV flashlight to inspect the structure for cracks or anomalies of any kind. Though he was freezing, he was at least out of the wind and protected from the abrasive volcanic ash; it felt like being sandblasted out there. He planned to get back to his company vehicle as soon as possible. Against company rules, he left the car running with the heater on, so that it would be warm when he got back in the car.

He checked the small turbine generator for vibration, leaks or overheating bearings. Everything looked OK. He started to leave the powerhouse when he noticed a package adjacent to the generator. "Kids," he said out loud, "This is not the first time they used the powerhouse as a love nest or to hide out and drink beer." William Partridge reached over to pick up the party debris. He noticed too late that it was wired to something.

The explosion evaporated Partridge, irreversibly damaged the turbine-generator and left the dam weakened. The Caribou dam fought back the hydraulic pressure exerted on its structure by the lake water pressure, but for only a few minutes. Cracks propagated from stress points and grew rapidly both in length and width until the dam failed catastrophically. The 32 plus Fahrenheit water broke through its restraints and forcefully overwhelmed the Aroostock River banks for twelve miles. The dam failure and aftermath took only 10 minutes; it was over quickly. Especially quick for Denise Partridge -- the cabin was swept off its foundation and crushed against a sturdy forest. Denise had heard the blast; she knew that William was in the powerhouse. She was watching through the kitchen window as the rushing water was approaching; she made no attempt to escape.

By the time the local "Search and Rescue" team got to the scene of the explosion, the only thing running was Ken's company car.

Though a small dam, the 900 kilowatts of electricity produced at the dam was important to the town of Caribou. It took days for the utility to redirect electricity from the grid to the town; it seemed that the grid was strained by regional demand, increased by the incredibly frigid fall. Most local Caribou veterans had wood stoves or fireplaces, and many had emergency generators. But not all Caribou residents survived the power failure; many elderly residents were unable to survive the combination of brutally cold weather, poor air quality and the loss of power.

Between the fatalities incurred as a result of the eventual collapse of the dam and the impact of the loss of electricity to homes depending on electricity for heat, 15% of the population would freeze to death in this deadly cold weather, before spring.

A call came in to the Governor of Maine on his private home land line. The caller, using a mechanical voice generator, claimed responsibility for the terrorist act on behalf of the *Society for Environmental Justice.* The caller said that if the governor didn't shut down the lumber industry in Maine that there would be more tragedies in the future.

CHAPTER 9

MIGRATING SOUTH
(ZERO+183 DAYS)

CHALK RIVER, ONTARIO, CANADA - OCTOBER 17TH: She jogged at a faster pace than normal just to stay warm; it was unusually cold for this time of year, even for Chalk River. Danielle tried to jog during her lunch hour almost every day; it helped her to relieve stress and be less of a type 'A' alpha-female at work. She was a health physicist for the Atomic Energy of Canada, Ltd. Laboratory (AECL) where, among other things, they manufactured medical isotopes.

She was jogging on Plant Road in the direction of the frozen Maskinonge Lake, wearing a surgical mask. The 33 year old single athlete generally jogged about 10 miles a day and was thinking about jogging in the gym on a running machine where she wouldn't need a mask. But she liked to be outside. She covered herself in sweats not only to stay warm but also so she didn't attract attention from unwanted males, unlike her 24 year old running mate, Sasha, who always wore spandex shorts to show off her long slender legs, no matter what the temperature or weather. Once a month or so, though, a vehicle would drive off the road while its driver strained to look more closely at Sasha. She looked very sensuous from a distance. Unfortunately for Sasha, her physique was not complemented with an attractive face. Danielle often had to console Sasha after an encounter with cruel men. So they became close -- like sisters.

Runners don't often carry on conversations while they run, but Sasha pulled down her mask long enough to ask Danielle, "Did you notice a decrease in the population of pterodactyls last summer?" This part of the Province of Ontario was home to trillions of very large black mosquitos, affectionately called pterodactyls by the local population because sometimes they seemed to be as large as flying dinosaurs. "Yes, I suspect the extremely cold spring and summer somehow disrupted their reproductive cycle. Wasn't it great not to be battling the beasts?" answered Danielle.

"Hmmmm," said Sasha. "I wonder what other biological changes we can expect with this unusual drop in temperature." As if on cue, the two runners simultaneously and shockingly observed a frightening looking pack of grey timber wolves. Sasha and Danielle had never before seen wolves; wolves didn't normally roam as far south into Ontario as Chalk River. Seven wolves were returning the gaze and observing the runners from a nearby field covered in gray snow. They were following the joggers' every move, heads tracking as if they were linked in some way.

Danielle said, "This might be a good time to turn around." Danielle reversed her direction and headed back towards Chalk River Labs. Sasha followed quickly, as did the wolves. The timber wolves moved in unison, in the direction of the runners. Danielle picked up speed and began leaving Sasha, the slower runner, behind. The faster Danielle ran, the greater the wolves' motion showed urgency. The apparent leader of the pack closed quickly and attacked Sasha from behind. The 175 pound timber wolf mauled Sasha's right leg before a bullet caught him in the chest and ripped through his heart. The rifle shot was heard an instant later. The dead wolf let go of Sasha's leg, while the other six wolves fled from the sound of rifle fire. A Good Samaritan in a pickup truck was passing by, headed in the direction of Chalk River Labs, when he observed the incident, grabbed his rifle off the rack, flipped the safety off and responded accordingly. The Good Samaritan ran to Sasha's aid; Sasha was in shock, sobbing in tremendous pain. Danielle arrived at Sasha's side at about the same time as the rifleman. The man said, "I'd heard rumors about the wolves migrating south because of the extraordinarily cold weather. This is the first time I've actually seen them. Help me get her in the truck and we'll get her to the emergency room."

The Good Samaritan drove as fast as possible to the emergency room of the local hospital with Sasha in the back seat and Danielle trying to apply pressure to her mauled leg wounds, to keep the blood loss to a minimum. The Silverado skidded to a stop in front of the emergency room and the Good Samaritan easily picked up Sasha and carried her to the ER front desk with Danielle right behind. Danielle said in a panic, "Please, help, she's been attacked by a wolf!" The ER team of four went into action and pushed Danielle and the Good Samaritan to the side as spectators.

One of the ER doctors looked at the Good Samaritan and said, "Mr. Kelly, sir, this is the first victim of a wolf attack to survive. Two other victims were not so lucky."

Danielle looked at the Good Samaritan and said, "You're Tom Kelly? Are you the Director of AECL?"

"Yes," said the Good Samaritan, "and if you will excuse me for a minute, I'm going to check on Sasha." The ER did not refuse the presence of Mr. Kelly in the operating and recovery rooms with Sasha. Sasha's care would be the best.

As grey timber wolves were driven south from northern Ontario by the deadly cold weather that was even too severe for them, they encountered more and more humans. Humans were everywhere; it was like a smorgasbord.

CHAPTER 10

THE SUN AND THE EARTH
(ZERO+196 DAYS)

HUNTSVILLE, ALABAMA – OCTOBER 30TH:
Murray Vest drove his 20 year old Porsche 911 up to the
gate of Marshall Space Flight Center with the top down,
even though it was unseasonably cold. His mid-life crisis
was in full bloom and the only thing he could think about
was last night's escapade with fellow solar scientist Melody
Hill. She had to be the most desirable woman he had ever
had the opportunity to entertain. He found her button; all
he had to do was push it. He had never before experienced
a woman who wanted to devour him like she did. Sex in
the front seat of the 911 was unbelievable, a position that
allowed for maximum penetration while nestling his face
between her plentiful breasts.

Because his mind was reminiscing about the previous
night, he almost missed that the gate guards were asking
him to pull over. This was a first. "What can I do for
you, gentlemen?" Murray asked. A female guard rolled
her eyes and said, "You really aren't paying attention,
here, Vest. Turnaround, head to the airport and meet

with Director Pasqua. You and the Director are headed to Reagan National where you will be escorted downtown to the Forrestal Building."

"Whoa, what does the Department of Energy want with me? I work for NASA."

"Don't shoot the messenger, Vest."

Eight hours later, Director Pasqua and Murray Vest sat in front of the U.S. Secretary of Energy, Sarah Plant, and surprisingly *also* the National Security Advisor, Dawn Carson. Though in her late 40s, Secretary Plant was a very attractive woman who obviously took good care of herself. She had a runner's physique, a flawless, unlined face, and short blond hair; never was a hair out of place. Pasqua and Vest had seen her on television and talk shows but had never before met her in person. Her left eye was a different color from her right eye; it was impossible to not stare at her, directly into her eyes.

Dr. Dawn Carson, a short pudgy woman with thunder thighs, never judged people by their appearance; she was only interested in their mental capacity. She observed the handsome solar scientist, Dr. Murray Vest, with no interest whatsoever in his charm, but she was anxious to hear him speak, to see if he was as impressive as his reputation predicted.

"Mr. Vest," Secretary Plant opened, "we invited you and Director Pasqua here to help us understand the full consequence of the recent solar activity on our weather. The president has asked us for a plan to deal with the possibility of an extended period of global cooling. Before we attempt to prepare a plan, we need to fully understand what is going on. We believe that we understand the impact of the dual volcanic eruptions on the weather. We even think we understand the impact we humans have had on the weather by limiting greenhouse gasses that would have helped hold the heat in the atmosphere. What we don't truly understand is the role of the sun on our predicament. In short, what effect can we expect from the sun over the next -- say, two years -- on the weather?"

"Sunspots," Murray said, "solar flares, coronal mass ejections, all have some effect on the earth's weather. A solar super-storm which occurs every 150 to 200 years would have a significant impact on the power grid and our communications systems. The last solar super-storm occurred in 1859, so we're due; it's possible that it could occur during the next two years. But the solar anomalies are minor compared to other earth related activities that we need to be concerned about."

Murray had everyone's attention. "The earth's orbit around the sun is cyclical. The earth's tilt toward or away from the sun in cyclical. The way the earth wobbles is cyclical. These phenomena are commonly known as Milankovitch cycles. There is strong evidence that these cycles affect the occurrence of glacial and interglacial periods within an ice age. The combined effects of the changing distance to the sun, the precession of the earth's axis, and the changing tilt of the earth's axis redistribute the sunlight received by the earth. It is important to note that changes in the tilt of the Earth's axis affect the intensity of seasons. The dominant pattern of glaciation corresponds to the 41,000-year period of changes in the earth's tilt on its axis."

"Mr. Vest," asked Secretary Plant, "are you saying that we are due for the next ice age?"

"If our models are correct," answered Murray, "we are overdue for a change in the tilt of the earth's axis. So, the answer is yes."

For the first time, Director Pasqua spoke: "Please understand that these models are developed by NASA using data that is very difficult to assess. We don't recommend the development of policy based on the accuracy of our models."

"That was quite a disclaimer," stated Dawn Carson. "What I want to know is what I should tell the president about our next course of action."

Without missing a beat, Murray answered, "As I see it, you have two options. Do nothing and hope that our model is inaccurate. Or prepare for colder weather."

CHAPTER 11

STRANDED IN ANTARTICA
(ZERO+197 DAYS)

**SCOTT BASE ON ROSS ISLAND, ANTARTICA –
OCTOBER 31ST:** The volcanic eruptions of Mount Mirapi
and Mount Nyiragongo occurred just before winter in the
southern hemisphere. Though, as it turned out later, they
should have been concerned, the polar scientists were *not*
overly concerned about their mission to Ross Island to
investigate the ravages of global warming on indigenous
penguins. Dr. Pamela Northamer and Dr. Omar Wong
were returning scientists, this their second tour of duty.
If truth be known, they volunteered because they became
lovers. Dr. Northamer was a UCLA graduate with post-
graduate degrees from Stanford. She was tall at 5'11",
weighed about 140 pounds, appeared awkward, all legs
with a large nose, and she perpetually carried a 50 pound
chip on her shoulder. Omar was the antithesis of Pamela.
He grew up in Tasmania, did his undergraduate work
in Australia, and post-graduate work in the U.K. He
was handsome, humorous, gregarious, and athletic -- a
racquetball champion. He was a couple of inches shorter
than Pamela and a couple of years younger. He saw

something in Pamela that no one else did, and knocked that chip right off her shoulder. She was a changed woman, and nothing was going to keep them from re-upping for another winter tour in Scott Camp.

Typically, winters on Ross Island got down to minus 40 degrees with wind chills dropping the effective temperature much further. The Grays, philanthropists from Wanaka, New Zealand, donated a MEG so that power for light and heat reduced the risk of winter research. But transportation of food and supplies to Ross Island was another story. If minus 40 degree weather persisted for an extended period of time, the Ross Ice Sheet would grow and thicken to the point that icebreakers could not reach Scott Camp.

Pamela, Omar and 15 other scientists landed in Scott Camp around the 30th of April (Zero+11 Days), long before the true hideousness of the severe cold weather was realized. The drop in temperature worldwide was uneven. The poles were impacted exponentially more than the equatorial regions. Scott Camp broke the historic low temperature on August 7th at a minus 77 degrees Fahrenheit. The Ross Ice Sheet completely surrounded Ross Island and extended 130 miles north of the northern shore of Ross Island.

Supplies were air dropped several times during the winter. During the coldest period, the reliable huskies and sled driver were forced outside to recover the packages. On one occasion the airplane missed the drop target by a quarter mile. Each scientist took turns as sled driver. The scientist who pulled the short straw for the longest run in the coldest weather met her fate with stoicism. She returned from the perpetual dark with the supplies, but 150 yards out the last of the exhausted and frozen huskies dropped in their tracks, leaving the sled driver stranded. The team of scientists collectively dressed for the occasion with base layer, mid-insulation layer, shell windproof layer body coverage, three pairs of gloves on their hands, fleece hats in wind-stopper fabric with fold down ear-flaps, multiple pairs of wool socks and boots. They went outside to save the scientist and recover the supplies. Thirty-two minutes later everyone and the supplies were inside the warmth of the research compound. Frost-bite took its toll on several scientists including Pamela. Three of her toes on her left foot turned black. But the most serious case impacted the sled driver; she lost her nose and right eye. Without the huskies, they were seriously challenged to recover the next supply drop. They could only hope that the drop was close to the laboratory.

Normally, when summer approached, Scott Base scientists typically enjoyed the operational flexibility which the warmer season in Antarctica affords. The Ross Island spring this year, however, was more like a typical winter with temperatures in the minus 30 to minus 40 range -- no summer break for the imprisoned scientists in Scott Camp.

A supply drop was due today. They all waited in anticipation for the sound of the P-3's engines. This time, they were told the supplies would include a special package that might help them survive the brutal elements until summer. They thanked God for the P-3 crew who dropped the supplies, skidding them to a stop not more than 50 yards from the front door of the lab.

The usual medical, mail, food and reading material supplies were accompanied by some pressurized spray cans without labels. Also included in the package was an envelope with an explanation of the purpose of the spray, the risks to users, a legal disclaimer and documents to sign that stated that they fully understood that it had never before been tested on humans.

The scientists universally decided to experiment with the spray, with the exception of the weak nose-less frostbitten scientist. They developed a test protocol that modified the quantity of spray per calculated skin surface area, time between applications, and outdoor wind-chill conditions.

Omar was the first to spray his entire body (Pamela enjoyed the task). He dressed in the normal attire for polar exposure including goggles. Omar went out into the minus 35 degree elements to a location where he could observe indigenous penguins. Omar was allowed 38 minutes in the severe conditions. Though he strangely did not see any penguins, when he returned he was thoroughly tested against 27 different parameters including heart rate, body temperature, blood pressure, and liver enzymes, to assess the impact of the chemical on his body.

Omar stood before the audience of scientists and said, "I never felt cold; in fact, one side effect is that I intermittently felt feverish. I actually wondered at one point if I had overdressed for the elements. My guess is that a little less spray per square inch should be considered for the next experiment."

And so, for the next two months (November and December) the team experimented with the spray until they were confident that they had the dosage range fixed. They prepared a final report and sent it off to New

Zealand's Department of Health with their satellite packet computer connection.

Though summer was only a couple of weeks away, the scientists were still trapped at Scott Base; no icebreaker could reach them nor get close enough to run helicopters back and forth from the icebreaker to the lab. But a British Antarctic Survey Canadian De Havilland Twin Otter could land and take off from a flat area two miles away. The Twin Otter could not seat many passengers at a time. Dr. Northamer and Dr. Wong were on the first rescue flight out. They were the guinea pigs to determine if they could traverse the two miles in the cruel winter-like Antarctic conditions. Without the new spray, they would not have survived.

When they were airborne, Omar and Pamela were looking out the windows in search of penguins, but saw none. This was a bit disconcerting. What they did see was an ice sheet that extended hundreds of miles further north than had ever been previously recorded.

The penguins of Ross Island instinctively knew to migrate north, when conditions on Antarctica became even too cold for them. Most of them made the long and difficult trek to Stewart Island, the southernmost island of New Zealand, and joined their indigenous brethren, the yellow-eyed penguin of Rakiura National Park. Those penguins which didn't make it became great snacks for killer whales.

Tucker and Maya Cherokee read the report prepared by the scientific team on Ross Island. They re-read the report out loud together. The smile on Tucker's face said it all. Even Maya couldn't help but smile as the news thawed her coldness toward Tucker; she had forgiven (not to be confused with forgotten) Tucker for his earlier transgression by conducting a test on himself without confiding in Maya.

They put in a call to Sanders at ENTROPY to share the good news, but the time difference prevented them from catching him. Star was in bed asleep. They opened a bottle of their favorite wine, a Pinot Grigio from Santa Marguerite, and celebrated -- long into the night.

CHAPTER 12

THINNING THE HERD
(ZERO+210 DAYS)

CHICAGO, ILLINOIS - NOVEMBER 13ᵀᴴ: "It is not my fault; I was born this way." He talked to himself constantly when nobody was around to observe him. He understood that he was mentally ill, but he was OK with it. "How many mentally ill people actually know their condition, as I do?" The killer knew and accepted that he was a psychopath. "It's good to know who you are."

The 'ghost' -- as the press liked to glamorously refer to him -- was freezing, a condition he and billions of others had endured for months now. He stood, knee joints cracking, walked over and grabbed the last wooden chair in the barren room and smashed it against the concrete basement block wall. He threw a piece of it onto the fire to keep it burning. He got close to feel the heat and rubbed his hands together. His makeshift chimney allowed the smoke to escape into the upper levels of the abandoned building. He'd have to go on the hunt soon to find additional burnable material to stay warm. He thought that he'd do that while he was out doing what he liked to call "God's work."

"The timing of my arrival on earth coincides with the onslaught of severe climate change," the 'ghost' thought. He had read that there had been numerous changes in the earth's climate over the past couple billion years, some of them severe. During each drastic change, entire species had disappeared. A previous ice age had caused billions of living creatures to die.

"I guess God needs to thin the herd. Maybe he's planning to do it again through this current severe weather cycle. Well, I'm here to help."

It's a thin line between genius and insanity. At the hospital for the criminally insane, his former case worker explained that he was well past that line into seriously uncharted territory. No one knew just how accurate the case worker's observations were. What the 'ghost' was planning was completely uncharted. He believed he was the smartest person on earth, with an IQ of 198. Unfortunately, he was well past genius into insanity.

"I am the smartest person in the world and a master of disguise. I can be anyone I want to be."

The 5 foot 7 inches tall, 160-pound plain looking Caucasian 'ghost' coated his nose and face with Vaseline, put on his ski mask, military-issued specially-designed arctic gloves, ear protection and night vision goggles.

He made sure before he broke into the house that the occupants would not be home tonight. He sent them an emergency text message that they thought was sent from a loved one. The 'ghost' was an expert at "breaking and entering" and disarming alarm systems.

The home was large with a spiral staircase up to five bedrooms on the second floor. The 'ghost' quickly found the child's bedroom, mounted a nano-camera with a wireless transmitter, inserted explosives into a stuffed animal and took some of the eight year-old's personal effects including panties. He had all he needed to successfully blackmail a powerful member of the current U.S. administration. "What a great tool blackmail is, when you need to gather critical information!" he thought.

The 'ghost' relished his unimpeded success at the tasks assigned him in Vancouver and Caribou. What the 'ghost' did, the role he played, and the tasks he continued to perform would be chronicled in history books as long as mankind survived.

CHAPTER 13

NATIONAL TREASURE
(ZERO+214 DAYS)

WANAKA, NEW ZELAND – NOVEMBER 17TH**:**
Five year old Star Li Cherokee could not contain her
excitement about the wildlife in Yellowstone National
Park. Every day for the past two weeks, she watched a
video about Yellowstone given to her by her dad, Tucker.
The precocious little girl surfed the internet about the
indigenous wildlife and Old Faithful. She read that since
1923 the land under Yellowstone has been swelling and
that it is very likely that a Yellowstone volcanic eruption is
imminent -- in fact, an eruption is estimated to be 40,000
years overdue. She also read that the "supervolcano"
under Yellowstone is more than 40 miles wide and 200
miles deep.

"Daddy, if we ever get to go to Yellowstone, will we be
able to take Ram with us?" Ram cocked his head.

A preoccupied Tucker was vaguely paying attention
to Star's question and said, "Of course, sweetheart; Ram
goes everywhere we go."

"What would happen if a volcano erupted in Yellowstone? Would all the wildlife die?"

Tucker stopped what he was doing and looked over at his special daughter. He knew that she had some sort of "gift." He thought about how best to answer the question but before he could answer, she began to cry. She said, sobbing, "What can we do, Daddy, to save all the animals?" She had done it again, read the answer in his mind before he said anything. He took her in his arms; she placed her head on his chest and they hugged. Tucker treasured the moment.

"Well, sweetheart, as long as Old Faithful keeps letting off steam and pressure, then maybe we don't have to worry about it in our lifetime." Star lifted her head up and stared intently at her Dad. Then she laid her head back down, apparently satisfied that he was being truthful and asked, "Will you take me to Yellowstone even though it is cold there?"

"Yes, someday," answered Tucker, "maybe Uncle Powers can give us a tour of Yellowstone by helicopter. That way we can see everything and stay warm. You know, Ram likes to stay warm."

"Can we leave soon, before the Yellowstone volcano erupts?"

With a broad smile on his face, Tucker said, "Sure, I promise to get us there before it erupts."

"Daddy, what do you mean 'sometime in the next couple of years'?"

Tucker's smile left his face. He was getting very concerned. She was showing her special skills more frequently, now. He was certain that sometimes, but not all the time, she read the thoughts of others.

Star said, "Don't worry, Daddy, I'm OK." She jumped off his lap and began playing with Ram.

Tucker wandered downstairs into Maya's research lab. She was focused on her work and didn't even see him enter. His presence startled her and she playfully threw a latex glove at him. "What are you doing down here?"

"I'm watching genius at work."

"Flattery will get you whatever you want."

"I'll keep the compliments coming then."

Maya looked at Tucker's forehead wrinkles and said, "OK, let's have it; what has you concerned?"

"Star read my thoughts again. She is getting better at it, and does it with greater frequency. I don't think we should just let it continue to happen without instituting some sort of a plan. We should be doing something, not just observing her special skill. But, I don't know what to do exactly. I don't want to have her tested and turn her into a guinea pig; I've watched too many paranormal movies to risk subjecting her to that. I know you must be thinking about it too so, what are your thoughts on the subject?"

"I think we need to learn the boundaries of her special talent. We need to confront her with our knowledge of her skills. You and I, with no outside help and in complete secrecy, need to work with her and understand the magnitude of her ability. What is her range, how close to us does she have to be to read our thought? Can she do it at will or do certain conditions have to exist for her to be effective? Can she do it with anyone or are there people whose thoughts she can't read? Can she read Ram's thoughts or feel his emotions? Can she read thoughts in multiple languages? Is there a way to block it? If we change her diet, can we modify her ability? Can she teach us how to read the thoughts of others? There are so many parameters to consider."

"OK, it sounds like we are in agreement. Let's go tuck her in bed."

Maya and Tucker went upstairs together and entered Star's bedroom.

Maya said, "OK, it's time to hit the sack, Jack."

Star said, "Daddy, Mom, Ram loves you. Both."

Maya looked at Tucker and said, "Well, that answers one of our questions."

CHAPTER 14

PRESS CONFERENCE
(ZERO +215 DAYS)

WASHINGTON, DC – NOVEMBER 18TH**:** The male-model-handsome Press Secretary Andy Snow sat in front of President Allen with a list of suggestions about what the president should say tonight to the people of the United States. Snow said, "It's been months since the Mount Merapi eruption. It became obvious weeks ago that the extremely cold weather is not likely to break any time soon. Oil and natural gas prices are way up and are likely to make home heating cost prohibitive for millions of Americans. The economy is weak; unemployment is up and that magnifies the problem of being able to afford home heating costs.

"Add to the problems that we already have, there's a terrorist organization out there somewhere trying to damage our nation's energy supply. Poor nations of the world are reaching out to the U.S. for our traditional disaster support.

"So, the big question is what are we doing about it?"

President Allen's Chief of Staff, Rocky Bishop, sat adjacent to Snow and said, "First, I think you need to come across extremely concerned about the health and well-being of the people of the United States -- in view of the impact the very cold weather is having on the weak, our children, and seniors."

Winston Allen said, "That should be easy since it represents how I feel. I don't need to come across that way; I feel their suffering."

"Yes, sir, I wasn't trying to be condescending."

"Rather than you two trying to tell me what I should say, let me tell you what I am going to say", President Allen said firmly and with body language that shut his two aides up.

"Fellow Americans, I come to you tonight to share with you a plan to deal with the serious issues that face us all as a result of the deadly cold weather and the unbreathable air the entire world is experiencing.

"First, I strongly urge you to stay inside unless it is absolutely necessary to go out. I am instructing all non-essential government employees to work from home and telecommute if at all possible. We will shut down non-essential government buildings to save fuel.

"If you must go outside, dress appropriately with no exposed skin. Wear a scarf or ski mask. The first sign of hypothermia is shivering uncontrollably. If you see someone in that condition, please, help them find warmth. We are setting up shelters in every major city in the country as well as in our territories.

"If your family completely loses its source of heat and you are at risk of hypothermia, call 911 or try to reach a government or Red Cross sponsored shelter.

"I have requested governors around the nation to mobilize the National Guard to facilitate transfer of senior and indigent Americans to shelters.

"I have declared 31 States as national disaster areas and authorized FEMA to provide adequate disaster support.

"Under the authority of Presidential Order, I have waived the recently published carbon dioxide air quality requirements for coal fired power plants in order to assure adequate electrical energy for heating.

"Under the authority of Presidential Order, I am making 35% of the Strategic Petroleum Reserve available to regions of the country most hurt by this brutal weather.

"With support from Congress, we are reassigning funds for the increase of production of MEGs, the neutrino based technology, to help the nation produce electricity for heat. This administration, under the management of FEMA, will transfer existing MEGs already acquired by the government to cover critical needs.

"The Attorney General and the Federal Bureau of Investigation are authorized to use Department of Defense resources to identify and stop the organization or organizations responsible for the energy infrastructure-related terrorism that has caused the death of so many U.S. and Canadian citizens. Anyone with knowledge or potential knowledge of the terrorists' identity or activities is urged to contact your local law enforcement authority. Stay vigilant.

"With the approval of Congress, we are redirecting the finest minds in the country, at our national labs, to develop technologies and methodologies to ensure our survival. Our fellow citizens are tough and ingenious and we will prevail.

"I also have great concern that some of our international friends will not fare as well as the United States. We will therefore need to help them to the extent that we can, and still keep the finest military in the world alert against foreign threats.

"My fellow Americans, we will get through this together."

"Ah, sir," said Andy Snow, "You just scared the shit out of me. Can you imagine what the average U.S. citizen will feel like after that speech? Hell, the suicide rate is going to quadruple and the Dow-Jones average is going to drop 20%."

"I'm going to tell the people of the United States like it is. I'm not going to sugar coat the situation," said President Allen.

CHAPTER 15

FORT RITZ
(ZERO+216 DAYS)

CHICAGO, ILLINOIS – NOVEMBER 19TH: The windy city has become virtually uninhabitable. The record-breaking cold summer has turned into a record-breaking frigid fall. Chicagoans feel like they are experiencing a surreal event, living in a science fiction story, like the Twilight Zone, as if Chicago has been teleported to Nome, Alaska. The thought of winter weather is frightening and depressing. The number of telecommuters over the last seven months has increased a hundred fold; people only want to work from home. Fewer and fewer people are willing to fight the elements, expose themselves to wind chill factors that have never before been experienced in Chicago, while suffering nose-clogging ash.

Exelon, the largest utility in the nation, is producing more megawatts than at any time in its history, to support demand. The demand is encroaching on Exelon's maximum production capacity -- Exelon will soon need to purchase power from other utilities. Except that there *are* no utilities with excess power; margins are down to zero. A drop in temperature of just another couple of degrees is going to force rolling blackouts, causing some areas to be without electricity for heat.

Powers was speaking late in the afternoon at the annual National Personnel Protection Conference being held at the Ritz Carlton in Chicago. Tank and Jolene were in the audience along with five of *White Knight Security*'s top protectors.

"And in conclusion, it is imperative that the hardware we use to protect our customers is suitable for the cold weather conditions. You don't want dysfunctional hardware when the life of your customer depends on you. Please remember that steel loses strength at lower temperatures; you should only expect 80% of the rated strength when it gets to 10 below, Fahrenheit -- and also, remember that wind chill does not count for hardware. Just for warm bodies like us. Thank you." The audience of around 100 gave Powers a decent applause. Powers stepped away from the podium and off the stage as the next speaker was introduced.

Tank and Jolene congratulated Powers for a job well done, and the three of them walked into the hotel lobby together. Powers said, "I need a drink. Let's go to the bar."

Tank said, "Sure, we'll join you for one drink, but we promised Maya's mother that we would come by and see her tonight, so we won't be able to stay for long."

At the bar, with a shot of Dewar's in his hand, Powers said, "You know, I almost forgot that Dr. Li lives in Chicago. What does she know about Maya or her whereabouts? Has she ever seen her granddaughter?"

"Virtually nothing, and yes. Tucker in his brilliance has figured out a way to Skype in an encrypted format so Dr. Li has gotten to, at least, see and speak with Star."

One of *White Knight*'s former Seals, Lucas, entered the bar and said to Powers, "Sir, they want you back on the podium to answer questions from the audience."

"Fuck!" Powers went back into the main conference room while Tank and Jolene caught a taxi to Dr. Li's spectacular lake view penthouse. The very refined and sophisticated psychiatrist opened the door to the Penthouse and invited Tank and Jolene into her home. Dr. Ingrid Li was a genetically slender 5 foot 10 inch tall 58 year old classy woman of Norwegian heritage. Her blond hair, showing threads of gray, her bluish hazel eyes, long fingers with long manicured nails and her wire rim eye glasses made her a very pleasant sight.

The view of a fully lit nighttime Chicago from the 20th floor was beautiful. Maya's mother asked the expected questions about how Maya and Star were handling their "incarceration" -- as Dr. Li referred to witness protection.

Suddenly, the lights of Chicago went out. It was pitch black everywhere. A few lights came back on at hospitals and in buildings with emergency generators. Lights never went out in the few facilities that had the new neutrino based power supply systems (MEGs). One of those places was Dr. Li's penthouse. She smiled and said to Tank and Jolene, "Well, there are some advantages to having a brilliant physicist as a daughter."

Tank asked Maya's mother, "What kind of firearms do you have here?"

Dr. Li said, "I beg your pardon; firearms are illegal in Chicago."

Tank didn't change his expression. After about 45 seconds, Dr. Li said, "357 Magnum in my nightstand."

Jolene said, "Within two hours the cold is going to create panic. Panicked people are going to look around and start migrating to the places that have light -- and therefore, heat. If they overrun your rent-a-cop security downstairs then you will be at risk of mob rule. One 357 isn't going to stop them."

"Though I believe that you are exaggerating the threat, I certainly appreciate your concern and I'm glad you are here. Can you stay until the city's lights come back on?"

Jolene said, "My guess is, there isn't a better place in the city to be right now than here."

Tank's cell phone rang. It surprised him because cell service had been terrible ever since the volcanic eruptions contaminated the air, and also because the city lights were out. "Yeah, Powers?"

"The Ritz Carlton has a diesel generator with a couple of days of fuel and the management has asked the conference attendees to protect the Ritz from looters. Do you want to come back and help out? Or do you want us to come to Dr. Li's and help out there?"

Tank said, "Can you send Lucas here, with some protection hardware? We have only one firearm. We have electricity here but we're the only ones within blocks with power. I expect that we'll have visitors."

"What do you need?"

Tank thought for a moment when Jolene said, "Shotguns would be best, Tasers if we have any, and a canister of teargas."

"Consider it done," said Powers. "I'll call the Chicago Police Commissioner's office and let them know we're here and what we're doing. They're going to have their hands full and may need us before the power failure crisis is over."

Tank asked, "Any news about how long they think power will be out? I suspect that this blackout is not a coincidence, based on the Vancouver and Caribou acts of terrorism."

Powers said, "We've heard no news yet from Exelon or the Mayor of Chicago."

"Tell Lucas to call up here when he gets to the building; he'll need an escort up."

Lucas was a serious guy. Never smiled, never joked, and never seemed to enjoy life. He was handsome in a rugged way but the scars were hard to hide. He was 5 feet 8 inches tall and weighed 225 pounds. Yet there was not an ounce of fat on him. He was as powerful as he appeared.

His humorless disposition was a reflection of his history. He had witnessed some pretty ugly things and was responsible for some of them. Though "unofficial" in black operations, he was one of seven seals sent into Africa to eliminate the head of an ethnic-cleansing civil war. The unspeakable horror of what some of the rebel soldiers did to women and children converted him into an anti-evil zealot.

Lucas had no confidence in mankind. At first meeting, he suspected that you were evil; guilty until proven innocent. After leaving the Navy, Lucas did a stint with Triple Canopy where he protected dignitaries for the State Department in Iraq.

Lucas couldn't get a cab from the Ritz Carlton so he decided to tough it out and walk. He was carrying the merchandise in an unmarked carrying case. He had to walk eight blocks to Dr. Li's penthouse building. When he was about three blocks away, Lucas was confronted by three young punks in ski jackets and ski masks.

"Hey, you, what's in the bag?"

Lucas responded, "None of your business."

Punk number one said, "We're making it our business."

"Listen guys, you really don't want to mess with me. Despite my charming and gentle appearance, I can be pretty difficult."

Punk number two said, "But there are three of us and only one of you. Besides, I also have an equalizer." Punk number two displayed a Saturday night special.

"Not really." Lucas threw the carrying case at Punk number two whose 32 discharged into the case at about the same time Lucas' knife penetrated the punk's solar plexus. Untrained Punk number one tried to throw a pathetic roundhouse punch, only to find his teeth caved into his mouth from a lightning-fast right foot. Punk number three couldn't run fast enough away from Lucas. Lucas saw no advantage in chasing him down.

Fortunately, there were no witnesses in this cold weather, so Lucas wasn't going to have to prepare a police report. He called Tank from the lobby entrance when he reached the building. Tank came down and persuaded building security to let Lucas in, but the rent-a-cop told Tank that security had to inspect the carrying case.

Tank said, "No." The building security guard looked Tank in the eye. Then he looked Lucas in the eye. He realized that there was no upside to continuing this line of questioning.

In the elevator (also powered by Dr. Li's Magnetic Electric Generator (MEG)) on the way up to the penthouse, Tank asked Lucas, "What's it like out there? Do you think Dr. Li might be in danger if we don't protect her?"

The laconic Lucas said, "Yes."

Outside the comfort zone of Dr. Li's heated and fully powered penthouse on Lake Shore Drive, life was less tolerable. Storefronts were being smashed, anger was being displayed by the freezing and hungry downtrodden, racial discourse followed, weapons were being displayed openly, and the Chicago war between Americans started. Life in Chicago became survival of the ruthless.

Eight blocks away from Dr. Li's penthouse, the fully lit-up decadent-looking Ritz Carlton became a magnet for anti-Exelon protests. The cold, hungry and frightened Chicagoans evolved from peaceful protestors demanding that their electricity be turned on, to attempts by protestors to enter the Ritz for food and warmth. No police arrived to quell the riot; the Ritz Carlton was on its own. The conflict, later dubbed the "Battle of Fort Ritz" lasted only seven minutes. Armed protestors and hotel invaders met 100 armed former Special Forces personal protection security soldiers. It was a one-sided altercation and the news spread fast through Chicago to leave the Ritz Carlton alone.

CHAPTER 16

MEGs
(ZERO+219 DAYS)

RICHMOND, KENTUCKY – NOVEMBER 22ND:
The largest manufacturing facility in the nation of MEGs (Tucker's Discovery) was in beautiful bluegrass horse country. Though the gray snow and gray skies dampened its beauty slightly, it was still truly God's country.

The manufacturing plant was already working multiple shifts to increase its capacity. Industrial engineers and logistics experts were trying to come up with operating methods, automation improvements, quality control activities, and supply chain refinements to increase production by 20% even before the on-going plant expansion was complete.

The plant managers, operators, and family all heard the president's news conference and learned that lives were actually at stake based on the work they performed -- that a production volume increase was critical. The plant manager was reviewing computer aided design blueprints when he was paged over the loudspeaker by his secretary.

They had a practice that when she announced that he had an incoming call over the intercom or the shop loud speaker, then it was code red. Code red meant it was his boss, Charles Washington, the CEO of Charleston Energy Holdings (CEH), the parent company.

The plant manager was expecting the call and the pressure Charles was about to apply. Charles could be quite persuasive. The well-dressed, imposing, sophisticated-looking African-American at 6 feet 2 inches and 235 pounds was handsome and muscular, with salt & pepper hair. His personality matched his former position as an all-American linebacker from Mississippi State University.

But the skype call was nothing like the plant manager expected. "Are you sitting down?" opened the CEO. The plant manager sat down. "Our supply of neodymium has just dried up. The California plant that provides us the rare earth metal has just been bombed by the same terrorist organization that claimed responsibility for the Vancouver and Caribou acts of terrorism. It appears that our supplier is likely to be down for eighteen months before they can restart production."

The plant manager said, "Are the Chinese likely to help out?"

"As you know, even though the People's Republic of China produces over 90% of the world's rare earth metals, they are using every ounce of neodymium internally and have no excess capacity. It is possible that President Allen can negotiate something, but it is unlikely to meet our demand."

"How much inventory do you have in Richmond?"

"About two weeks' worth, at present production levels."

Charles Washington was noticeably upset and said, "Well, that's more than most of the rest of the plants around the country have on site. I'll get a message to President Allen somehow and get back to you."

The heavy concentration of ash in the contaminated atmosphere made cell phone and satellite phone connections unreliable. After multiple tries, a frustrated Charles Washington reached Stephen Sanders, CEO of ENTROPY. Sanders was working out of his home office in Exeter, New Hampshire, when he picked up the phone without paying attention to who the caller ID. "Yes, this is Stephen Sanders."

"Stephen, this is Charles Washington, Charleston Energy Holdings; do you have a moment?"

"Of course, Charles, I've been expecting your call ever since I heard on the news that your neodymium supplier's production plant was sabotaged. How can I help you?"

"Do you know how to reach Tucker and Maya? I think I need their help. And do you have access to the president in any way? Can you get a message to him from me?"

Stephen Sanders said, "I have no idea where Tucker and Maya reside, but I do have a way to reach them. What message would you like me to convey to the Cherokees?"

Charles said, "I need a neodymium substitute."

Sanders said, "Good luck with that. What message do you want to get to the president?"

Charles Washington said, "If the *Organization for Environmental Justice* is responsible for the destruction of our nation's only rare earth metal production facility, then we have to assume one of its other targets is a MEG production plant. We need protection; I'm thinking the National Guard. The president might be able to persuade governors to deploy them; I don't have that kind of influence."

THREE HOURS LATER -- Charles Washington was on the phone with his 'K' Street lobbyist trying to garner support for utilizing U.S. government stockpiled neodymium when his secretary buzzed him that there was another call which he might want to take. He apologized to his lobbyist and took the other call.

"Mr. Washington, I am calling from Australia. I am the CEO of the largest supplier of rare earth metals in Australia and the third largest supplier in the world. Apparently, the President of the United States and the President of Australia had a joint conference call with a Mr. and Mrs. Cherokee, the famous discoverers of the MEG technology which you manufacture. I have been strongly encouraged by our president to supply you with as much neodymium as possible. I will have to break existing contracts to support this request for the metal, but I have never been contacted by my president before. It must be urgent. So I'm here to help."

Charles said, "This is wonderful, and thank you. However, I strongly recommend that you call your president back and ask for physical protection."

CHAPTER 17

THANKSGIVING
(ZERO+222 DAYS)

CHICAGO, ILLINOIS – NOVEMBER 25TH:
Electric power had been out in Chicago for six days
running. Facilities with emergency generators were
scrambling for fuel. The Ritz Carlton guests had also
helped secure fuel for their backup power. It was
Thanksgiving, and most Chicagoans didn't feel the love.
But Dr. Li, Maya's sister Suzanne, Tank and Jolene made
the most of it. They had food, power and heat -- what else
could they ask for?

Powers, Lucas and the other hundred or so personal
protection agents attending the conference remained in
what was now referred to as Fort Ritz. The manager of
Fort Ritz requested that Powers come to his suite. Powers
could have declined, but it's not like he had much else
to do.

Powers knocked on the door of the manager's suite.
The door opened and the manager invited him in. Inside
were three men who might just as well have had neon

signs on them -- they were Feds. The agent-in-charge for the Chicago field office held out his badge and introduced himself as Vinny DeLuca. Vinny DeLuca was a never-been-married 38 year old, 5 foot, 11 inch tall, 220 pound hawk-nosed Caucasian with an unpleasant disposition. Vinny looked directly at the Ritz manager with malice -- the manager excused himself and exited his own suite.

With an edge of sarcasm in his voice, Vinny said to Powers, "You and your boss have quite a reputation. You are well thought of by the Director of the FBI. He asked me to contact you directly." Powers was a little unsure where this was going, so he remained silent waiting for the other shoe to drop. Vinny continued, "You might wonder why the lights are still off in Chicago."

Powers said, "I assume because Exelon can't fix whatever is wrong."

Vinny continued, "My guess is that even a well-connected guy like you might not have been informed about why the lights are off. What exactly caused the power failure? Was an electrical transformer blown up? Did a power line come down? Did a power plant overload the grid? What's your theory, Powers?"

"My theory is that a terrorist organization blew something up."

"You'd be half right. A terrorist caused the power failure and even took credit; it's the same organization that took credit for Vancouver, Caribou and the rare earth metal plant in California. No, the terrorist used a computer as his tool. And every time Exelon tries to bring the power back up, the cyberterrorist takes the grid back down."

"Agent DeLuca, I think there is a misunderstanding. I have no cybersecurity skills. I'm old school. But there might be some other guys here at the Ritz who can help."

Vinny smiled a knowing smile. "What I need is some old school help. The FBI is constrained by all sorts of rules. We don't have the interrogating freedom which a private company might have. The terrorists who are keeping the lights off in Chicago are freezing God knows how many innocent people to death here. We know exactly where the cyber-attacks are generated. If we take them into custody, we are unlikely to be as persuasive as, say, a *White Knight* might be. I understand that you and Tank Alvarez can be quite persuasive. You have a reputation of gathering information in a timely fashion."

"You want us to apprehend and interrogate on your behalf."

"Oh, no; not on our behalf -- we'll show up after the fact."

"What's the plan?" asked Powers

Vinny smiled; the hook was firmly planted.

CHAPTER 18

THE SMARTEST PERSON IN THE WORLD (ZERO+222 DAYS)

ZION, ILLINOIS – NOVEMBER 25TH: "It's not my fault; I was born this way." He wondered why God made him this way. "Does God have a purpose for me?" He did not pretend to be religious, but he liked to think that maybe God made him the way he was for a reason. This idea reinforced his rationalization for doing what he did. "Why did God make Joseph Stalin, Pol Pot, Adolph Hitler, or Mao Tse Tung with their psychopathic or sociopathic disorders?" He had given that question a lot of thought when he was a guest at one of the nation's highest security hospitals for the criminally insane. In total, the four most famous mass murderers had killed more than 90 million people. He theorized that God needed mass murderers to "thin the herd." Man "thinned the herd" when the deer population got too high. He liked to think that his enjoyment in killing people had a purpose. There were over seven billion people on earth, and populations were still growing. "I'm here to thin the herd."

He viewed himself as a sportsman, not much different from a fisherman or a hunter. Sportsmen loved applying tactics to attract bass and the thrill of pulling the fish in. Some fishermen actually ate their catch, but it's wasn't why they fished; they fished for the enjoyment of outsmarting the fish. Most hunters enjoyed the kill; they didn't hunt because they needed the food. He was not that different from hunters and fishermen, except he enjoyed killing *people*.

He truly enjoyed the concept of mass murder; he enjoyed the planning, the attention to details and the thrill of victory. He enjoyed the hunt and he enjoyed getting away with it. He planned to kill more people than Joseph Stalin, Adolph Hitler, Mao Tse Tung and Pol Pot combined, without anyone knowing his name.

Zion, Illinois used to be the site of a large nuclear plant. Lots of operator training services for the nuclear plant were conducted in Zion. Nuclear power plant control room operators got their training on a simulator provided to the utility by Computer Simulation, Inc. Later, the nuclear plant was converted to a fossil fuel greenhouse-gas-generation power plant -- go figure. But the old control room simulator was still operable. It made a perfect site for a cyber-terrorist, for him, the smartest person in the world.

But the smartest person in the world had left a cyber-footprint. He was surrounded by the entire *White Knight* contingent. Tank casually walked in the front door. The terrorist knew immediately that he had been caught. Tank said, "The heat signatures say you are here alone. Where are the rest of your compatriots?"

The cyber terrorist said, "Don't you need to Mirandize me?"

"Nope." About that time the rest of the team came in the building in full battle gear, holding extremely intimidating weapons.

CHAPTER 19

TANK INTERROGATES
[ZERO+223]

CHICAGO, ILLINOIS – NOVEMBER 26TH:
Tank asked the *White Knight* team to return to Dr.
Li's penthouse. He didn't want any witnesses to his
interrogation technique. Special agent DeLuca didn't
want any of his agents within miles of the place. The
former tool shop in the abandoned metal fabrication plant
made a great place to conduct an interview. Tank moved
a kerosene heater into the small 15 foot x 18 foot room
in order to keep the temperature tolerable. A couple of
Coleman lanterns came in handy, but he didn't need too
much light for the discussion.

The unknown person in Tank's custody was almost
charming. He was hard to be angry with, and hard to
feel animosity toward. But Tank's instincts were almost
always on the mark. He knew in his gut that this guy was
guilty of more than the cyber-attacks. He wasn't exactly
sure about this guy's role in all the energy infrastructure
terrorism, but Tank was sure that he had an important
role.

The guy was small, roughly 5 feet 7 inches tall, weighing 160 pounds. Tank, at 6 feet 7 inches tall and 295 pounds was not worried about any aggressive action the guy might take. But Tank could tell by looking in the guy's eyes that his mind was formulating a plan, that he was calculating, strategizing, observing, and assessing the risks of potential actions.

So, Tank loosely tied him to a chair with duct tape wrapped around his chest. Tank briefly went outside the tool room and brought back a Samsonite case with equipment inside. He opened the case while making eye contact with the "alleged criminal." Beads of perspiration started to form on the small man's face. Tank pulled out a FLEX-BAMMER portable gas powered nail gun. Without hesitation or expression, Tank placed the gun on the man's right foot and drove a nail through his shoe and foot into the tool room's wooden floor.

The man screamed for 45 seconds, non-stop. When he finally regained some composure, he said, "Why? Why in the world would you do this to me? You're a monster!"

"You are not the first to call me a monster. I've been called worse. A lot worse. But I'm just a harmless little friend, here to make your acquaintance. The paradox is that when one monster battles another monster, which monster will win?"

The prisoner asked, "Why are you referring to *me* as a monster? I'm not the one who just nailed an innocent person's foot to the floor."

Tank said, "It is an interrogation technique to first demonstrate that I will follow through with my threat. Now you know that if I threaten to nail your other foot to the floor, I'll do it. You believe me now, don't you?"

The suspect remained silent.

"As you have no doubt observed, I am not constrained with your Miranda rights or 'rules of engagement.' And since I am a quote "monster," you know that I will follow through with my threats to torture you if you don't answer my questions honestly. Let's start with a simple question. What is your name and social security number?"

Without hesitation, the prisoner said, "Robert Grainger, 121-77-5159."

Tank pulled out his cell phone and made a call to Jolene and Powers who were on standby. Tank gave them the information and asked them to check it out while he continued the interview.

"OK, Robert, you're off on the right foot, pun intended." It was difficult for Tank not to smile at his own joke but he needed to keep his game face on. "Next question, who are you working for?"

"I am self-employed, a consultant; I work when and where I can find it."

Tank asked, "What kind of consulting work?"

"I am an Information Technology consultant and provide computer forensic services."

"OK, I don't know exactly what that means, but I get the general idea. But what I don't understand is why an IT guy is attacking energy sources and freezing innocent people to death. What kind of monster does that?"

"I'm the innocent person here; I have done no such thing. You're torturing the wrong person."

Tank looked this guy in the eye, stared in silence for maybe two minutes, until his cell phone rang. Tank answered, "Yo."

Jolene said, "The social security number checks out, matches the name, Robert Grainger, last address 750 South State Street, Elgin, Illinois. Tank, that is the address for the Elgin Mental Health Center for the criminally insane. It is the last address for Robert Grainger because Grainger died there, brutally murdered."

Tank looked in the direction of his prisoner; they made eye contact, and a chill went up Tank's spine. There was no fear in the prisoner's eyes, even though he knew that he had just been found out and he was tied to a chair with his foot nailed to the floor. Tank took a photo of the perpetrator with his cell phone and forwarded it to Jolene. Tank picked up the FLEX-BAMMER and started to place the nail gun over the prisoner's left foot.

"Stop. I'll talk. There is an abandoned iron mine in Soudan, Minnesota. It was converted into an underground laboratory operated by the University of Minnesota. One thing about being a half mile underground is that the temperature never drops below 55 degrees Fahrenheit. You'll find that the leaders of the *Society for Environmental Justice* have taken over the lab."

Tank pulled out his cell phone again, and related to Powers the information he'd extracted from the prisoner.

Powers said, "Vinny is patched into this call and he already has Blackhawks scrambling. The FBI invited us to join the bust."

Tank said, "Go, but two of you need to stay and protect Dr. Li"

"Roger that."

Lucas and Jolene stayed to protect Dr. Li while Powers and the rest of the team jumped in the FBI Blackhawk helicopters and headed to Soudan, Minnesota.

Tank turned back to the prisoner and decided to continue the interrogation. Tank asked, "What is the mission of the *Society for Environmental Justice*? What purpose does it serve to freeze seniors, children, the homeless, and the weak to death?"

Tank picked up the FLEX-BAMMER and started to place the nail gun over the prisoner's left foot again.

When he regained consciousness, Tank was in excruciating pain, lying flat on his back with his knees up, arms stretched out in a crucified configuration, with both feet and both hands nailed to the floor.

CHAPTER 20

DISINFORMATION
(ZERO+223 DAYS)

SOUDAN, MINNESOTA – NOVEMBER 26TH:
Above ground, late at night, it is scary-silent in Soudan.
The unincorporated town with a population of only 446 is
located adjacent to the Soudan Underground Mine State
Park, but far enough away to be undisturbed by anything
that happens there. There is virtually no light pollution,
and at these extremely cold temperatures, there is little
water vapor in the air, only ash. The artic-like cold had
silenced all flying insects, and the 12,000 hibernating
little brown bats that call the mine home, as well -- until
the sound of rotating blades cracked the peace. The closer
the Blackhawk helicopters come to Soudan, the louder
the shock wave.

Located a half mile below the surface is a University
of Minnesota research laboratory where Dark Matter
research is conducted. The intrusion of noise on the
surface doesn't penetrate down to the lab. Unless you
are a bat, the only way into the laboratory is a wire cage
elevator.

University of Minnesota physics professor Dr. Carl Volpe runs the lab. At 10:15 PM, he is the only person still in the lab and working. He will spend the night on his cot in his office. He doesn't want to leave the relative warmth of the mine lab and expose himself to the subzero weather. It hasn't been unusual for him to spend the night on his cot in his office. It is quiet below ground except for the classical music in Carl's iPod earpiece.

Carl felt a vibration from the elevator cage motor. He pulled his earpiece out and listened to the elevator climbing 2,500 feet to the surface. "What the hell," he mumbled. "I thought I locked the elevator in the down position." He put his clipboard down, where he was recording measurements, and walked over to the elevator. Sure enough, someone was here and was overriding the controls. Though a pacifist, he was pragmatic and kept a gun in his office for his protection at the urging of his late wife. The elevator stopped; it had reached the surface. After less than 15 seconds the motor started, which signaled that it was on its way back to the lab level. Someone was on their way back down. If someone he knew was coming to the lab this late at night Dr. Volpe would have received a land line call. He quickly checked his voice mail in case he missed a call while listening to Bach.

No voice mail; he was getting anxious.

He switched his gun's safety off, and held it behind his back. He hid himself behind a circulating water pump for protection.

After a short wait, the elevator reached the laboratory level.

"Jesus Christ" he said out loud, "I surrender!"

Five fully armed FBI agents in full combat gear emerged from the elevator. "Thank God that they had FBI jackets on," Dr. Volpe thought. "I might have foolishly fired my gun, otherwise."

Special Agent Vinny DeLuca yelled, "Put the gun down; get on the floor; spread your legs and keep your hands where I can see them." DeLuca proceeded to kick the gun out of reach of Dr. Volpe, now an FBI "person of interest."

The trembling 62 year old scientist did as he was told. He didn't utter a word. He did soil his pants.

"Where are the others?"

Dr. Volpe said, "I am here alone."

"What is your name?"

With a courage he didn't know he had, the scientist asked, "May I see your credentials?"

Special Agent DeLuca presented his credentials as the Dr. turned his head to see.

Volpe said, "I am the lab director. My credentials are in my office in the top drawer of my desk."

Vinny nodded to Powers. Powers entered the scientist's office, opened the drawer and found the lab director's wallet. Powers said, "Dr. Carl Volpe, Director of Soudan Labs for the University of Minnesota. Picture ID shows the guy we are questioning."

"Dr. Volpe, are you or have you ever been member of the *Society for Environmental Justice*? Do you know anyone who is a member of the *Society for Environmental Justice*?"

"No and No."

"Keep your hands where I can see them, and you can stand up now. Dr. Volpe, please give us a tour of the lab, every nook and cranny."

Feeling sure that the FBI agents would not violate his constitutional rights, he said, "You could have gotten an official tour during normal working hours and without forced entry."

DeLuca said, "Every nook and cranny."

45 minutes later, Special Agent DeLuca was satisfied that the lab was not occupied by the *Society for Environmental Justice* as the guy Tank interrogated claimed. Vinny said, "All right, I am convinced the lab is secure and that there is no evidence of forced occupation."

Powers said to Vinny, "That little son-of-a-bitch lied to us. I want to put a nail in the other foot myself."

"Dr. Volpe, do you have a hard-wired land line down here? I assume that cells don't work a half mile underground, surrounded by iron ore."

"Of course."

"Powers, we need to inform Tank that we have been duped. I wouldn't want to be the little guy when Tank hears about this."

Powers walked over to the hard-wired phone and called Tank's number. No answer. Powers called Jolene and asked, "Have you heard from Tank lately?"

"No. I haven't tried." She yelled over to Lucas and said, "While I'm on the line with Powers, would you call Tank?" Lucas called, with no success.

"I know that cell phones are unreliable due to the volcanic ash in the atmosphere, but you guys better head over and find out why Tank has broken communications protocol."

CHAPTER 21

STARVATION
(ZERO+223 DAYS)

UNGGI, DEMOCRATIC PEOPLES REPUBLIC OF KOREA – NOVEMBER 26ᵀᴴ: Twenty-two year old Soon-Bok's precious 3 year old daughter Mi-Hi was both starving to death and freezing to death in the town of Unggi. The little girl's fate was sealed the day she was born into the family, there in Unggi. You couldn't get any further away from the supreme leader and still be in North Korea than Unggi, as the town occupied the farthest point from Pyongyang.

It was not unusual for children to starve to death in Unggi, or for that matter anywhere outside the palace in Pyongyang. The people of North Korea suffered under a regime which allowed its citizens to live in conditions considered to be about the worst of all nations of the world, in terms of standard of living. Further, the workers in Unggi suffered a standard of living close to the worst, compared with all of North Korea.

Unggi's gray weather was predictably very cold for five months out of the year. The state-issued coats and uniforms only marginally managed to keep the peasants warm. But the cold was worse this year than during any other year in Soon-Bok's memory. The will to live among her relatives and friends had never been high, but it was worse this year. Older family members were intentionally giving their rationed food to their offspring, in the hope that they would die and their younger loved ones would live.

Of the 20,000 people who lived in Unggi, most either labored in a chemical plant or in the uranium mine, or were fishermen who caught codfish, pollock or herring in Unggi Bay. Some, however, were employed by the state to guard the border. Unggi was only 16 miles from the Russian border. Trade between Russia and North Korea primarily passed across the rail bridge over the Tumen River. Soon-Bok's father, Ha-Ung, had been a border guard there for 27 years, inspecting rail cars that ran across the bridge. Not once in all that time had he discovered immigrants trying to cross the border into North Korea. However, he frequently had discovered North Koreans trying to escape into Russia.

The Russians didn't want North Korean immigrants. If captured by the Russians, the North Korean peasants were returned. The Democratic People's Republic of Korea discouraged any attempt to escape their Stalinist paradise. If a worker was caught attempting to escape, the Government would incarcerate not only the escapee, but also the escapee's family, in a forced labor camp. Conditions and survival rates in forced labor camps were even worse than conditions in Unggi.

The people of North Korea were prohibited from contact with the outside world, to "protect them from contamination and corruption." There was virtually no electricity available to the people of Unggi, and therefore, no TV, no radio, and no internet. Anyone discovered to have smuggled a radio into the country received a death sentence. Thus, the peasants of Unggi were unaware of the reasons (the recent volcanic eruptions) that the weather had gotten unbearably cold. The colder weather translated to a shorter growing season for the state-run agriculture cooperatives. Rice and potato crops this year were pathetic. Most of the fish caught were shipped south under guard. This was a sordid return to the conditions of the 1990s, when famine took millions of proletariat lives.

Soon-Bok's husband, Mi-Hi's father, had worked in the chemical plant. An industrial accident mauled his right arm. The lack of antibiotics in Unggi was often fatal. The infection eventually spread into his internal organs. He died at the age of twenty-one.

Soon-Bok's father experienced an epiphany. Though he was no rocket scientist, he was logical enough to know the reason no one ever tried to illegally enter North Korea was because no outsider wanted to *be* in North Korea. It was a lifelong feeling, building for years, but this epiphany caused him to reach a breaking point. At 49 years of age, all the years insufferable, he felt an obligation to provide a better life for Soon-Bok and his granddaughter Mi-Hi. He had no idea if there was a better life on the other side of the rail bridge or not. But he knew that a tragic and horrific life was inevitable on this side of the bridge. As a senior guard, Soon-Bok's father, Ha-Ung had the only set of keys to a well-stocked Sonbong armory. The paranoid supreme leader wanted to make sure that if the Russians came across the border, the Unggi guards would be able to resist until the military arrived.

Ha-Ung knew that his life was wasted if he didn't take Soon-Bok on a journey across the bridge into Russia. Ha-Ung's epiphany came with a plan. He had never discussed his plan with anyone. But he didn't want his extended family to suffer because of his brazen act of selfishness. So he proceeded to go from family member to family member to secretly tell them what he was going to do. It was a potentially fatal flaw. One family member could turn them in and get his daughter and granddaughter killed.

No one turned them in. Rather, they all wanted to join in the escape. Twenty-seven family members of all ages followed Ha-Ung into a rail car headed northwest into Russia and eventually on to Vladivostok. At the border, Ha-Ung's uninformed fellow guards inspected the "empty" box car. The guards opened the doors to the boxcar to face twenty weapons, all pointed in their direction. The head of the guards looked in, smiled and said, "Good luck Ha-Ung. We'll pretend to shoot in your direction, so please don't return fire."

Shots were fired when the box car had penetrated a good half mile into Russian territory. The shots were fired at the Russian guards to keep them preoccupied and distracted so that they didn't inspect the boxcar that was now an escape vehicle for the downtrodden family of Ha-Ung. One round from the Unggi side accidentally killed a Russian guard. The Russians returned fire and three North Korean guards were injured. An international incident ensued, but the family of Ha-Ung continued their journey.

The lead North Korean guard called in for reinforcements, claiming that they were under attack from Russian soldiers. Within 30 minutes, Russian Sukhoi SU-35s from the military naval base in Vladivostok were strafing North Korean soldiers and armament in North Korean territory.

The supreme commander of North Korea called the President of Russia and warned him that if they didn't cease their aggression, he was going to launch a nuclear weapon into Vladivostok.

Vladivostok was Russia's most important port. It was the center of Russia's Pacific fleet and the primary service center of the Russian nuclear submarine fleet. There were a thousand more nuclear warheads in Vladivostok than the entire nuclear arsenal possessed by North Korea. Russian President Karloff did not hesitate. He called the commander of the Pacific Fleet and told him to arm warheads and program them to destroy the North Korean nuclear silos.

President Karloff knew that if he launched a nuclear attack on North Korea, Russia would feel the wrath of China. He wasn't concerned about the U.S. He knew that the war would be over before the U.S. would make a decision about what to do. Not so with the Chinese. So Karloff called the premier of China and advised him of the status of the confrontation.

The People's Republic of China didn't really care about North Korea. But they didn't want millions of refugees flooding the border. China mobilized 300,000 soldiers to enforce and empower border protection.

President Karloff ordered the Russian Air Force TU-95 Bear-H bombers to drop bunker busters on the North Korean nuclear silos from 36,000 feet. The bombers were escorted by MIG-29s with heat seeking missiles to protect them from anti-aircraft fire.

By the time the Ha-Ung family reached the Russian city of Kraskino, North Korea no longer had nuclear weapons. An irrational supreme leader ordered the entire North Korean military to the far northern corner to overrun Vladivostok. The North Korean Military was the largest military on earth, with over 9 million members -- nearly 40% of the entire population. Military leaders of North Korea's National Defense Commission warned the supreme leader of the consequences, and strongly urged a different strategy. But the supreme leader was convinced that Vladivostok couldn't resist the influx of 9 million soldiers and sailors. The supreme leader had experienced a brief dream about taking control of Russia's nuclear submarine fleet.

As the North Korean peasants observed the military abandoning the DMZ between North and South Korea to engage combat on the north corner, there was a rush of literally millions of North Korean civilians into South Korea.

In less than two days, an unintended consequence of the extremely cold weather was a change in geopolitics. The DMZ moved north to within 10 miles of Pyongyang. South Korea controlled the port of Wonsan. Russia claimed the provinces of North and South HamYong, including the warm water ports of Hamhung, Kimchoek and Changjin. Ha Ung's family became Russian citizens before they reached Vladivostok. And China protected its borders.

Many Korean families were reunited and many millions of North Koreans were saved from starvation.

A military coup ensued. The long reign of the Kim family ended. The first geopolitical impact of the extremely cold weather manifested itself.

The first; maybe not the last.

CHAPTER 22

RELISHES CAFÉ
(ZERO+227 DAYS)

WANAKA, NEW ZEALAND, NOVEMBER 30TH: Tucker, Maya and Star Cherokee (known to the locals as Brinton, Catherine and Star Gray) were enjoying a rare dinner at Relishes Café. Few people in Wanaka were willing to venture out into the freezing spring night and volcanic ash soup. At the dinner table, they were trying to come up with an acronym for each of the two research projects they were working on. They weren't worried about being overheard because the three tables surrounding theirs were occupied by *White Night* veterans assigned to maintain protective vigilance.

"Let's play a game while we're waiting for dinner to be served," said Tucker excitedly. "Let's come up with an acronym for the lotion or spray we're trying to develop that will help prevent people and wildlife (making eye contact with Star) from freezing to death. I wish we had played this game before the Defense Department dubbed our last discovery NEUREM -- for Neutrino Electricity Using Rare Earth Magnets. What a cumbersome acronym! I think it was smart of Charles Washington of CEH to rename NEUREM with the acronym Magnetic Electric Generator -- MEG." With a broad and playful smile he continued, "I'll start. How about 'Cold Resistant Application Protection' or CRAP? No one would forget that. A person could ask, 'Would you spray some CRAP on me?'"

Maya rolled her eyes, shook her head, but couldn't stop a smile.

Tucker continued, "Or we could call it 'Safe Heat Innovative Treatment' and a user could say he sprayed some….."

"Stop, I get it -- but we have a young lady here who doesn't need to hear this," Maya interjected.

Star spoke up and said much too loudly, "You mean you don't want me to hear Daddy say 'Shit'?" Maya hung her head, put her hands over her face and started to laugh uncontrollably. The six *White Knight* guys in close proximity began laughing and before too long the entire restaurant got caught up in the contagious laughter.

While laughing, Tucker asked, "How about 'Thermal Innovative Treatment' or 'TIT' or 'BM' for Bodyheat Maintenance?"

Maya said out loud, but to herself, "My husband is undeniably sick."

Tucker was on a roll and said, "Or we could call it the 'First ENTROPY Cold Escape Spray' or 'FECES.' I also like 'Applicator for Safe Survival' or ASS."

"Stop. Please stop. Your mind scares me sometimes."

"OK. But I have two serious acronyms to present. 'Safe Topical Applicator Reflective Spray' or STARS. However, my favorite serious acronym is Safe Topical Undercoat for Freaky Frigid temperatures or 'STUFF.' You know, spray some 'stuff' on yourself. Or on me."

"Let's take a vote." I see we have one for STUFF, one for CRAP and one for HAPPY. Maya, I'm surprised at you. Star, HAPPY wasn't one of the options"

Star said, "Well it should be, we need to put some Happy on them."

"OK. So we'll call it 'Heat Application Protection Innovation' or HAPI until a better idea pops up."

Their meals were brought out and they were enjoying every delicious bite. As they were eating, Tucker smiled and said, "Do you want to play the same acronym game for the discovery you have been tasked to perform for ENTROPY?"

Without hesitation Maya said, "No."

"So you don't want to know that 'CAN' is an acronym for 'Clean Air Now'?"

They ordered some more wine and "relished" their opportunity to be outside the Gray Compound.

CHAPTER 23

SITUATION ANALYSIS
(ZERO+223 DAYS)

CHICAGO, ILLINOIS, NOVEMBER 26TH: He lay flat on his back, arms fully extended, no bend in his elbows -- two nails in the palm of each of his hands. Despite his strength, Tank had no leverage with his arms fully extended. He knew that pain was a mind control game. Powers had taught Tank how to manage pain through denial. "Make your mind think of something else besides the pain you are currently in." Tank was thinking about his feet. His knees were up, so that his feet were flat on the wooden floor.

"Can I ease the nail out of one foot by rocking back and forth without pulling the head of the nail back through the foot?" he asked himself. He rocked left to right and then right to left. No dice.

"OK", he said to himself, "If I am going to lie here, I'm going to have to deal with the pain by thinking about anything but the pain. So, I'll take advantage of this downtime to analyze the situation I'm in."

"One, why don't I have any recollection about what happened? Analysis -- drugs must have been involved somehow.

"Two, why didn't he kill me? Analysis -- he derived greater personal satisfaction by having me regain consciousness with nails through my hands and feet than just by killing me. Plus, he expects to kill me later anyway.

"Three, how was the drug introduced. Analysis -- airborne.

"Four, why didn't the airborne chemical affect him? Analysis -- damn, I can't come up with anything.

"Five, the heater and lights are off; does he expect me to freeze to death? Analysis -- no, but he does expect me to suffer."

The cold hit him like a sledgehammer. Suddenly, he was shivering. Tank suspected that loss of blood through the nail penetrations was beginning to take its toll. He became nauseous and his head started to spin. He felt suddenly hot. Then he realized he needed to urinate. A shadow fell over his face in the dark; that is impossible but he felt it. Maybe it was a "sound" shadow. . And then, the shadow spoke.

"I have to leave now, but I did enjoy your suffering," said the cyber-attack terrorist. "We will meet again when I have more time to 'interrogate' you."

He paused for effect, "And Jolene."

The 'ghost' was gone, and hate filled Tank's heart.

Less than five minutes passed before Jolene entered the tool room with an LED flashlight to survey the room and Tank's condition. She threw herself onto Tank and said, "Oh my God, are you all right?"

Tank said with a panicked inflection, "He's here Jolene; don't let down your guard." Jolene sprang from Tank and immediately took a defensive position with weapon drawn, moving the flashlight, surveying everything. The room was too small to hide anything, so she locked the door from the inside and returned to Tank and said, "What happened? How did that little guy get the advantage on you?"

Tank said, "I have no recollection, but would you please get the nails out of my hands? Now I know some of the pain Christ must have felt, but I'm having a tough time forgiving anyone." Jolene tried to remove the nails without crushing Tank's hands but was unsuccessful.

Finally, Tank said, "This is a tool shed in an abandoned metal fabrication shop. Surely, there are crowbars around here somewhere."

Jolene said, "Yes, I'm sure there are -- and if I use one, it will crush every bone in your hand."

Tank asked, "And the option is.......?"

Each nail was embedded approximately one inch into the wooden floor, so when Jolene placed the end of a crowbar under the head of the nail and began to exert pressure onto Tank's left hand, Tank silently grimaced. The nail didn't move.

Jolene had been Tank's "significant other" for nearly ten years now. Jolene was just about as tough as is Tank. As a marine, Jolene Landrieu did two tours in Iraq. She, too, trained under Powers, but not at the same time as Tank. Tank and Jolene met at a private firing range where they hit it off, enjoying each other's company. Tank always had difficulty courting women because of his intimidating size; he didn't appear to be very gentle. Jolene did not like to fraternize with fellow marines, but they were the only people who "hit" on her. She intimidated most other men with her military bearing and her hand-to-hand combat training. Jolene worked hard not to be very feminine in outward appearance, to avoid unwanted sexually aggressive male marines; her hair was short; she wore no makeup, and her breasts were always restrained in a sports bra. That was the outward appearance; behind closed doors in the privacy of their bed, she was quite feminine and Tank was quite gentle. She loved Tank to death. She could joke with Tank without risk of hurting his feelings; in fact, she found Tank's self-deprecating humor endearing. Tank loved Jolene's smile and infectious laugh; it put the world in perspective. Jolene retired from the marines and joined *White Knights* as a personal security specialist. She now had to translate her love for Tank by hurting him -- not an easy concept to absorb.

She put her strength and weight to the crowbar, pivoting on a block of wood she had found, and ignored the pain in Tank's face. Tank eventually passed out in pain. When Jolene was through with the four nails in the palms of Tank's hands, she wiped the tears out of her eyes and took advantage of Tank's unconsciousness to remove the nails from Tank's feet. She called 911 but got no response -- apparently she was 95th in line.

There was no way to pick Tank up or move him to a hospital without help. He needed a tetanus shot and antibiotics. Maybe, even some blood. She called Lucas and asked for help. She called Powers and DeLuca and briefed them. The FBI forwarded a photo of the 'ghost' to the Chicago police. They energized the entire FBI field office and Chicago police force to apprehend this guy, the 'ghost.'

No one ever saw even the slightest sign of him -- the 'ghost' had earned his name once more.

Lucas and Jolene together were able to get a semi-conscious Tank into a vehicle to take him to Dr. Li's penthouse. The hospital ERs were in panic mode, so they decided to bandage and medicate Tank themselves until a professional could see him. As they carried him into the building lobby, they were surprised to see that there was no building security on hand. Lucas mumbled under his breath, "damn rent-a-cops." They caught the elevator to Dr. Li's apartment and yelled out for help to both Dr. Li and Maya's sister, Suzanne. There was no answer. They moved Tank into the bedroom to rest. When they were done, they found a note on the dining room table. It said,

"You're a day late and a dollar short."

CHAPTER 24

KIDNAPPED
(ZERO+223 DAYS)

CHICAGO, ILLINOIS – NOVEMBER 26TH:
An intelligent, sophisticated, refined, resourceful, and graceful Dr. Li -- Maya's mother -- lay on an odorous unsheeted twin mattress restrained and blindfolded, with duct tape over her mouth and eyes. On the floor not 15 feet from her was an intelligent, educated, less resourceful and equally frightened Suzanne Li -- also restrained and blindfolded with duct tape over her mouth and eyes, but lying on the filthy concrete floor. A wood fire was burning in the room to maintain roughly 50 degrees Fahrenheit; the trace smell of wood smoke lingered under their noses like Vick's Vapo-rub. Suzanne was tall and slender like her sister, Maya, and three years younger. She was nowhere near as stunning as her sister, but still pretty. The women did not know that they were in each other's company. It was silent in the room. The room smelled old and musty. Dr. Li figured that it had to be a basement.

A door to the room opened and someone walked in, straining while carrying something. A loud noise scared both the Dr. and Suzanne Li half to death, as though they had been shot, but the noise was the wacko who kidnapped them dropping wood scraps he had collected, to keep the fire going. You could hear him breaking furniture apart and throwing pieces onto the fire. Finally, he sat down on the floor in the space between Suzanne and Dr. Li.

He spoke, "So, my dear Ingrid, do you recognize my voice?"

Dr. Ingrid Li, a respected psychiatrist, thought long and hard about the thousands of patients she had treated over the years. She couldn't place the voice. She shook her head, "No."

"Good, because if you did recognize my voice I was going to have to kill you. I may kill you anyway, after you and your daughter here serve your purposes. Your daughter is here to make you talk. When she starts screaming in pain and begging to make it stop, you'll talk."

Dr. Li was as tough as she was sophisticated. She shook her head in the affirmative direction making sure he knew that she understood. The mellifluence with which he spoke and the obvious pleasure he exuded when he spoke of hurting Suzanne triggered her recognition synapses.

She knew who he was. "Oh, my God, let it be anyone but him," she silently prayed.

WANAKA, NEW ZEALAND – NOVEMBER 27TH: Maya's anger at just having been tested again by Tucker and *White Knight*'s trainer was being replaced with a smorgasbord of emotions which she was having trouble separating. She had just awakened from a nightmare and was surprised by Star who had been able to read Maya's thoughts even when she was in the middle of the nightmare; then, the two masked intruders broke into the study and opened fire. Maya responded to the drill perfectly, but was nonetheless upset by the timing and her perception that it was unnecessary. She said, "Tucker, I know you would not have put Star and me through this test and defensive response exercise without good reason. So, I'm patiently waiting for an explanation."

Tucker calmly approached Maya and extended his hand, palm up. She handed him the 9mm Beretta with blanks, grip out. Tucker turned and handed the automatic paint gun and Beretta to the *White Knight* trainer and asked him to leave. The grim and sad expression on Tucker's face coalesced all her emotions into anxiety; something really bad was happening.

"I received communication this morning from Tank. He's been seriously injured but that isn't what the communication was about. Your mother and your sister are missing and may have been kidnapped by the same guy who injured Tank. Anyone who can get the best of Tank is someone to be feared. Tank and the FBI think that the people who have your mother and sister are the same people who are responsible for the Chicago blackout and other acts of terrorism. As a precaution, we need to assume that they are also after you and Star."

For a good 30 seconds, Maya said nothing, as tears ran down her cheeks. Finally, she asked, "What in the world would the terrorist want with Suzanne and Mom? What is the connection? And where were Powers, Tank, Jolene, and all those *White Knights* in Chicago when this psycho abducted Mom and Sis?"

"I don't know, sweetheart," said Tucker as gently and understandingly as possible, "but the FBI is all over it and investigating all possible motives for the kidnappings."

Maya said emphatically, "It is time we shed our witness protection persona and go home. I'm not going to stay here and 'hope' that someone else saves my mother and sister." Maya stood up and said, "I'm out of here."

CHAPTER 25

DETERIORATING CONDITIONS (ZERO+227 DAYS)

WASHINGTON, DC – NOVEMBER 30TH: A prime-time news conference was requested by President Winston Allen. The press room in the White House was packed, "standing room only," with nervous activity and fearful expressions. President Allen shuffled to the podium without his usual confident gait, wearing a heavy winter suit. His eyes were swollen and dark from evident exhaustion. Lines were visible on his face which was not there when he was last seen by the public. He had not rehearsed the briefing he was about to give.

He opened with, "My fellow Americans, I said a silent prayer for all the people of the earth who are suffering as a result of this extraordinarily harsh weather. I stand before you and vow to use all of the substantial resources at my disposal to mitigate the impact on you, and to apprehend the terrorists who are multiplying your suffering for reasons difficult to understand.

"It is obvious to all of us that the Chicago blackout, the destruction of the Caribou Dam, the bombing of the California plant, and the acts of terrorism in Vancouver are coordinated and related. The FBI, the Department of Homeland Security, and our civilian intelligence agencies are working 24 hours a day and seven days a week to apprehend and bring the terrorist perpetrators to justice.

"To help all citizens of our nation and the world endure the frigid weather, this administration reached out to the current administration of New Zealand to develop a method of allowing all of you to deal with the brutal elements. I've invited New Zealand Prime Minister Samuel Snyder to share some rare good news with you."

The Prime Minister of New Zealand was unknown to the world. It is estimated that a billion people worldwide were listening to what the President of the United States was going to do about the current crisis. This was an extremely fortuitous opportunity for the nation-state of New Zealand.

Prime Minister Snyder moved to the podium and began: "New Zealand has not been immune from the extremely cold weather. New Zealand's southern islands are as close to the South Pole as Nova Scotia, Canada is to the North Pole. The citizens of New Zealand are as vulnerable to continued frigid weather as Canadians or citizens in the northern United States.

"New Zealand also has a territory, Ross Island, in Antarctica where research is conducted. American, Canadian, British, and United Nations scientists have been trapped in weather that reached minus 77 degrees Fahrenheit." Snyder paused for effect.

"Under the leadership of President Allen, the United States initiated a program to develop a lotion or spray that can be applied to the body, much like lotion or spray used for sunburn protection, but with the single purpose of keeping heat from escaping from the human body.

The brave scientists stranded on Ross Island have performed human studies that have now proven the effectiveness of this new product."

"Thank you, Prime Minister Snyder," said U.S. President Winston Allen, as he reassumed the position at the podium. Looking directly into the camera, President Allen said, "The U.S. is mobilizing its enormous manufacturing infrastructure to manufacture the spray and lotion in very large quantities so that you will have access to the material as soon as possible.

"Also, as you may have discerned, the production of MEGs was seriously curtailed by the terrorist attack on the California supplier of the element neodymium, used in magnets. Fortunately, the U.S. Government has been stockpiling neodymium for military applications. I have issued an executive order to make our neodymium stockpile available to facilitate the accelerated production of MEGs for the domestic production of electricity without fuel. Additionally, the President of Australia has authorized the re-direction of their neodymium production to support additional manufacturing of MEGs.

"With the support of Congress, I have instructed the national laboratories of the United States to work with the scientific experts in New Zealand to develop technology to accelerate the precipitation of the dust released by the Merapi and Nyiragongo eruptions. They will devote every effort so that the earth can once again receive the full warmth of the sun, and to clear the air so that we can breathe without masks. This will also contribute to the restoration of wireless technology which depends on satellites and cell phone towers.

"The Governor of Illinois has, with my blessing, called on the National Guard to patrol the streets of Chicago. We understand the anger, fear, and disappointment Chicagoans are feeling -- you're cold, hungry and frustrated. We get it, and we're doing everything we can to end the blackout and return full electric power to your homes and businesses."

President Allen empathetically connected with his audience. His face was distraught. A genuine and natural tear rolled down one cheek. He said, "The greatest minds in the world are focused on solving our tragic weather situation. You are in the best place in the world to survive the onslaught of both severe cold weather and terrorism. And I know that you, that *we*, are strong enough to make it through this difficult time."

The president paused for a few seconds.

"The brutal rogue nation of North Korea was not operating in the best interests of the people of North Korea. The Stalinist government operated in the best interest of the Kim family. The already sad and pathetic conditions in North Korea had worsened as a result of the tragically frigid weather. Starvation was inevitable for thousands if not millions.

"The United States' best interest and maybe the best interest of the world was to observe the conflict and not take a boots-on-the-ground approach. We lost enough brave Americans during the Korean conflict in the early 1950's. We didn't need to lose more.

"What we are doing is providing humanitarian aid to help South Korea manage the overwhelming influx of millions of North Korean refugees. The lesson learned here is that nations which do not take care of their citizens will be faced with anarchy. The government of the United States will take care of its citizens. God bless you all … and God bless America."

CHAPTER 26

JET STREAM
(ZERO+227 DAYS)

ATLANTA, GEORGIA – NOVEMBER 30TH:
Polar jet streams generally meander at elevations between 23,000 to 39,000 feet above sea level. Wind speeds can run between 50 and 250 miles per hour. The debris in the atmosphere resulting from the volcanic eruptions modified solar heating of the atmosphere, which translated into a drop in jet stream elevation from 23,000 feet to 10,000 feet. Normal wind velocities at the earth's surface of 5-8 miles per hour were increased to 21 to 29 miles per hour. Wind chill factors increased. If the temperature was 10 degrees Fahrenheit, a 5 mph wind made it feel like 1 degree. The drop in the polar jet stream increased a 5 mph wind to a 30 mph wind. At that wind speed, a 10 degree Fahrenheit temperature condition felt like minus 12 degrees.

The Director of the National Weather Service called the president to advise him about these sustained trends.

Hearing this news at his desk, President Allen said to his secretary, still on the line, "We just can't catch a break. Please get General LaSalle in here."

Soon after his request, Brigadier General Ray LaSalle and the Chairman of the Joint Chiefs of Staff, Admiral Maxx Longstaff, sat before the President of the United States in the Oval Office, with the Secretary of Defense, Jane Bolton.

"OK," said President Allen, "please give me your assessment of the impact of the jet stream dropping in elevation. What does your algorithm tell us?" Ray LaSalle was unhappy about continually being the bearer of bad news, but he opened with, "More people will freeze to death, and it will take even longer for the ash to settle out of the atmosphere. In other words, the wind chill effect will be worse and it will last longer."

"Wonderful," said POTUS sarcastically, "and your recommendations?"

"Ask Congress to apply federal funds to help electric utilities reopen formerly closed coal fired power plants." Ray waited for a response but got none. "Ask Congress to apply federal funds to help electric utilities protect the grid by guarding the most critical substations and transformers. Both of these recommendations would help employ the unemployed." Again, he waited for a response but got none. "Offer Japan access to the MEG technology before they act out of desperation and do something drastic." This time, Ray got a response.

POTUS looked at Chairman Longstaff and SecDef Bolton and asked, "Any thoughts on that subject?"

Chairman Longstaff said, "They need much more than electricity, but it may stave off their desperation in the short-term."

SecDef Bolton said, "We should sell them the technology or get something in return."

President Allen looked at General LaSalle and asked, "Anything else?"

"Pray for Global Warming."

CHAPTER 27

REVERSE IMMIGRATION
(ZERO+227 DAYS)

NOGALES, ARIZONA – NOVEMBER 30TH:
Jack and Karen Graham were attending a computer recycling conference in Tucson, Arizona. From Tucson, the Mexican border was a short but easy drive. The normally clear blue skies over the desert contained a disappointing grayish-brown volcanic ash haze that could literally be tasted. They were looking forward to the warm, dry desert weather after months of even more dreary overcast and miserable weather in Endicott, NY. But like the rest of the world, instead of its average 74 degrees Fahrenheit, Tucson was 25 degrees below normal. Still, it was better than the subzero weather they were experiencing at home.

Karen convinced Jack that they should take advantage of their proximity to Mexico and have dinner on the Mexican side of Nogales where they could enjoy being serenaded by a Mariachi band. Karen further convinced Jack that they should experience Mexico stoned.

About 15 miles south of Tucson where the Saguaros dominated the landscape, Karen lit up a joint and shared it with Jack. A little while later, after the marijuana achieved its maximum effect on Karen, she became unbearably horny and began fondling Jack as he tried to concentrate on an unexpectedly high volume of traffic. She fully undressed in the car and aggressively went down on Jack as he continued to drive. Jack was trying to make it to the next exit; not an easy feat. But he made it, pulled over into the desert and made passionate love with his wife. As the pot was passing its peak effect, they laughed uncontrollably at what they had just done. After redressing, they searched the car for a snack. They found some chips and snacked and remembered silly jokes for a few minutes, trying to sober up a little. Then, Jack started the car to get back on the interstate and head out, looking forward to the dinner with the serenading Mariachi band. The wheels spun in the sand. He put it into reverse, then forward, then reverse. Jack could get no traction.

He got out of the car to assess his options. His options were limited. He had no room to back out of their spot under an old piñon tree. Just then, a family of five appeared out of nowhere. A hard-looking migrant worker said, "Can we help you, señor?"

Jack, still not fully recovered from the influence of pot, said, "Maybe you'll have more luck getting this rental car out of the soft sand than me." Jack gestured that the man could take his place in the driver's seat. The family patriarch hit Jack as hard as he could, with a set of brass knuckles. Jack hit the sand like a sack of potatoes. The matriarch merely stared into Karen's eyes. There was no question about the meaning of the look: "The same will happen to you if you resist."

Karen slid out of the car and sashayed over to her fallen husband. Jack's pulse was strong; blood was oozing out of a cut below his left eye, but despite remaining unconscious, she was sure that he would be all right. Karen removed the cell phone hidden in her back pocket and dialed 911. Jack and Karen would talk about the adventure for the rest of their lives.

The Mexican family had gotten into the Grahams' rental car, and after some rocking back and forth, had finally gotten traction and driven away. They drove another 20 miles until traffic forced them to slow down to a crawl. Forty minutes later, they observed a sign that displayed the distance to the border, another 22 miles. The migrant worker family was not alone in trying to re-enter Mexico. The horrible cold weather and ash had ruined the growing season in California. It was impossible to find a job, and difficult to survive legally. They were cold, sick, hungry and disillusioned. They were moving south to warmer weather. They were going home.

CHAPTER 28

BEHAVORIAL FORENSICS
(ZERO+227 DAYS)

QUANTICO, VIRGINIA- NOVEMBER 30TH**:**
Special Agent Magnus Glass received encrypted
correspondence from Special Agent Vinny DeLuca
of the Chicago Field Office. It was a photo. The text
that accompanied the photo said simply "the terrorist."
Magnus maintained the FBI database on the criminally
insane and was a specialist on tracking their whereabouts.
He kept the pressure on the field offices to re-capture
escapees. He was investigating the current residents of
the Elgin Mental Health Center when the photo arrived.

He cross-referenced the photo with the center's
current and past occupants but did not get a hit. He
cross-referenced the photo with other criminally insane
hospitals in the region but did not get a hit. He then
initiated a global facial recognition search. This could
take hours. While the computer was searching for a
match to the photo, he continued a second task -- that of
investigating all the registered members of the *Society for*

Environmental Justice, to correlate membership with any ties to the criminally insane.

The over-educated Agent Glass got started on his career late in life. He was a perpetual student because he never fully understood what he wanted to be when he grew up. He first got a liberal arts degree from Lehigh. He got a master's degree in mathematics from the University of Virginia. He went on to get a law degree from UVA. After getting his law degree, he went back to school at William & Mary to get a degree in psychology and another degree in computer science. Finally, he secured a position with the FBI in a niche that suited his attention deficit malady. At 35 years old, he finally grew up. His passion for his job was a joy to watch.

He heard a ping. He looked over to find that the search for a match to the photo was complete. The photo matched the name of a Robert Grainger, a psychopath who enjoyed observing victims' fear of poisonous snakes. He murdered 18 people on separate occasions while videotaping their horrid demise. Grainger was reported to have watched the graphic videotapes over and over.

But Robert Grainger was murdered two years ago at Elgin Mental Health Center.

Agent Glass called Vinny DeLuca and shared with him what he had found. "Listen, Glass; don't you think a guy smart enough to hack into Exelon's network and keep Chicago's lights out might be smart enough to switch his photo with a deceased person? Hell, on Election Day he probably votes a bunch of times. Go back through Elgin's records and see if you can find any kind of an anomaly. Also, see if there is a connection between anyone at Elgin and the *Society for Environmental Justice*.

"While you're at it, see if there is some kind of connection between any patient at Elgin and Dr. Li. I'm going to subpoena Dr. Li's patient history."

CHAPTER 29

SURVIVAL
(ZERO+228 DAYS)

SAPPORO, JAPAN – DECEMBER 1ST: Japan, the third largest economy in the world, is a nation of 127 million proud and hardworking people. Japan is also a nation with virtually no natural energy resources, and therefore is obliged to be the world's largest importer of coal and Liquefied Natural Gas (LNG). The imports are required to provide the energy to sustain Japan's economic engine. With the onset of unusually cold weather, Japan's need for energy had increased at a time when the worldwide demand for heating fuels made energy increasingly difficult to secure. The terrorist crisis in Vancouver didn't help, as Japan, Inc. was depending on energy imports from the Canadians and Americans. The editorial pages of most major newspapers in Japan suggested that the Vancouver act of terrorism was an attack on Japan as much as an attack on Canada. The Japanese social media were abuzz about conspiracy theories supporting that position.

The Yamada family had lived all of their lives in Hokkaido, on the northern and traditionally the coldest-weather island of Japan. The harsh winters toughened the island residents, who were thus more prepared to deal with the unusually frigid weather. The local government of Hokkaido, located in Sapporo, had been able to keep the energy flowing to the local fuel distributors in the community so that all its citizens were able to stay relatively warm -- until now.

Inventory in Sapporo's fuel storage tanks was at an all-time low, and the island was unable to beg, borrow or steal fuel on the open market. The Hokkaido Electric Power Company cut back production of electricity as its stockpile of coal rapidly diminished. The rationing of energy and institution of rolling blackouts was now inevitable.

The cold weather, coupled with the ash contamination, also seriously diminished the nation's supply of rice. The ability of the nation of Japan to import rice from other Southeast Asian nations was seriously impacted due to the worldwide reduced production of rice and the competition, mostly from China, for the limited rice being grown. The seafood availability had been maintained, but with other food sources weakened, the demand for fish products was stressing the fishing industry.

Silver-haired Akio Yamada was honored to be a member of the House of Councillors within Japan's version of Congress, the Diet. His seniority within the Diet gave him access to the Prime Minister of Japan. But the Prime Minister was not answering the phone. This was disconcerting and reflected the seriousness of the situation. This was a sign; Yamada-san called his brother, Hiroshi, in Tokyo.

"It is time, my brother, to finally put 'Operation Fugu,' into action, the senior Akio said in a monotone voice, showing no emotion. "We need to assemble the leadership in Oarai within five days. I'll inform all members here on Hokkaido. The other leaders need to do the same for their corresponding prefectures."

"Yes, Grand Master," said younger brother Hiroshi.

The Freemasons of Japan were as powerful in Japan as the Freemasons of the western world were glamorized to be. The most powerful people in the Japanese Diet, in Japan's largest corporations, in the Japanese National Guard, and in the Ministry of Agriculture, Forestry and Fisheries, were members of the Freemasons of Japan. Corporations like Mitsubishi, Toyota, Hitachi, Mitsui, Fujitsu, Toshiba, Kawasaki Heavy Industries and many other powerful, major Japanese entities were embedded with the Freemasons. Secrecy was paramount for members, and younger members were not trusted with information known to the senior leadership.

For the past nine years, the Freemasons of Japan had been preparing for the inevitable event -- that Japan would have to defend itself against foreign aggressors. In theory and by treaty, the United States had promised to defend Japan in return for Japan agreeing to never rearm itself and for payment to the U.S. Treasury for protection. About 10 years ago, it had become evident to the Japanese majority that the U.S. might not actually honor its commitments to protect its allies, including Japan, from foreign aggression as promised. Fear of an aggressive People's Republic of China (whose population still did not forgive Japan for its past sins) and an irrational and unpredictable North Korea with nuclear weapons, drove the senior and powerful elite in Japan to plan for a morally weak and unreliable friend in the United States.

Operation Fugu was launched in secret, with the blessing of the Prime Minister of Japan, nine years ago. Over that period, the powerful Freemasons of Japan, using both taxpayer and corporate funds, had assembled a shadow military. The Japanese Defense Minister, a high-ranking Freemason, secured taxpayer funding for two Aegis destroyers. What Japan lacked in numbers of military hardware, they made up for in strategic planning, tactical methodologies, and scientific genius.

The Freemasons of Japan secured propulsion technology from Australia that was incorporated into ships secretly manufactured at Kawasaki and Mitsubishi manufacturing plants.

The implementation of Operation Fugu would permanently alter the world balance of power. As Grand Master, Akio Yamada was often quoted, "The well-being of the Japanese people comes first. Everything else comes second."

The era of pacifism was over.

CHAPTER 30

WHERE'S DR. LI?
(ZERO+228 DAYS)

CHICAGO, ILLINOIS – DECEMBER 1ST: Tank was really hurting; both his feet and both his hands had become infected despite the heavy dose of antibiotics he was taking. He remained in Dr. Li's penthouse where, at least, there was electricity -- one of the very few places in the Chicago metropolitan area. Jolene was playing nurse to Tank and actually enjoying taking care of him. But Tank was in a foul mood -- as long as his wounds were raw, he couldn't operate on all cylinders, and therefore would be unable to help track down Suzanne and Dr. Li. Tank felt responsible for their kidnapping. If he hadn't allowed the prisoner to escape, Maya's mother and sister might not have been kidnapped. He felt like he let Maya and Tucker down. Tank couldn't control his anger about getting outsmarted and beat by some untrained guy 150 pounds lighter than him; how embarrassing.

His cell phone rang; he picked it up and said only, "Yo."

Vinny DeLuca said, "What, were you in the Navy or something?"

"I hope you're calling with some good news."

"Well, the good news is that you are alive."

"Tell me something I *don't* know," Tank said impatiently.

"As you are painfully aware -- yeah, yeah; I know -- one second you're in control and the next thing you know, you are nailed to the floor. Tank, you inhaled a chemical, a spray, called FLPC3. It's an acronym for some unpronounceable compound. The chemical, in this spray, nearly instantly causes unconsciousness. It's a good thing you're a big bastard because anyone with a body weight under 250 pounds would have never awakened, considering the dose this guy released.

"It was developed by the Defense Advanced Research Project Agency -- DARPA -- for the purpose of making interrogated terrorists completely forget what they told us under advanced interrogation techniques. It is difficult to control the dosage, so the Army manufactured mini pressurized aerosol containers with a pre-set amount based on the body weight of the interviewee. To administer the aerosol, the interrogators would don gas masks before they sprayed it under the nose of the interrogated terrorist. The spray has to be released close to the target; otherwise, it just falls out of the air and becomes inert, within a minute.

Tank said, "So, all this guy had to do as I was bending over to nail his other foot to the floor was reach back and pull the mini aerosol out of his back pocket and hold his breath for a minute."

"Correct, but the real question is how did this 'ghost' or his organization get their hands on a top secret formula, or vials which are guarded by the military in a top secret facility?"

Tank said, "I don't think I'm going to like the answer to that question."

"Me either," said Vinny, "and at this point we are nowhere close to finding the answer."

Neither Vinny nor Tank wanted to talk any further. They were both thinking hard about what they should do next. Finally, Tank asked, "What are you not telling me, Special Agent DeLuca?" More silence. "Are you still there?"

"Yeah, yeah. OK, we think that the *Society for Environmental Justice* is being **set up** by whatever the real perpetrator organization is, for the dual purpose of distracting law enforcement and to exact vengeance on the **real** *Society for Environmental Justice.* So we're trying to narrow down the competing organizations which would hate the Society enough to put them under an FBI microscope. We think that the organization responsible for all the terrorism is much more insidious and that the jerk holding Dr. Li and Suzanne will not let them live. Time is of the essence, and we don't have a clue where to find this guy."

The smoke in the room was burning her eyes, even under a duct tape blindfold. The temperature was beginning to drop in the damp and odorous basement. With duct tape over her mouth, she was unable to tell the kidnapper that she needed to go to the bathroom. Suzanne Li, Maya's sister, had been formulating an escape plan. She had lain on the floor for 18 hours and could do nothing but plan. She hadn't heard any movement by him for hours. The diminishing smell of smoke and the temperature told her that the fire was starting to burn out and smolder. Still, no sound from him. Her mother was in the room and her first task was to free her mother; together, they might be able to overtake the guy. The temperature was dropping quickly, so she needed to do something soon -- but what? The plastic ties around her feet kept her ankles together. The plastic ties around her wrists, behind her back, were too tight; they hurt with the slightest movement of her arms. Duct tape was over her mouth and eyes. She was somehow tethered to the concrete block wall. She could move in a radius of only about three feet. She hadn't been fed or given water since she arrived. Suzanne concluded that it was his intent to starve them or freeze them to death after he got whatever information he needed from her mother.

"He knew my mother," she thought to herself. "So, he must have been a patient of hers. I've got to get Mother's gag off somehow. She may have some insight on him that would be useful."

Dr. Ingrid Li, Maya's and Suzanne's mother, was thinking hard, real hard, to remember all the personality disorders that the kidnapper possessed. The two things she remembered most about him were, first, how absolutely unremarkable looking he was. You would never guess this guy was the monster he is. When she testified in court against him as the expert psychiatrist on criminal sociopaths and psychopaths, he showed no expression at all -- no anger, no fear, no apprehension, no nothing.

The second thing she remembered was that he had the highest IQ on record at 198. A genius sociopath needs to be incarcerated forever. Dr. Li was afraid that he wanted revenge on her. "But what does his hatred for me have to do with the Chicago blackout and other terrorist acts his organization is inflicting? Where do they intersect? Oh, my God; I wonder if it has something to do with Maya and Tucker's Discovery."

CHAPTER 31

NUCLEAR WINTER
(ZERO+228 DAYS)

**THE PENTAGON, ARLINGTON, VIRGINIA –
DECEMBER 1ST:** The Chairman of the Joint Chiefs
of Staff, Admiral Maxx Longstaff, summoned General
Ray LaSalle to his office. This time, W3 escorted LaSalle
into the Chairman's secure office where they could have
a one-on-one discussion. The Chairman was much more
personable than one would expect from someone in his
lofty four-star position. He was small in stature but large
in presence; he commanded your respect the moment you
looked into his brilliant eyes. You'd swear they produced
light and sparkled.

"I called you here to educate me. My next meeting
with the Secretary of Defense may determine our
geopolitical path forward. The more I understand our
options, the more convincing an argument I might be able
to make, to do whatever is the right thing. I recall that 30
years ago, when we were seriously preparing for a nuclear
confrontation with the Soviet Union, that a scenario
dubbed 'Nuclear Winter' was considered. Are the scenario

impacts delineated in the old study of any value to our situation today? Are there any valuable lessons which we learned from the preparation for 'Nuclear Winter'?"

"Ah," said Ray LaSalle; "The good ole' days of the Cold War. The Nuclear Winter scenario was based on the assumption that a large-scale nuclear war could produce such conflagrations that smoke from nuclear detonations and burning forests would create debris and ash in the atmosphere similar to what we are currently experiencing from the volcanic eruptions. It was theorized 50 years ago that the smoke would absorb enough of the light from the sun that there could be serious and prolonged reductions in photosynthesis and temperatures over the northern hemisphere, resulting in a catastrophic agricultural failure.

"Carl Sagan was the most visible of the scenario investigators who, on the basis of quantitative modeling, concluded that a large-scale nuclear war would cause temperatures to drop an incredible 65° Fahrenheit, and remain below freezing for several months. Their work was heavily challenged, but provided the basis for a number of other publications which appeared bearing Sagan's name and the expression 'nuclear winter,' which they coined to describe the phenomenon. Some of the apocalyptic visions which arose included a claim that a major nuclear exchange would produce 'the greatest biological and physical disruption of the planet in its last 65 million years' -- a period which includes four great ice ages, -- and that the number of survivors would be reduced to a fraction of 1% of those now alive.

"Some argued that even if there were doubts about the phenomenon, it would be wise to base policy on the 'worst-case analysis.' That sounds familiar, doesn't it? Biologists said that if significant surface darkening occurred for many weeks, coupled with freezing land temperatures persisting for several months, that such a climatic catastrophe could cause the extinction of a major fraction of the plant and animal species on the Earth."

The Chairman asked, "Is that scenario possible here?"

"Yes, I think it is possible that there will be the extinction of some plant and animal species."

The Chairman asked, with penetrating eyes, "What do you think is our current worst-case scenario?"

General Ray LaSalle said, "We have run hundreds of scenarios with probability analysis and consequence assessments. A low probability scenario with an extremely high consequence is the scenario that NASA scientist Murray Vest presented to the Secretary of Energy and the National Security Advisor, where the earth may be entering a tilting and wobbling cycle and we're headed for the next ice age. If that is the case, sir, there is not much we can do about it except build underground complexes and grow mushrooms.

"If this historically cold weather continues for, let's say, more than another year, there will be mass starvation; the seas will be fished out; there will be war between nations over farm lands; there will be war over energy sources; the masses will migrate toward equatorial regions, and riots, looting, disorder and lawlessness will prevail. We calculate a worst-case scenario where 1 billion, 700 million people will not survive. It gets worse if the current weather conditions persist for more than another two years."

CHAPTER 32

MOTHER RUSSIA
(ZERO+228 DAYS)

MOSCOW, RUSSIA - DECEMBER 1ST: Siberians are a tough bunch. A weak Siberian is a dead Siberian. They've been living the unbearably frigid life while the rest of the world has experienced what someone once described as to them as 'warmth.' It takes a lot of antifreeze -- vodka -- to keep Siberians going without freezing to death. Boris Molotoff, an ugly bear of a guy, was a superintendent for the East Siberian Oil and Gas Company at the fields located in the Katangsky district of the Irkutsk Region, approximately 261 miles to the northwest of Ust-Kut.

There was nothing to do there but work, eat, drink and sleep. When the temperature reached minus 37 degrees Fahrenheit on November 28, the drilling equipment became difficult to keep going. The maintenance crew couldn't work for more than a few minutes at a time. Boris' job as operations superintendent was to make sure that the drilling continued non-stop; they had production volumes to achieve. If he didn't make his production target, he'd never get the vacation he was promised in the Canary Islands.

Today, when the temperature dropped to minus 42 degrees Fahrenheit, almost nothing worked including his crew. Without Boris' persuasive encouragement, the workers would spend today playing cards or chess in the mess hall. Boris walked over to the mess hall from his office trailer, a short 20 yards but still a long way, in this weather.

"What the hell," said Boris out loud as he reached the mess hall; "why is this door open?" He passed through the threshold to observe a shocking and nauseating site; he was looking at a war zone, a massacre of his crew. Blood and tattooed body parts were everywhere. Tables were overturned, food and vodka was smeared on the floor. The odor in the mess hall was horrendous, smelling of blood and feces and vodka, and there was something else he didn't recognize. Boris finally recognized it, just before the huge paw of a polar bear decapitated this tough and hardy superintendent.

Polar Bears had never before come this far south into Siberia.

President Karloff sat with his inner circle in a city accustomed to disasters, tragedy and cold weather. But Muscovites were not used to the cold persisting for this long when winter hadn't even arrived ... yet. Siberia was having weather similar to weather you'd expect at the North Pole. Moscow was having Siberia weather and the dachas on the Black sea were having Moscow weather. Neva Bay and the Gulf of Finland were frozen solid, making the port of St. Petersburg worthless. Sixty percent of the operating Siberian oil and gas fields had been abandoned, awaiting more tolerable weather in order to restart production. Many mining towns east of the Ural Mountains had been discovered with hundreds of residents frozen in place and the rest gone, having migrated south.

Mass migration south was difficult for the Russian hierarchy to stop. President Karloff's only consolation was that the countries on Russia's southern border were not garden spots either. "Where are they going to go," Karloff mused to himself -- "Mongolia, North Korea, Kazakhstan, or Azerbaijan?"

The inner circle consisted of the Prime Minister, the head of Gazprom, the head of Razneff, the head of the SVR (the Russian Intelligence Agency) and the head of the Russian Military apparatus.

"We are in a Catch-22 as westerners say," started President Karloff, "our neighbors and eastern European customers want and need more natural gas and oil to keep their citizens warm. But our internal need has increased because of the unusually cold weather, and our production is way down because our equipment and workers can't deal with the artic-like conditions. Our revenues are down, so we don't have the resources to acquire agricultural products at exponentially increasing prices. Alex, can you add anything to my statement?"

Alexander Sversk was the head of the SVR, the modern-day version of the KGB. Alexander was an evil looking man with rotten teeth, a pock-marked face from childhood acne, beady eyes, a full fu-manchu mustache, cauliflower ears and a severely broken nose. But no one ever underestimated the guy; no one was better at getting even. Alexander said, "One -- The Ukraine is desperate for natural gas; you can negotiate any terms you want. Frankly, we need to consider a trade for wheat and other agriculture products in exchange for natural gas. Two -- NATO will not get in our way. Whatever military move we want to make will be met with only rhetoric; all northern hemisphere countries are just trying to survive. Three -- As you know, our recent takeover of a large part of North Korea provides us with a new source of coal and valuable minerals, so that we'll eventually be able to replace lost revenues with natural resource sales to Japan and South Korea. And Four -- Of the warmer climate OPEC nations, the most vulnerable for military takeover are Algeria and Angola."

President Karloff looked in the direction of the Prime Minister and said, "Do you have a preference?"

The Prime Minister had never been caught smiling. He wasn't going to be caught smiling today, either. But he was smiling within himself. "Angola."

President Karloff looked over at the heads of Gazprom and Razneff and said, "Would our gas and oil field workers enjoy a trip out of Siberia?"

"At this point, I think they would ***pay us*** to get out of Siberia," said the head of Gazprom.

"OK, General Schtoll," said Karloff, "what is the downside of invading Angola and what are the consequences?"

General Schtoll wasn't just sucking up to the President and Prime Minister; he believed what he was going to say: "None."

"How long before you can mobilize the military?"

"About eight minutes, Comrade President."

"How long will the invasion last?"

General Schtoll said, "Eighteen hours to secure control; decades to end the resistance. Like Afghanistan. The only difference is that Angola will be worth it."

The Prime Minister said, "President Karloff and I will address a private session of the Politburo in the morning. Be ready, General Schtoll; you may get the go-ahead as early as tomorrow."

The Prime Minister looked over at Alexander Sversk and asked, "If you know any reason why we shouldn't proceed with this operation, you need to speak now."

Sversk said, "From an intelligence perspective, you could conquer both OPEC countries simultaneously, without NATO or U.S. resistance."

President Karloff said, "We're depending on the accuracy of your intelligence. We don't want a bad intelligence situation here like Bush had with Iraq and the WMDs."

Alexander Sversk stared President Karloff down and said, "You, of all people, know that Bush's intelligence was accurate. I believe you were in charge, at that time, of moving Saddam's chemical weapons into Syria." An angry President Karloff turned bright red. The heads of Gazprom and Razneff knew that they just heard something they shouldn't have. They suddenly worried about their own personal longevity.

CHAPTER 33

COMPOUND SECURITY
(ZERO+230 DAYS)

WANAKA, NEW ZEALAND – DECEMBER 3rd:
Tucker was packing his suitcase; there was no way he was
going to let Maya go home to Chicago and search for her
sister and mother alone. Also, there was no way he would
be able to talk her out of going, nor did he really want to.
He felt compelled to "do something" besides sit around in
witness protective custody and hope for the best.

Tucker was having a one-way discussion with Ram.
Laugh all you want, but Ram understood every word
Tucker said to him. His instructions to Ram were simple;
under no circumstances was he to allow any harm come
to Star. It was silly for Tucker to have this talk with Ram,
because there was no way Ram would let anyone harm
Star anyway. But Tucker wanted to reinforce Ram's sense
of duty and responsibility.

Maya was hugging and talking with Star, trying to
explain to her why Star couldn't go to the United States
with her parents. Star pleaded, "Tank and Jolene are in

Chicago. Grandma Li and Aunt Suzanne are in Chicago; even Powers is in Chicago. Who is going to stay with me? I'll be here all alone with just Ram."

"You won't be alone, sweetheart; your au pair, Mammy, will be here to take care of you; Chef Rhino will cook for you, and six of your *White Knight* buddies will be here. Your dad and I will be back before you know it."

Star cried un-consoled, and Ram leaned against her to reassure her. Tucker came in to hug Star and walk out to the car with Maya as one of the *White Knights* carried Maya's bags. Maya was also crying, as she had never before been separated from Star.

It is not easy to go anywhere from Wanaka, but, then again, that's the purpose of living there under witness protection. It's a five and a half hour commute just to get to the Auckland airport, and a three hour flight to Sydney, Australia. The flight from Sydney to San Francisco takes forever. In San Francisco, they would have to wait in a long line to get through customs, and then check-in again and fly on to Chicago. All in all, the trip would take close to 30 hours from door to door.

The driver and the man sitting shotgun on the drive to Auckland were both *White Knights*; that left four *White*

Knights guarding the Gray compound. The scenery from inside the Volvo XC90 was spectacular, and they were warm; even the seats were heated. The digital outside temperature gauge on the driver's console panel read 2 degrees Fahrenheit. The drive required navigating winding roads; around each turn there seemed to be another dark blue lake or a breathtaking mountain view. About 20 minutes out, the driver started looking too frequently into the rear view mirror. The man in the front passenger seat switched the safety off, on his weapon. Maya and Tucker reached under the seats in front of them in unison, as they were trained to do, and removed the prepositioned Berettas with hollow point rounds in their clips. Tucker spoke first, "What's the threat?"

The driver said, "Maybe nothing, but the Lexus behind us slows down when I slow down and speeds up when I speed up. I also saw a glint of a reflection that I would bet my left testicle was metallic. So, here's the plan. I'm going to make an evasive 180 degree maneuver. You two need to be on the floor until I tell you you're safe. I'll give you a one or two second warning before I make the maneuver. Junior here will be prepared to unload his semi-automatic Mossberg. There is a cross-road coming up in a quarter mile; I'll roll left -- hang on tight."

The driver did not slow down, he gave no indication that he was going to deviate from his steady driving. The roads were icy in spots and lined with ash; he worried about the maneuver if he hit an ice patch in the process. The driver said loudly, "Two, one, action." The Volvo made a drastic turn to the left at roughly 50 miles per hour; the tires screeched; the vehicle started to roll over with its passenger-side wheels off the ground -- when the driver reversed the direction by turning his steering wheel clockwise as hard as he physically could. When the wheels touched ground they were stopped, but headed in the opposite direction, and a Mossberg peered out the passenger side window plus an M16 out the driver's side window.

The black Lexus RX350 had no chance whatsoever to react in time. It drove on by as if nothing happened. The *White Knight* driver said, "Stay down." Tucker and Maya did as they were told but were ready if need be. The Volvo did not move. Junior pulled a pair of field glasses out, to be ready if the Lexus returned. The driver waited.

Reaction time was going to be important because you could see less than 100 feet of roadway before the next curve. The Lexus came out of the curve at lightning speed; it must have been moving over 70 miles per hour, with both windows down on the driver's side, the short barrels of AK74s hanging out the window, strafing at 100 rounds per minute. The *White Knights* returned fire, but were inaccurate and ineffective due to the speed of the Lexus. The deafening sounds stopped as quickly as they started. Junior looked over to see the driver slumped over, bleeding profusely from the neck. The Volvo's windshield was blown out and the radiator was releasing steam. The rear window was split wide open. The 2 degree air with an 8 mile per hour wind overwhelmed the car almost instantly. Junior said, "We need to prepare for their return. Get out of the car and go hide in the forest until I determine that it is safe. I think they will be back." Junior handed Tucker the Mossberg and said, "Take this; you might need it." Tucker and Maya crossed beyond the side of the road on the left, while Junior grabbed the dead driver's M16 and rolled right.

When the Lexus returned, it slowed down. A grenade was accurately lobbed into the Volvo. The Volvo had a full tank of gas and exploded in a fireball that rose 50 feet into the air with black smoke outlining the boundaries. Junior was more effective this time with his M16 and was able to take out both passenger side tires. The driver of the Lexus lost control and buried the car in a pile of large boulders.

It turned out that there were four occupants in the totaled Lexus. The driver and the guy riding shotgun were saved by the airbags, but they were temporarily disoriented. The two in the backseat were propelled through the windshield into the boulder -- they died instantly.

Junior took advantage of the slow recovery of the two living shooters and closed in cautiously. The passenger-side shooter regained alertness first. Before Junior could disarm the guy, he pulled his Smith & Wesson handgun out of a shoulder holster and was within a fraction of a second of discharging it into Junior when a hollow point exploded through his ear and sprayed blood all over the front seat of the Lexus. Blood also covered the driver who had not fully recovered from his trauma. Tucker had vigilantly followed Junior by ten yards or so and shot the passenger side shooter; Maya had followed Tucker, about ten yards back, also with her Beretta drawn.

Junior grabbed the driver, dragged him out of the Lexus and disarmed him. The driver was screaming in pain as Junior was putting handcuffs on him with both hands behind his back -- one of the driver's arms was dislocated at the shoulder from the accident, and the other arm was broken at the wrist. Junior didn't seem to care. They were all going to freeze to death anyway. Maya's teeth were chattering; Tucker was rubbing his arms to stay warm. Junior was staying warm on adrenaline only, but it was going to wear off soon.

Tucker said to Junior, "You want me to do it, or do you want the honors?"

Junior said, "Tucker, you just saved my life so I'll spare you the chore and I'll make use of my *White Knight* interrogation training techniques." I'd like to suggest that you and Maya go back to the remains of the Volvo and see if there is anything left of your luggage that might keep us warm. If nothing else, you can get warm from the fire until it burns out. And see if cell phone service is good enough to call in some reinforcements to pick us up."

From the time the *White Knight* driver made his auto diversion move until the Lexus' passenger side killer's head exploded, only 12 minutes had elapsed. During that time many rounds were fired, an explosion occurred and a ball of fire projected into the sky. Yet no other vehicle passed by, no nearby residents showed up to see what was going on, and no police sirens invaded the silence. Maya had her smart phone out, trying to determine the GPS coordinates, while Tucker rang up the Gray compound to have someone come get them ASAP in case the bad guys had reinforcements too.

Seventeen minutes later, a black Escalade with tinted windows pulled up and two men got out, armed with automatic weapons. Tucker and Maya recognized the men as *White Knight* guards. Maya said, "There are now only two guards protecting Star. We need to hurry back to the compound."

At about that time, Junior strolled up from the totaled Lexus without the driver whom he was interrogating. Junior's head was hanging and said, "My technique needs some improvement and refining. He's dead and I didn't learn enough to identify who hired them to assassinate you."

Tucker said to Junior, "Go ahead and get in the car; we're headed back to the compound. We'll listen to your story during the drive back." The Escalade drove off with the three survivors and two guards. The five who didn't survive the ordeal were left at the scene of the devastation.

On the way back, Junior related to everyone what he had learned from the Lexus driver during his "interview." He had not learned much other than that the killer spoke with an Eastern European accent.

When they got back to the compound, the impossible had happened. The gate to the compound was open; one of the *White Knight* guards was lying immobile in the driveway, and there was no sign of the remaining guard. Maya and Tucker jumped out of the Escalade and ran full speed into the house without caution, screaming Star's name at the top of their lungs. They found blood in the hallway and saw someone's feet with combat-type boots extending out of the doorway to Star's playroom. Tucker reached the doorway first, only to see that the victim on the floor was the last of the *White Knight* guards. Blood splatter was everywhere in Star's playroom; Star was not there. The door on the other side of the playroom led into Star's bedroom. The door was open, and on the floor in Star's bedroom were the remains of another person, who once had been a large adult.

Star was sitting on her bed -- legs crossed, tears running down her face and shaking uncontrollably, but untouched.

Next to her on the bed with blood all over his snout was Ram, panting.

CHAPTER 34

THE UNITED NATIONS
(ZERO+230)

NEW YORK CITY, NEW YORK – DECEMBER 3rd: An emergency meeting of the United Nations Security Council was called to assess the seriousness of the disaster which extremely cold weather had created worldwide. The Security Council's greatest concern was world hunger. The population in the countries besieged with poverty was increasing at an alarming rate, at a time when the rise in agriculture yield was growing more slowly than the birth rate. That was *before* the current disaster.

The Chairman of the Council on World Hunger stood at the podium to announce the findings of their study. A very serious, dour and professorial doctor of sociology from a European Union nation opened the emergency meeting by stating that "Conditions are worse today than at any time in modern history. The extremely cold weather disaster has impacted the poor and hungry the most. The wealthy will be able to find food; the poor are left with only what remains after the wealthy take their share.

"Agricultural productivity in the breadbaskets of the world is down roughly 30% compared with last year's production rate. In this ***capitalist world***, the unit price of agricultural products has increased by approximately 150% over the same time period. Less food for more people at higher costs is a formula for world disorder.

"We recommend that the wealthy find a way to share their wealth by donating ***more*** food to the impoverished countries of the world, so that the disorder I'm warning about doesn't reach their doorstep. Please donate food to the 'World Health Organization' so that we can distribute the food to the truly starving masses."

As the doctor paused, the lights went out in the famous building. New York City was experiencing a rolling blackout. Consolidated Edison couldn't produce or buy enough electricity from the grid to meet the increasing demand which the frigid cold weather created. The blackout extended from Greenwich Village through 110th Street in Manhattan without warning. Hundreds of thousands of people were not only thrust into the dark, but thrust into the cold. New Yorkers are not known for putting up with a lot of shit. This was no exception.

Within an hour, a crowd formed in protest, in front of Consolidated Edison's offices on West 34th Street. A spontaneous show of anger about the whole government response to the cold weather crisis erupted; Con Ed was just the messenger -- the place where the anger was expressed. New York's finest showed up to protect Con Ed's offices from the mob. This made the protestors even angrier. By daybreak, two cops were dead and 135 protestors were injured. And the power was still off.

The mayor of New York City received a call from a mechanical voice identifying itself as the *Society for Environmental Justice*, taking credit for the blackout and demanding the shut-down of Wall Street.

CHAPTER 35

FULL DISCLOSURE (ZERO+230 DAYS)

CHICAGO, ILLINOIS – DECEMBER 3RD: "I won't have long to live, now, if I don't do something drastic," Suzanne mumbled to herself under the duct tape across her mouth. She wondered if there was any food value in duct tape. She had not eaten or had water in three days. She had soiled herself a couple of times now and was sure that she was about to freeze to death. She unfortunately understood the Coyote concept where you might chew your arm off to survive (and the joke that goes with it). It was the sound of the rats that really gave her a wakeup call. She contorted herself, used her long legs to provide leverage and dislocated her shoulder. It hurt like hell, but it put her in a position where she could rub the plastic ties behind her back against the raw concrete wall. It was slow going, but eventually she was rewarded with a free hand. The hand on her dislocated left side was useless.

She ripped the duct tape off her eyes and immediately searched for her mother while she pulled the tape off of her mouth. Dr. Li was only fifteen feet away, lying motionless on a twin size mattress. Suzanne said, "Mom, if you can hear me, I'm coming for you. Please, hang in there." There was no sign of life from Dr. Li, and no indication of recognition. Suzanne, already panicked, began a desperate attempt to free herself. With her newly acquired eyesight and a free hand, she was able to grab a piece of broken glass from the concrete floor and slowly cut through the ties that held her feet together. She was then able to stand, and it felt damn good. She was able to free herself from the tether, because it was secured to her belt.

Suzanne was completely free. She approached her mother with apprehension and feared that she was dead. She ripped the duct tape off her mouth. Suzanne was sure that she saw her mother's blue lips move. She proceeded to remove the duct tape from her mother's eyes. They were not her mother's eyes. They were the eyes of someone else, someone who used to be her mother. But her mother's blue lips moved again. Suzanne put her ear down to her mother's lips. Dr. Ingrid Li whispered into Suzanne's ear with her last breath.

CHAPTER 36

GRID OVERLOAD
(ZERO+230 DAYS)

CHATTANOOGA, TENNESSEE – DECEMBER 3RD: Rusty Murphy was doing his civic duty by donating blood early this morning to the Red Cross through a Tennessee Valley Authority (TVA) sponsored drive. Rusty worked as a transformer inspector for TVA's power distribution group. TVA is a corporation owned by the U.S. government which provides electricity for 9 million people in parts of seven southeastern states. Rusty had the universal donor blood type, O negative, and was encouraged -- rewarded with a day off -- if he gave blood every 90 days. The nurse-phlebotomist did the usual preparation, applying Betadine to his arm prior to inserting the needle into a prominent vein. Rusty gave his pint, held his arm up to coagulate the blood, pressed the dressing over the needle hole, and went to the food counter to get hydrated and eat Fig Newtons. After five minutes, he began to feel nauseated, which was very unusual for this blood-donating pro. After seven minutes, he began vomiting uncontrollably and perspiring like he was in an oven. After nine minutes, he was unconscious and they rushed him to a hospital.

The Red Cross nurse exited the blood drive center with a TVA badge that allowed access to all TVA transformers. The nurse limped seven blocks to a stolen truck owned by the Soddy-Daisy Landscaping Company. The nurse (the ghost) had a list of TVA's largest transformers and their locations. One by one, the nurse would locate a critical transformer; open the access gate to the transformer using Rusty's transformer inspection badge -- and then strategically place Willy Pete under the transformer oil reservoir. Willy Pete is white phosphorous which auto-ignites and burns at 5000 degrees Fahrenheit. The "male nurse" had been able to secure M34 Incendiary Grenades which the army had manufactured at the Rocky Mountain Arsenal during the Vietnam War. He wired a timer to each grenade fuse. When the fuse created a spark, the Willy Pete burned a hole in each of TVA's most critical transformers, igniting the transformer oil which drained from the transformer, causing the copper coils to heat up for the lack of oil, so that they warped and got close enough to arc, which resulted in a powerful explosion.

By 10:00 PM that evening, after Rusty died of cyanide poisoning, six of TVA's most critical high voltage transformers simultaneously exploded; the TVA grid was compromised and 5 million of the 9 million people serviced by TVA were without power.

The Governor of Tennessee received a computerized call from the *Society for Environmental Justice* taking credit for the blackout and demanding that TVA shut down all its coal-fired power plants, or face more reprisals.

CHAPTER 37

THE SNIPER
(ZERO+230 DAYS)

MUNICH, GERMANY – DECEMBER 3ᴿᴰ: Harold Pfeiffer was an Iraq and Afghanistan veteran. He was a decorated sharpshooter and had assassinated more people than he would like to admit, as a U.S. Army soldier.

For what? He had a bitter taste in his mouth about U.S. policy in the Middle East; too many of his buddies had died over there only to be forgotten when the next administration came in. His bitterness, his disappointment in his country, his hatred of politicians warped his thought process and allowed him to rationalize his conduct. He was just a killer now.

It surprised the hell out of him when his largest moonlighting contract of all time was not to discharge his weapon in the direction of a human being, but to shoot inanimate objects. The pay was fantastic and the risk was infinitesimal, compared with killing people.

The instructions included a map of the targets for the month of December. Only one target a day. What a piece of cake.

Pfeiffer was on R&R from the Wiesbaden Army Garrison.

By the end of December, after discharging ten well placed shots into transformers each day, 75% of Munich was without power.

The Chancellor of Germany received a call from a mechanical voice at her private residence from the *Society for Environmental Justice*, taking credit for the attacks and demanding that Germany withdraw from NATO.

CHAPTER 38

ANGER MANAGEMENT (ZERO+230 DAYS)

CHICAGO, ILLINOIS – DECEMBER 3RD: Tank was still not 100%. But when he received a call from Suzanne, Tank's pain was not an issue -- he was one mad and bad MF. Though he was very happy that Suzanne was alive and well, the passing of Dr. Li devastated him. Even Jolene couldn't quell his anger. The best thing anyone could do was get the hell out of Dodge. His anger, his rage was so palpable that you didn't want to be in the same universe with him. Despite his unpleasant disposition, you still wanted him on your side -- you didn't want to be exposed to Tank's wrath.

Maya's mother, Star's grandmother, was dead because of Tank. He blamed himself because the person who killed Dr. Li was in Tank's control when he was interrogating him. The guy, the 'ghost,' had been his responsibility.

Tank's mind started racing, "I'm not going to just catch this guy, but I'll be as cruel as humanly possible to this piece-of-shit murderer responsible for the death of Dr. Ingrid Li."

Tank's adrenaline was pumping to the point where his hands and feet no longer hurt from his having been nailed to the floor by this nameless guy, the 'ghost.' "Who is this guy?" Tank picked up his cell phone and called Special Agent Vinny DeLuca. Without an introduction, Tank asked, "Any progress on identifying who the killer is and what organization he works for?"

"Well, hello to you, too!" Vinny was in an equally bad mood. "No new intelligence has been derived by fingerprinting or gathering more DNA other than to say it is the same guy that you had in custody in the tool shed. And both DNA and fingerprints keep leading us back to a guy who has been dead for years. Our specialist at Quantico, Magnus Glass, has not been able to link anyone from the local hospitals for the criminally insane with the *Society for Environmental Justice*. The Director of the FBI is on my ass, and about to pull me as the lead agent-in-charge if something doesn't happen soon."

Tank asked, "Did you debrief Suzanne? Did she provide any leads?"

"Yes and Yes. The best lead we have is that the killer knew Dr. Li. Suzanne said that he called her by her first name and acted like he knew her from the past."

"What, you didn't think that was important enough to tell me unless I pried it out of you?"

An angry and blustering Vinny said, "Tank, you ungrateful bastard; I don't have to tell you shit. Be grateful that I share anything with you; it's the FBI culture. We're chasing it down. I subpoenaed her patient list and we're going through each one meticulously."

"I assume someone at the FBI is smart enough to cross-reference her patient list with the universal population of the criminally insane. What we need is actionable intelligence, not desk jockey stuff."

"Listen, smart ass, one name keeps coming up, Robert Grainger, the dead guy. He was on Dr. Li's patient list. The killer is a fucking ghost."

Vinny continued, "Because I'm such a nice guy, I'm going to share something with you that I would like you to keep confidential. That means for you less cerebral types, don't share this with anyone. The late Dr. Li's husband, Henry Li, left Dr. Ingrid Li, and now her two daughters, an estate worth over a billion dollars. We're investigating Henry Li's past. Where the hell did that much money come from? Is there something in Henry's past that triggered hatred by the 'ghost' toward Ingrid?"

"Do you think either Suzanne or Maya knew their mother's net worth? I wonder, if either of them had even the slightest clue about their potential inheritance."

"I don't know, but what I do know is that we have a couple of new leads to follow," said Tank.

"What do you mean 'we,' Kemosabe?"

Tank's cell phone was receiving another call. He said, "We'll talk later." He disconnected Vinny and opened the new call, knowing that it was Tucker. "Hey, bud, where are you? Have you arrived here in Chicago?"

"Tank, on our way to the airport, we were attacked. The compound was attacked and compromised. Three of your men were killed in the line of duty. If it weren't for Ram, I think Star would have been kidnapped -- or worse. Maya and I are all right, but you need to call the Director of the FBI to let him know that our witness protection broke down. We're exposed, and someone or some nation is after us. See if your team can get back here soon. We are getting military protection from your friend the Prime Minister until you and your team get back."

Tank thought, "My God, the world is falling apart." He said, "We'll be back ASAP. Tell Maya that her sister is safe."

"We know. Suzanne called Maya. I don't know what Suzanne said to Maya, but Maya has practically been in a trance ever since, though; it could be the trauma from everything that has happened in the last two days."

"Tucker, do you have any theories about whom or what is behind these attacks?"

"The Wanaka police and New Zealand Bureau of Investigation have lots of manpower collecting evidence, DNA, fingerprints, and the usual stuff. They are fairly certain that the attackers were Australian immigrants from Russia -- in other words, the Russian mob. So now the question is, was it state sponsored or hired Russian mobsters? My guess is the latter. If it were Russians, they would have hired American thugs to deflect suspicion from themselves."

"Are they following the money?" asked Tank.

"They may need some help with that. Gee, do we know anyone who can help?" Tucker asked sarcastically.

Tank said, "Consider it done. But first, Tucker, I need to contact all the next of kin of each of the fallen *White Knights,* and contact the coroner in Wanaka for instructions. What a sad and gruesome task."

CHAPTER 39

OUT OF CONTROL
(ZERO+232 DAYS)

CHICAGO, ILLINOIS – DECEMBER 5th: During daylight hours, the sky remained hazy like the highest smog-alert days in Los Angeles or Shanghai. A dry gray ash coated everything, making you feel dirty two minutes after you'd bathed, if you went outside. Most people who braved the frigid weather were wearing paint masks over their noses and mouths to keep from choking on the ash. It got into your hair, your nose, and into your mouth. But the only people who were outside were the desperate or the criminal -- people with nothing to lose, or thieves. *They* could either freeze to death outside or freeze to death inside.

Looting was prevalent in stores where items were sold that kept people warm; items like ski jackets, socks, gloves, hats, and wool coats were gone. Establishments that sold propane, kerosene, kerosene heaters, Coleman stoves, fire starters, alcohol, emergency generators or butane were looted days ago.

Food warehouses and restaurants were unable to protect their stock. Grocery stores, sadly, were obliged to maintain their own security forces. But the biggest prize of all for would-be thieves was a MEG. To have your own electricity without fuel in a town without power in the frigid cold was precious. The black market value for a MEG was 100 times the actual purchase price.

The truly pathetic were even fighting over dumpsters. Dumpster diving became socially acceptable and required for the survival of the truly desperate.

Theo Bussey had great leadership skills. At the prime age of 19, he commanded respect. If that didn't work, he demanded respect. If that didn't work, he commanded fear. He was 6' 2" tall, 175 pounds, unshaven, with poor hygiene habits and narrow eyes and irises as black as his pupils. He commanded a small army of criminals. The Panthers, as they called themselves, "recovered" MEGs and sold them on the black market. Lake Shore Drive residents were, on the average, more affluent than, say, residents of South Chicago. It was easy to locate MEGs -- residents with MEGs had lights on after dark.

Theo's strategy was simple; use "shock and awe" by overwhelming owners with force. The Panthers had lost a soldier or two over the last week, but Theo's gang had a

100% success rate at securing MEGs. Theo's target today is the penthouse of the deceased Dr. Ingrid Li. Fifteen armed "soldiers" forced their way into the building lobby with crowbars and mauls, and then offered the guard his life if he didn't resist. They forced the guard to give them access to the penthouse elevator. Eight heavily armed gang members aged between 17 and 25 followed Theo Bussey into the elevator.

As the door opened on the penthouse floor level, Powers threw a canister of tear gas into the confined space and slid out of sight. The Panthers discharged their weapons but hit nothing. Theo stepped out of the elevator, choking from the tear gas, and leaned in the wrong direction -- directly into Tank's massive right forehand; the bridge of Theo's nose cracked like a twig and he dropped like a bag of sackrete. The seven other Panthers, who followed Theo out of the elevator with burning eyes, choking for a breath of clean air, were no match for Lucas and the other *White Knights* who were former Navy Seals or Army Rangers. Within three minutes, all the gang members were secured. No one was killed. Tank instructed Powers to clear the lobby in the event that there were more gang members prepared to guard their compatriots' escape.

A little reconnaissance would have gone a long way for Theo's team; maybe they would have discovered that they were targeting a residence where a *White Knight* planning meeting of twelve elite fighters was underway. One day later, and Theo's plan would have worked.

Tank opened the door to Dr. Li's penthouse, strolled into the study, and sat down on the sofa next to Jolene and Suzanne Li. Tank said, "Would you consider coming with us; you could visit with your sister, Maya. I don't think it is safe for you here as long as Chicago is without power."

Suzanne had lost her smile after the ordeal she had gone through, and the loss of her mother. She sat stoically with her arm in a sling and said without emotion, "Tank, just where is it safe in the world right now?"

CHAPTER 40

SUBTERFUGE
(ZERO+234 DAYS)

JUBAIL COMMERCIAL PORT, SAUDI ARABIA – DECEMBER 7TH: *The Yen*, a 74,000 ton cargo vessel landed in port two days ago from the Port of Kobe, primarily carrying heavy machinery, structural steel, fabricated vessels, pumps and electrical substations. And two unmarked sea-land containers which were off-loaded onto a trailer hitched to a Mercedes diesel tractor. As soon as the containers were secured, the captain of *The Yen* -- who was watching the transfer through binoculars --notified the Japanese Ambassador to Saudi Arabia. The Captain said, "Step three is complete."

The Ambassador was actually excited; he expected to be anxious and apprehensive about his role in the operation. Instead, he felt surprisingly elated. The success of the operation now wholly depended on him. Everyone else had done their job, and compared with the difficulty of the tasks others had to perform, his job was simple. The trip to the warehouse was roughly 45 minutes, by the route which this truck was taking. The Ambassador called his driver and told him to have his car ready in 10 minutes. He packed his gym bag with a change of clothes, four security access cards, a Beretta 92 with silencer, and a disguise in the event that he needed to escape.

He reached the warehouse five minutes before the tractor-trailer. The diesel tractor backed into the loading dock and with hoists and roller conveyors; the eleven men waiting in the warehouse slid the sea-land containers onto the floor. The locks on the sea-land containers had to be removed with an acetylene torch, as planned. There were three smaller containers in each of the two sea-land containers. Around them was a lot of packing material to keep them dry and elevated, in the event that water invaded the containers.

The first of the interior boxes was carefully opened. An even smaller container, a vessel roughly 12 inches in diameter and five feet long, was removed from the interior box. The vessel weighed 500 pounds, so a winch with a cable and fabric-mesh saddle lifted the vessel. At one end of the vessel was a keypad. A limousine with diplomatic plates was driven up adjacent to the first vessel. The back seat of the limousine was removed to reveal saddles designed for the vessel. The vessel was transferred to the limousine and the hollow back seat was repositioned.

The Ambassador casually and excitedly kneeled down, pushed numbers on the keypad and programmed the vessel to activate at a specific time and date. The process was repeated five additional times. Each time, a limousine with diplomatic plates would leave the warehouse to be positioned at a specific predetermined set of coordinates.

The first limousine was driven to and located in the parking garage of the Al Faisalaih Hotel, not too distant from King Abdullah bin Abdulaziz Al Saud's palace in Riyadh. The driver booked a room, but stayed in the limousine to guard against possible intruders.

The second limousine was parked one kilometer from King Abdul Aziz Air Field, not too distant from the port of entry and 500 km from Riyadh. The driver parked at a movie theatre in Dahran, where royal family members were known to be entertained.

The third limousine was placed 1500 meters from the entrance to Riyadh King Khalid Air Base. The fourth limousine was placed a kilometer and a half from the American Eskan Village Air Base. The fifth limousine was parked in front of the King Fahd Air Base.

The final limousine traveled 840 miles on Route 40 to Mecca. The passenger in the back seat was dressed in traditional thobe and tagiyah. He had been on a satellite phone speaking with Akio Yamada, the Grand Master of the Freemasons of Japan. Operation Fugu was on schedule. The chauffeur opened the rear door for the royal visitor who came to pay his respect in the Holy Shrine in the Great Mosque that honors the birthplace of the Prophet Muhammad.

King Abdullah bin Abdulaziz Al Saud was enjoying a rare private moment with his favorite granddaughter. She was a joy to be around; she was always so happy and inquisitive. He did not want anyone to know about his love for her. Otherwise, she would be at greater risk of kidnapping and extortion. It was their private secret. So he was angry when he was disturbed by his private secretary. His private secretary was a large and fierce looking man. To meet with the King, you had to first convince his secretary that you were worthy of a meeting. He was a most intimidating man, and it had to be important to even want to get past the gatekeeper.

"What is it, Abdul; you know the rules?"

"It is an emergency of the highest kind, Your Excellency."

King Saud grabbed the phone extended to him by his secretary and said, "Who is this?"

"Your worst nightmare has arrived, *former* King Saud. I regret to inform you that your reign as King of Saudi Arabia is at an end. As of this phone call, you are dethroned and are now a territory of Japan. This is the Prime Minister of Japan and I am, hereby, declaring war on the nation of Saudi Arabia. You may stay in your palace; you can retain your existing wealth, and you can save the lives of the Saud family. All you have to do is surrender to Japan.

"Before you say a word, you should know that we have strategically located six nuclear weapons in your country. One is located not too far from you in Riyadh. A second one is also located in Riyadh at the Riyadh King Khalid Air Base. You make one attempt to mobilize the Royal Air Force and I will order the detonation of both nuclear bombs.

"There are four more nuclear weapons located in your country, one in the Great Mosque in Mecca. It is too bad that you drove the Americans to Qatar, they might have protected you. But you are naked, vulnerable, and weak. If you would like, I will detonate one of the bombs to prove that this is not a threat."

King Saud finally spoke and said, "Why? We have given you trillions of dollars of business over the years. We have never been enemies. We have provided you with oil and refined products. I thought we were friends."

The Prime Minister of Japan said, "It is our destiny."

King Saud surrendered without a shot being fired.

Within four weeks, the Japanese military completely occupied all oil wells, refineries, industrial production facilities, and the operation of the ports and the airfields. The Royal Family was not mistreated. Not a single death occurred during the "war."

The Prime Minister of Japan had actually committed suicide days before the call between the alleged Prime Minister and King Saud was conducted. But Akio Yamada sounded just like the late Prime Minister. Part 1 of Operation Fugu was complete.

Akio Yamada picked up his satellite phone, contacted his accomplice and said, "You are free to let the other shoe drop."

CHAPTER 41

FOLLOW THE MONEY
(ZERO+236 DAYS)

WANAKA, NEW ZEALAND – DECEMBER 9TH:
Tucker Cherokee sat in the comfort of his desk chair in his office, staring at his satellite phone. It was time to violate protocol and expose his whereabouts. Your first clue that witness protection is no longer working is when you're ambushed. He picked up the phone and called his old boss at ENTROPY, Stephen Sanders, in Exeter, NH.

Sanders answered the phone and said, "Tucker, you have never once before called me at 3:30 in the morning. I love your encrypted phone system though; this time is says you're calling from New Zealand. So, what's the emergency and how can I help?"

"I **am** calling from New Zealand. My cover is blown. We were ambushed, and we lost *White Knights* in the process. Maya's mother is dead; Maya's sister was kidnapped, and someone tried to kidnap Star. Other than that, everything is fine here." There were no words which Sanders could utter, so Tucker went on, "Do you still have that highly classified contract with the Treasury Department?"

Sanders said, "I'm sorry, Tucker; I don't know what you are talking about."

"Yeah; okay. Well, let me ask the question differently. Is Jimmy Ma still an ENTROPY employee?"

"I'm sorry," Sanders said; "Jimmy who? No, but we do have a John Smith who still works with us. He lives in the Watergate Hotel in Washington, DC. Could he be of assistance?" Without further communications, they both hung up.

Tucker called Tank and said, "Can you send Powers to Washington, DC? I would like for Powers to 'protect' someone at the Watergate Hotel. His name is Jimmy Ma, though he may be registered as John Smith. I think he would be safest here in Wanaka."

Two days later, December 11th: Jimmy Ma sat in Tucker's office at the compound in Wanaka. Though the temperature in the room was around 60 degrees Fahrenheit, Jimmy was sweating. On one side of him was Powers; on the other side was Tank. In front of him was Tucker. No one smiled. This was serious stuff. Jimmy thought, with good reason, that his life depended on his cyber skills. Jimmy, a third generation Chinese-American was a genius with a 145 or so IQ. He earned a PhD in computer science from the Massachusetts Institute of Technology (MIT). He was snatched up by ENTROPY, based on the recommendation of the Dean of Engineering. He'd been contracted to the U.S. Treasury Department for over 13 years. No one was more competent at following the money. He tracked the flow of money into terrorist organizations, tracked counterfeiters and tax evaders with accounts in Belize, the Canary Islands, Switzerland and the Cayman Islands.

Tucker asked, "Jimmy, do you know who I am?"

Jimmy said, "Yes."

"Who am I?"

"You are Tucker Cherokee. You and your wife, Maya, formerly Maya Li, are the primary inventors of the Neutrino Electricity Using Rare Earth Metals -- NEUREM -- generator technology. You are here under FBI witness protection from state-sponsored terrorists. The alleged terrorists are primarily funded by OPEC nations. You have a special child named Star. You are a former and current employee of ENTROPY. You are a billionaire with philanthropic tendencies. You recently invented a spray to protect people from freezing to death that is being beta-tested in Antarctica. You and your wife are currently under contract to develop a technology to shorten the duration of this extremely frigid, and I may add, unpleasant weather. You employ *White Knight Personnel Protection Services* to defend you against the potential OPEC-funded terrorists. You have a dog named Ram whom I do not want to meet."

Six eyes stared at Jimmy Ma with incredulity.

After a full minute of stunned silence, Tucker finally asked, "How can you know all that?"

"Mr. Cherokee," Jimmy Ma said, "You kidnapped me because I **know** shit. There is almost nothing I can't learn through hacking. I know that you also know that I am employed by the National Security Agency -- the NSA -- to test whether or not I can break through their firewalls. I always succeed. I'm also used to test the Pentagon firewalls. I also know that the only way you could have found me is through Sanders. For Sanders to expose me means whatever you want me for is damned important. So just tell me what you want. I am your loyal servant."

Tucker said, "You are on the clock. I'll double whatever ENTROPY is paying you, so please don't consider yourself kidnapped. I have several tasks for you.

"The first task is to find out who paid the guys who ambushed Maya and me, when we were on our way to the Auckland Airport. Tank and Powers have been working with the forensic scientists with the Wanaka Police and the New Zealand Bureau of Investigation. We have names or aliases as a starting point. What do you need from us to do your thing?"

"I need access to a supercomputer."

"I thought you might," said Tucker. "Two *White Knights* will escort and protect you during your tour of duty at New Zealand's National Institute of Water and Atmospheric Research (NIWA) where you will have access to an IBM Power 575 supercomputer, known as FitzRoy. Here is a satellite phone. Call me once a day. All your expenses will be paid. Do you have a 'significant other' whom you would like us to bring to you?"

"The last thing I want is for anyone to know that I have a significant other. She would be at risk of being kidnapped."

"So, you don't want Delilah to be with you?" Tucker asked.

Jimmy Ma hung his head. "I've tried so hard to protect my privacy. I guess what is good for the goose is good for the gander. OK. I'd love to have her here with me. I'll call her and see if she is willing to come."

"One more thing before you go." Tucker nodded at Tank. Tank got up, walking gingerly, and opened the door to Tucker's office. In came Star and Ram. Star approached Jimmy Ma and looked into his eyes. Jimmy was shaking uncontrollably and seemed damn near paralyzed with fear.

Star said to Ram, "Good, <u>Good</u>." Ram would now protect Jimmy Ma and not consider Jimmy a threat. Star, reading his thoughts, said to Jimmy Ma, "Don't worry; he will also protect Delilah."

CHAPTER 42

THE GOOD OLE DAYS OF GLOBAL WARMING (ZERO+238 DAYS)

DES MOINES, IOWA – DECEMBER 11TH: The breadbasket of the United States runs through Iowa. The farmers and farmlands of the United States are the most productive in the world. Through science, technology, fertilizers, irrigation, and rich soil, the amount of food produced in the States per acre of land is phenomenal.

Or, it was. The cold weather brought on by the volcanic ash cloud in the atmosphere, and the ash that smothered plant leaves reducing plant capacity to absorb carbon dioxide, shortened the growing season, resulting in a 35% reduction in the food supply. The permanent ash cloud prevented sunshine from reaching the crops. One beneficiary of the alleged "global warming" crisis had been the breadbasket of the United States.

Until the eruptions of Mount Merapi and Mount Nyiragongo, satellite measurements showed that our planet was greener than it was prior to the onset of global warming. The rising carbon dioxide concentrations in the atmosphere dramatically increased overall global food production. The presence of more carbon dioxide had a fertilizing effect on the growth of plant life.

Warmer weather meant a longer growing season, and thus translated into the potential for greater agricultural output. This, combined with fewer frosts and more precipitation, greatly benefited all of the agricultural economic sectors. "Global Warming" also had a positive impact on forestry and recreation. In addition to the dramatic increase of land available for cultivation, made possible by warmer weather, natural resources were much easier to extract from the unfrozen earth. The overall economic impact of global warming on the U.S. economy was actually positive and created a measurable increase in Gross Domestic Product.

As the ice retreated at the poles, more arable land became available for agricultural purposes. Large land-masses in the northern hemisphere, near and just south of the Canadian/U.S. border, became more habitable and the land more arable. Most Canadians lived in a belt running along the southern border with the United States. All of Canada welcomed agricultural growth with longer growing seasons. Heretofore uninhabitable land became inhabitable. Evergreen vegetation, woody plants, and other plant life had increased across Australia over the past 200 years as a result of carbon dioxide enrichment, from gradual global warming.

The bread baskets of the United States, Canada and the Ukraine in the northern hemisphere were now suffering from the unusually frigid weather. Less food available as a result of the shorter growing season meant that there was less food for the masses; it drove up prices and made food less available to the poor.

Riots were inevitable, anarchy probable, and civil wars distinctly possible.

It took 15-year old Leon Adams three days to hitch-hike from south Chicago to West Des Moines, Iowa on Interstate 80. Eighteen-wheelers were the only vehicles which would stop for him. Leon's mother had packed him only one meal and had given him just ten dollars. She dressed him warmly, gave him her only paint mask, made him a sign that said "Des Moines," and gave him the address to his cousin's home. The cousin was an agricultural field hand. Before she sent him on his way she said, "Leon, this is no place to grow up. I have no job, no electricity, no food, and not much kerosene left for the heater. If you stay, you'll end up in a gang, and probably in jail or worse. Your cousin has a job working in the fields. I figure, if nothing else, you'll be fed well in Iowa. So go now, before I start crying and change my mind."

A truck driver continuing on to Omaha fed the underweight Leon a peanut butter and jelly sandwich before he dropped him off in West Des Moines. Leon had to walk 17 miles in the subzero weather to reach his cousin's rented one-bedroom home. Leon banged repeatedly on the front door but got no answer. Leon wanted to get out of the cold so he tried the front door knob -- it was open. He stuck his head into the house and yelled for his cousin, but instead of getting a verbal answer, he was brutally assaulted by the unmistakable smell of death.

Leon's search of the small house easily resulted in his finding the remains of his poor cousin, a Saturday night special on the floor, and a note on the living room table. Leon read the note: "I was laid off; I'm out of money, out of food, out of fuel, and out of luck. Tell Mama that I love her."

Leon checked the gun to see if it had any more rounds. The deadly cold weather had claimed two more victims.

CHAPTER 43

GOLD (ZERO+238 DAYS)

SPOKANE, WASHINGTON - DECEMBER 11ᵀᴴ: The average temperature over the last week dipped to minus 13 degrees Fahrenheit with an average wind velocity of 17 mph from the north. Steven Stewart said to his lovely wife Sheila, "It's too fucking cold to do anything but lie in bed under the covers." The temperature in the house was 45 degrees. They had to preserve their propane. Out here in the country, it was getting harder and harder to get propane delivered to their 500 gallon storage tank, regardless of the price Steven was willing to pay. The cost of propane had risen by 150 percent over the past three months.

On paper, Stephen was doing very well financially. Stephen was a stock broker and didn't have to leave his home to do his job. He traded precious metal mining stocks; stocks were sky-rocketing with the weather crisis and the on-going geopolitical dramas. North Korea had collapsed; Japan had conquered Saudi Arabia, and some organization was attacking the U.S. and Canadian energy infrastructure. Gold, silver, platinum, and rare earth metals were skyrocketing; Stephen was cashing in.

Sheila said to Stephen with a sensuous smile, "I'm OK with staying under the covers all day." They cuddled and turned on the TV to see that every station was covering a Presidential address. The President of the United States, Winston Allen, was addressing the nation and saying, "Ladies and gentlemen of the United States, one of the duties and responsibilities of the Government of the United States is to protect you -- protect you not only from foreign aggression but protect you as much as possible from disaster. The disaster we are currently enduring is the first weather disaster to affect all 50 states and all U.S. territories. We have exceeded the capacity of FEMA to respond.

"I am hereby asking that the Department of Defense be tasked to support FEMA in dealing with the impact of the extremely frigid weather on the citizens of the United States. I am also hereby proposing that defense forces be made available to the National Guard to support the cities of Chicago and New York City in an effort to control riots and crime in those cities. It is with great sadness and my deepest sorrow that we must declare Martial Law in the City of Chicago. A curfew is hereby established between sunset and sunrise until power is restored. I am asking

Congress to temporarily suspend the 'Posse Comitatus Act' that prevents the use of the military for domestic law enforcement until power is restored in these affected cities.

"The U.S. Government, by the power vested in me, is fully committed to bringing the people responsible for the heinous acts of violence against our energy infrastructure to justice. We ask that you help us and call our hot line if you observe anything suspicious; please, stay vigilant.

"The recent world events, partially resulting from the unusually cruel weather, could be expected. The downtrodden people of North Korea are much better off today under the democratic government of South Korea, and with Russia. The fact that we are no longer under the threat of nuclear aggression from a terrorist supplier of weapons of mass destruction makes the world a safer place.

"Japan, on the other hand, has disappointed us, violated our treaties, and reversed almost 70 years of peace. It is with a heavy heart that we witness the Japanese military offensive against the nation of Saudi Arabia which strains a solid relationship with the United States. We understand their predicament, the impact that the frigid cold weather has had on their country, the destruction of needed energy resources as result of the terrorist attacks in Vancouver, and the scarcity of energy on the free market. But we do not accept that the nation of Japan had to resort to military aggression to save its people.

"We also understand that the nations to whom Saudi Arabia has supplied oil are now at risk, and may become as desperate as Japan was, before this military action. As a result of the unprecedented attack on the sovereign nation of Saudi Arabia, the United States will sanction Japan by ending trade as a Most Favored Nation.

"Finally, I'm asking congress to convene a special session to allow the release of up to 60% of the Strategic Oil Reserve to help communities like yours to have access to methods of heating your family dwelling.

"God Bless you, and God Bless the United States of America."

After President Allen signed off and before the pundits told you what you just heard, Stephen Stewart said to his wife, "That was depressing. He said they don't have a clue how to stop the impact this incredibly cold weather is having on Americans. He said they don't have a clue who is destroying our energy infrastructure and that they don't have a clue when or if the lights are coming back on in

Chicago, New York, the TVA region, or in Maine. People are freezing to death, for crying out loud. Say what you want, but the Japanese Government took care of business and protected their people. Our Government is asking us for help to identify the terrorist organization.

"God, I miss our country." They stayed warm under the comforter and heated blanket and hugged each other. Until other ideas filled their heads.

Afterwards, Sheila went to the bathroom. She looked out the window at a depressing gray sky where the sun was barely visible. Twelve eyes were looking back at her menacingly. She was trembling when she called out to her husband and said, "Honey, please, I'm frightened. Where is your hunting rifle?"

At that statement, Stephen jumped up, ran to the walk-in closet, pulled the rifle out of the overhead rack and sprinted to the bathroom to protect Sheila. He looked out the bathroom window to see wolves. He'd never seen wolves close up.

The extremely cold weather continued to drive wolves south, a new risk to livestock and humans.

CHAPTER 44

PIPELINE
(ZERO+240 DAYS)

FAIRBANKS, ALASKA – DECEMBER 13TH: Harold Pfeiffer, the army sniper, stepped off the plane in Fairbanks and thought he'd freeze to death just walking from the plane to the concourse, and that was *inside* the jetway. It was minus 28 degrees Fahrenheit outside and the sky was dark, in the early afternoon. The job was easy if it were not for the inclement weather. Only now did he conclude that taking this assignment might not have been such a good idea. But the money was too good. For the first time in his life he was going to be wealthy. After all, the job in Munich was a piece of cake, with no repercussions.

Sergeant Pfeiffer strolled out of the airport lobby to the taxi stand, and after only a few seconds of being outside was grateful for a taxi with heat.

"Where to?" asked the native Alaskan taxicab driver. Harold explained to the driver what he wanted. They spent the next 3 hours getting supplies and securing services, starting with a rifle and jacketed rounds. The guide with huskies and a sled was more difficult to secure than the warmest clothing available in all of Alaska. But he was successful -- he had an unlimited budget.

The next morning, Harold, the guide, the huskies and a sled ventured out into the coldest weather Harold had ever experienced, with winds at 12 miles per hour. Though he had no bare skin or eyes exposed to the elements, he was still at risk of freezing his extremities. Harold told the guide that he was a pipeline inspector and despite the weather conditions, he was required to perform these inspections. The guide didn't care; he was being well paid. The native Alaskan Indian guide escorted Sergeant Pfeiffer to the closest point that the Alaskan Pipeline came to Fairbanks. Once there, Harold asked the guide to go north. After roughly 2 miles of rough mushing, Harold pulled his Remington rifle and put five .45 ACP Highway Master police armor-piercing ammo holes into the pipe through its jacketing. The pipe immediately began leaking profusely.

Sargent Pfeiffer looked in the direction of the guide and said, "We're going to do this ten more times -- every 5 miles -- do you have a problem with it?"

The guide said, "The problem will be living long enough to get back to Fairbanks. We cannot go another

45 miles and return with all our toes." Harold used one of his armor penetrator bullets on the guide. He was going to have to kill him anyway. Harold took control of the sled and headed north. He accomplished his mission and put a total of fifty holes in the Alaska Pipeline, forcing the pipeline to close for two months until it could be repaired. The continued assault on the energy infrastructure of the U.S. and Canada translated to an additional 9,000 deaths attributable to freezing of citizens around the world.

The seven Huskies and three Malamutes were spotted by an Alaska Highway Patrolman on the outskirts of Fairbanks, dragging a sled. The man in the sled, later identified as Sergeant Harold Pfeiffer, was frozen solid.

CHAPTER 45

SISTERS
(ZERO+242 DAYS)

WANAKA, NEW ZEALAND – DECEMBER 15TH: After a great dinner of sautéed scallops, asparagus, and snow peas, the ladies sat with glasses of wine and finally had a chance to talk about Suzanne's and her mother's ordeal. Maya said, "You're one tough little sister to have survived that kidnap. As tough as Mom was, she was just a little too old to endure the cold and starvation. I am **so** grateful that you survived. Star needs her aunt Suzanne.

"What mom whispered in your ear at the end -- could she have been delusional and not known or meant what she was saying?"

"Possible, but unlikely. She seemed her usual confident self."

"Did mom ever tell you much about dad or what dad did when he wasn't at home? I remember him being loving, and fun. He was a pretty good cook, too. But he was away a lot. Mom used to say he was an accountant when we were young, but as we got older and figured out that he could not have bought mom the stuff he did on an accountant's salary, she clammed up and would never speak of his profession.

Suzanne said, "His murder was a strong signal that he was not a simple accountant. I wonder who he really was. I hope we're not descendants of criminals. How could Mom know that the guy who kidnapped us was the same guy who killed Dad? How could she know that?"

Maya jumped in and said, "And what in the world do mom and dad have to do with the group called *Society for Environmental Justice* that is destroying energy infrastructure, for the apparent purpose of freezing people to death? What's the connection?"

Suzanne asked Maya, "Have you told Tucker about dad? Does Tucker know that dad was into something shady?"

"No," Maya objected; "until we know otherwise, I'd like to think that Mom and Dad were honorable people. They never taught us anything but to be honorable. Did Mom ever tell you about the details of her exposure to the 'ghost'?"

"As best as my memory serves me, the story goes like this: *The guy she was testifying against and whom we now refer to as the 'ghost' never had a real name. He was referred to as Gamma-C-3. He was on trial for brutally murdering his social worker who came by the hospital for the criminally insane to help rehabilitate him. The cause of death was so horrid that even the jurors never heard the full truth. Mom was often called upon as an expert witness when the criminally insane were on trial. She almost always testified on the side of the prosecution. She had interviewed the 'ghost' through a plate glass window. She said that he couldn't carry on a conversation without suddenly trying to shock Mom with something so evil and off-the-wall that she couldn't continue the discussion without showing signs of anxiety.*

"The time came when the prosecution called her to testify. She apparently was extremely accurate in describing the guy's condition. He got so upset that he tried to attack her in the courtroom, even though he was shackled and handcuffed to two extremely large Chicago policemen. He yelled in the courtroom that he would torture her and kill anyone she loved. I understand that he was pretty graphic about the way he was going to torture her.

"To the best of my knowledge, Mom never knew that he had escaped from the highest security prison for the criminally insane in the country. If she knew, she never told anyone."

Maya said, "I didn't know that Mom was so wealthy. I guess Dad made a lot of money and left her a ton. Our very large trust fund that he left us when he died was just a pittance compared to his total wealth, though it was more than I needed. I have to know, Suzanne, who our father really was. Are you with me? Let's take some of our huge inheritance and find out who he really was."

Suzanne smiled and said, "Though I don't have your scientific brain, we think alike."

With that response, Maya pushed a button on the intercom and said, "Tank, if you or Powers can hear this, would you come in and visit with Suzanne and me?"

It was fifteen minutes before Tank strolled in and said, "Sorry ladies; I was on a call with that idiot Special Agent Vinny DeLuca. He's not making much progress; I'm beginning to question his competence."

Maya said, "Please, have a seat, you walk like your feet are killing you. We, Suzanne and I, or rather the Li Estate, want to hire *White Knight*. We will expect that you will keep our request as confidential as you would treat any other customer. That means keeping our request confidential from Tucker."

Tank said, "Whoa right there. I will not investigate Tucker or betray him in any way. It would be a conflict of interest and a personal impossibility. I can recommend another firm which I trust."

Maya interrupted Tank, "*White Knight* offers private investigation as one of its services, correct?"

"Yes."

"Before you reject our business, isn't it prudent to hear what the request is? All I'm asking is to keep the subject of the request from Tucker; this has absolutely nothing to do with him."

"OK."

Suzanne spoke up and said, "We want you to find out how our father made all his money. We want to learn who he really was. *If* we learn that our father -- and maybe it was *with* the complicit knowledge of our mother -- was doing something inappropriate, or illegal, we'd like the option of sharing it with Tucker ourselves. Is that asking too much?"

Tank said, "Someone else is already investigating your father." Both Maya and Suzanne's eyes widened. "Special Agent Vinny DeLuca, in his investigation of your mother, discovered your parents' wealth. He was trying to determine if something in your mother's past triggered the 'ghost.' In that investigation, he uncovered the fact that your mother's net worth was over a billion dollars. That, in turn, triggered a side investigation as to how she accumulated such wealth."

"And what has he uncovered?" Maya asked, hopefully.

Tank took a deep breath, tried not to let his frustration show and said, "Nothing, so far."

Suzanne asked, "So do we need to find another P.I. or can you handle it?"

Tank looked into Suzanne's eyes, knowing what she had been through, and discovered that he couldn't possibly say "no."

CHAPTER 46

LNG
(ZERO+244 DAYS)

LUSBY, MARYLAND – DECEMBER 17ᵀᴴ: Over the past several years, after the discovery of the scientific advance called hydraulic fracturing or fracking, the United States had become a net energy exporter of natural gas -- in the form of liquefied natural gas or LNG. Natural gas is difficult to transport from one point to another without changing it from a gas to a liquid. By cooling the natural gas to minus 260 degrees Fahrenheit, the gas can be reduced to 1/600ᵗʰ of its volume in the non-compressed state. Dominion Cove Point's natural gas pipeline is connected to Dominion Transmission's interstate pipeline, as well as to other interstate pipelines which have access to the growing natural gas supplies in the region. The Cove Point plant is used to export LNG globally and provides extra energy security to the United States. One supertanker of LNG shipped from Lusby, Maryland is enough energy to keep 50,000 homes warm for a full year. Europe and Japan are desperate for the energy which this LNG provides.

"Three for the price of one," thought the 'ghost.' An LNG export terminal down for repairs would hurt the U.S., Japan *and* the European Union.

There is nothing more inconspicuous than a brown UPS truck. He picked out a driver leaving the UPS distribution center who was roughly his size. When the driver made a delivery to an office complex, the 'ghost' slipped inside the truck. He could have just knocked the driver out when he returned to the truck, but that wasn't as much fun as garroting him. He always liked the sounds garroting made. He was careful not to get blood on the driver's brown uniform. The driver's body fit nicely into one of the boxes in the back of the van.

The ghost put on the brown uniform and drove to a Public Storage facility and entered the code (recently acquired under the name Robert Grainger) to pass through the gates. He drove down to his storage unit, backed the van up close to the door and opened the rolling overhead door. He grabbed the dolly in the van, removed the box that contained the garroted driver and replaced the box with another box eight feet long by two feet square. The ghost removed additional boxes in the van to make space for his next item. He started up and drove a Kawasaki Ninja motorcycle into the back of the UPS van. He closed the roller door, locked it, drove the van to the gate, opened it and drove in the direction of the Dominion Energy's Cove Point LNG Export facility.

The 'ghost' didn't have to get that close. The rocket propelled grenade (RPG) he was carrying had a decent range. All he had to do was get within 200 yards of the natural gas pipeline entering the Cove Creek facility. He already knew where he needed to aim the RPG. He had hacked into the plant computer-aided-design drawings and determined the point of greatest vulnerability. He pulled the van into position so that his escape on the motorcycle was out the back. He changed clothes again, took off his UPS driver uniform, and replaced it with another outfit. He sat in the passenger side of the van, both doors open, with the RPG launcher outside the van facing his target. He had a ski mask on in the event he could later be identified on some unknown surveillance camera. He let it rip.

The rocket flew at a speed of 230 miles per hour; in less than three seconds it hit its target. The 'ghost' dropped the launcher, grabbed a helmet, jumped on the Ninja and blew out of the back of the brown van within 15 seconds of the launch. He turned off the main road, ditched the motorcycle under pre-prepared branches, and casually blended in at the local shopping center. He selected a grocery cart and was wandering the aisles as if he belonged there.

The RPG grenade had exploded at the valve prior to the LNG pipeline entrance to the plant. It created quite a fireball, a war-like display including shrieking sounds, black smoke, lots of excitement -- and the attack activated several automatic firefighting systems and response protocols. The plume of flame reached 100 feet into the air. But the fire was quickly placed under control; backup valves before and after the destroyed safety valve closed automatically and the impact was minimized. After the damage was assessed, it was determined that it would take roughly sixty days to get the plant back on line. This was just as the 'ghost' had planned.

CHAPTER 47

YOU CAN'T ALWAYS GET WHAT YOU WANT (ZERO+244 DAYS)

LOS ANGELES, CA – DECEMBER 17TH: Over the past three weeks the average temperature in Los Angeles had hovered around freezing. Though warm by Fairbanks, Caribou, Chicago, New York, and Des Moines standards, it felt cold to the natives who were not used to, and were unprepared for, an extended period of cold weather. Los Angeleans expected their city, state and federal governments to do something about it. Where were the citizens supposed to go to get government-supplied coats, gloves, heating fuel, and earmuffs? The 911 emergency call exchange was already overwhelmed with calls for home delivery of McDonald's Big Macs and Chicken McNuggets.

Too many residences in L.A. lacked heating systems, whether electric, natural gas or propane-fueled. But almost all residences had a television, usually a wide-screen. They could see the drama unfolding around the world. The depressing volcanic ash mixed with LA's natural smog, made their usually wonderful weather intolerable and the depressing news even more depressing. They gathered around the courthouse, at first, demanding warm clothing or warm shelter.

Then, the crowd grew larger and started demanding access to soup kitchens and government-supplied blankets.

The crowd grew even larger; it attracted the press and the troublemakers who enjoy seeing themselves on TV. Before long, the cold weather became a racial issue. As soon as race was mentioned, Rodney King's and Michael Brown's names were blasted over the loudspeakers, and it was on.

Storefronts were smashed in; looting for clothing and food spread to a radius of twenty miles. Weapons were drawn by people of all races trying to defend their property. As soon as the first death was announced by the media with a racial overtone, the violence grew.

When rioting and looting finally settled down, thirteen days later, 45 police officers had been killed in the line of duty, 14 firemen had been killed by the mob as they were trying to save people from burning homes, and 1,712 others -- both the innocent and the violent -- were dead.

The deadly cold weather continued; no one got government-provided blankets, clothing or food, and the depression grew worse. Sporadic violence continued, erratically, as time wore on.

CHAPTER 48

JIMMY MA
(ZERO+245 DAYS)

WANAKA, NEW ZEALAND – DECEMBER 18TH: Delilah, Jimmy Ma's girlfriend, was playing with Star on the floor, under Ram's constant watch. Ram never took his eyes off Delilah, but at the same time was not intimidating to her, with his chin on the floor. Delilah was reading a book about Yellowstone National Park to Star for the third time.

Tucker, Tank, Jolene and Powers were all in the study anxiously awaiting a complete debrief by Jimmy about the status of his findings. Maya was down in the lab talking with her sister, while trying to discover a way to reduce the duration of the extremely cold weather, under contract with ENTROPY. The people in the study were expecting Jimmy Ma to have followed the money and divulged the secret about who had ambushed the Cherokees and how the killers knew where to find them.

"I'll give you my status report verbally. The thugs who ambushed you, Tucker, and tried to kidnap Star

(Ram's head lifted up as he stared at Jimmy) were not Australian or Russian. Tucker, would you say something to that dog?"

Tank said, "That is not a dog; he's family, and if you call him a dog again things may get worse for you." Tank looked over at Ram and with the slight movement of one finger, Ram put his head back down … but he kept his eyes on Jimmy.

Jimmy swallowed hard and continued, "Two of the thugs were Serbian and the rest were Kurds. The Serbs and Kurds don't normally associate with each other, so that raises a flag. Following a link to their homeland, I discovered that they each had bank accounts with deposits from the same source, a bank in the Cayman Islands, under the name SFEJ, Inc."

"Deposits into the Cayman Island bank were made from a Swiss Bank with the name SFEJ, LLC. No deposits have been made into the Swiss Account for over 15 years. The account's name was changed to SFEJ, LLC this year."

"So," Tucker asked, "What was the name originally on the Swiss Account?"

Jimmy Ma knew his answer was going to cause all sorts of commotion. He took a deep breath and started to say something. Before he could answer the question, Star cheerfully and happily said, "Henry Li."

Everyone stared at Star with their eyes wide. Ram stood up and sashayed over to Star and stood beside her, daring anyone to be aggressive with her. Star said, "My middle name is Li, Suzanne's last name is Li and so was Grandma's." Everyone continued to stare at Star.

Jimmy Ma's mouth was open wide enough for a Boeing 777 to use it as a hangar. Jimmy thought to himself, "What the fuck just happened?"

Tucker understood immediately by looking at Jimmy Ma that Star had just read his thoughts. Tucker thought to himself, "Oh, fuck, how are we going to keep it a secret that Star has these special skills?"

Star amplified the situation by asking, "What does 'fuck' mean?"

Except for Jimmy Ma and Tucker, the room burst out in nervous laughter. Jimmy Ma knew for certain, now, that Star had read his thoughts. He and Tucker made eye contact for several seconds. Finally, a quick thinking Tucker said, "It's an acronym, sweetheart, for "Formerly Utilized Containers from Kansas." Everyone else in the room laughed even harder but Star dropped her head slightly and looked at her daddy as if looking over the top of a pair of glasses -- she knew that he was lying by reading everyone else's thoughts.

After reading and digesting everyone's shocking thoughts, Star said to Delilah, "Would you read to me again?" At that moment, at the wise age of five, Star Li Cherokee made a life-changing decision; she would no longer let people know that she was intercepting their thoughts or that she could experience the emotions of animals. She would pretend that she had lost, or had out-grown, the ability to read the thoughts of others.

Tank said to Tucker while looking at Jimmy Ma, "Based on everyone's reaction, I assume that what Star said is correct. If so, you might want to call Maya and Suzanne up here before we go on with Jimmy's status report."

Tucker got up and said, "I'd better explain this to them in person." Tucker left the study while Tank continued the discussion. "Who would have the right to alter an account's name from one entity to another?"

Jimmy Ma said, "That's out of my area of expertise."

Jolene said, "It could only be done by the Executor of the Estate or someone with the Executor's Power of

Attorney. You know, ***it is possible*** that SFEJ stands for the *Society for Environmental Justice,* and that the same group that killed Dr. Li also stole an old account owned by Henry Li."

Suzanne and Maya walked into the study at about the time Jolene finished her comments. Maya said, "And possibly the same people who murdered our father." Both Maya and Suzanne were staring at Tank, as if he had betrayed some secret, but Tank shrugged it off.

After Maya and Suzanne were completely brought up to speed by Jimmy Ma, Maya asked, "How much money are we talking about in this Swiss account?"

Jimmy said, "It started out with roughly $12 million but is down to $7.5 million after the withdrawals to the bank in the Cayman Islands. That account has had several withdrawals. There was a cash withdrawal of three million dollars. There were bank transfers to accounts that led to the Serbs and the Kurds and there is a bank transfer to a Sergeant Pfeiffer in Wiesbaden, Germany.

Suzanne said, "So, as I see it, this 'ghost' who works for the *Society for Environmental Justice,* kills Dad, hacks into his account, uses his funds to attack the energy infrastructure of the United States, Canada, and

Germany, kills my mother, kidnaps me and continues to use the funds in an attempt to murder Maya and kidnap Star. All this because he hated my mother for testifying against him?"

Tank's anger returned at the thought that he had the asshole in his grip and somehow was outsmarted by him.

"We need to locate the legal entity that had the right to change the name on the account in Switzerland," Tucker said.

"It's time for my buddy, Special Agent Vinny DeLuca to do something. This may be the lead he needs to pull himself out of a career nosedive. I'll go wake his ass up." Tank left the room and made the call.

Maya looked at Powers and asked, "How could this ghost know who to call to have us ambushed? How could he know who to call to get a sniper to shut down power in Munich and shut down the Alaska Pipeline? Who's running the *Society for Environmental Justice*? Jimmy, can you track down where funds come from for the *Society for Environmental Justice*? Powers, can you do a little PI on these guys?" Both of them nodded their heads affirmatively.

CHAPTER 49

ANGOLA
(ZERO+247 DAYS)

MOSCOW, RUSSIA – DECEMBER 20TH**:** The Prime Minister of Russia, the President of Russia, the Russian Director of Intelligence, and the highest ranking military general were in the Kremlin war room watching twelve separate wide screen monitors, each screen monitoring a different element of the military operation. Satellite visibility in the normal light wave-lengths was poor, but fortunately the microwave cameras could penetrate the ash clouds and software converted the data artificially back to an animated screen. It allowed them to monitor the operation.

The Pentagon – 4887 miles away, the Secretary of Defense and the Chairman of the Joint Chiefs of Staff were in a room similarly endowed. The Russian military was on the move. P3s had identified four Russian attack submarines off the west cost of the Republic of Angola. Russian TU-95 bombers were in the air flying over central

Africa. Three hundred Ilyushin Il-18s were progressing from Saudi Arabia's Riyadh Air Field in the direction of Luanda, Angola, the capital.

Moscow --The Prime Minister of Russia said to President Karloff, "You know, taking off from Riyadh telegraphs to the west that we are co-conspirators with Japan, that we turned our eyes away from their aggression if they supported our aggression. The U.S and NATO know that by now. So it will be interesting to see how they react."

Alexander Sversk, the Director of Intelligence, the head of the SVR, the modern-day version of the KGB said, "No worry; the President of the United States is preoccupied with disasters and crises of his own. He won't have the temerity to defend an unimportant country like Angola. And without the support of the United States, NATO is harmless."

President Karloff said to Director Sversk, "I hope your intelligence is correct, because we have 15,000 paratroopers in the air right now. They'd be sitting ducks against American fighter jets."

The Pentagon – The Chairman of the Joint Chiefs of Staff, Admiral Maxx Longstaff, said to the SecDef, Jane Bolton, "Well I see from the satellite photo on screen seven that the Russian Aircraft Carrier *Admiral Kuznetsov* is within range of Luanda. It won't be long now. It is time to inform POTUS." The SecDef took a deep breath and called President Allen in the oval office. He had been briefed earlier and knew the seriousness of the situation.

The President picked up the encrypted phone but did not speak; he waited. Secretary Bolton said into the conference room speakerphone, "There is only bad news, sir. First, Russian bombers are in the air, 300 Russian IL-18s are airborne, four attack submarines are in position and the *Kuznetsov* is ready to launch the fighter jets. If there is anything you can do to affect a change, now is a good time to call President Karloff. The other bad news is that the IL-18s took off from Riyadh, so the Japanese must be complicit."

"What would you have me say, Jane, 'please stop'?"

"No, sir."

"Would you have me make an idle threat?"

"No, sir."

"Would you have me engage in war with Russia at the risk of a huge number of American lives?"

"No, sir."

"Well, I'm all ears; what would you and the Chairman have me do? Do we have a defense agreement with Angola that I'm not cognizant of? Is the sovereignty of Angola a national security issue? Just what are we risking if we intervene? What are the consequences?"

The Chairman of the Joint Chiefs said, "Sir, silence from the United States is tantamount to approval. An unchecked Russia will lead to further aggression. At some point we're going to have to stand up to Russian -- and for that matter Japanese -- aggression. We can do it now or we can do it later."

"What I want from you, Admiral, and the SecDef, is a counter move. Get General LaSalle engaged and propose to me a duplicitous move that will surprise even them."

Moscow – Alexander Sversk watched the progress of the operation and said to President Karloff and the Prime Minister of Russia, "No movement by NATO; it is too late for them to do anything. We are past the point of no return; the MIGs have left the *Kuznetsov*. If the General agrees, you might consider calling The Republic of Angola's President Santos. How is your Portuguese, Mr. President?"

"Of course, it's not as good as yours, Alexander. Possibly you can act as a translator."

"It would be my pleasure." Alexander nodded to a Russian communications engineer. The engineer nodded back. In Portuguese, the Director of Intelligence said, "This call is from President Karloff of Russia. He is hereby declaring war on the Republic of Angola. To prevent unnecessary death to your people, we ask that you surrender. To prove my claim, a MIG-29 will strafe your palace in 30 seconds."

As claimed, a MIG-29 harmlessly strafed an area in the palace yard with gunfire.

"The next time around, the pilot will not be so gentle. Do you understand? Do you surrender? We will not kill you or your family if you surrender. We will kill many, many Angolans including you and your family if you do not. Your choice."

President Santos finally spoke, and said in Portuguese, "Why?"

Sversk answered in Portuguese, "The opportunity presented itself."

President Karloff leaned over in the direction of the Prime Minister of Russia and whispered, "To use a vulgar American expression, I hope we didn't just shit in our mess kit."

The Prime Minister's response was, "Only dead fish go with the flow."

Angola, its oil wealth, its warm water port and warm climate was now a territory of Russia; it was another geopolitical impact of the deadly cold weather.

CHAPTER 50

WE'RE OUT OF HERE
(ZERO+248 DAYS)

NORTHERN LATITUDES – DECEMBER 21ST: Eight months after the eruption of Mt. Merapi in Indonesia and seven months after the eruption of Mount Nyiragongo in Africa, the deadly cold weather continued its downhill slide without mercy, in all regions of the world. If there was any improvement in the darkened sky it was imperceptible; there was no indication that the ash and dust was settling at a meaningful rate. The sky showed no signs of brightening, no sign that a brilliant sun would ever peek through the haze and warm things up; it was the same everywhere on earth.

The winter solstice was today, in North America and Europe. The fall months this year were harsher than last year's winter. During an average or normal winter, weather conditions in places like Lillehammer, Norway; Vaasa, Finland; St. Johns, Newfoundland; Winnipeg, Manitoba; Nome, Alaska; Rugby, North Dakota; Tallinn, Estonia; Linz, Austria; Cheyenne, Wyoming; Maysville, West Virginia; Enterprise, Oregon and Walden, Colorado were brutally harsh. The forecast this year was for the winter months to be record-smashing -- the coldest in modern history.

It wasn't obvious to all at first, but people had started migrating south. People didn't believe that they could endure the upcoming winter, as forecast, under deteriorating conditions. Surviving winters with temperatures that occasionally drop to 10 below zero Fahrenheit was one thing; surviving winters where the potential for sustained temperatures at minus 35 degrees is quite another. People started winterizing their homes and heading south. Many of the courageous had no idea where they would end up; they just had to head south.

The more affluent northerners contacted various cruise lines and bought passage -- from Amsterdam to Aruba, Baltimore to the Bahamas or Tampa to Trinidad. When they arrived at their final destination, they just did not return to the cruise ship. Other affluent people were sailing on their seaworthy boats moored in places like Bath, Maine; Providence, Rhode Island; Copenhagen, Denmark; Dover, United Kingdom; Portland, Oregon; or Cape May, NJ. They would just stock up on food and clothing and hope for the best; they hoped that there was somewhere in the warmer weather world where they would be accepted.

On this day, December 21st, the high temperature in North America was in Panama City, Panama at 69 degrees Fahrenheit. In South America, near Rio de Janeiro, it rose to 75 degrees Fahrenheit. Europeans were swarming to Brazil, the French Guianas, the Cayman Islands, Trinidad and Tobago, Suriname, the British Virgin Islands, Martinique, Guadalupe, Saint Martin and Cuba where temperatures were alleged to rise to a balmy 50 degrees Fahrenheit. Americans were flocking to Miami, Puerto Rico, the Virgin Islands, Cabo San Lucas, Belize, Costa Rica, Cancun, Key West, Honolulu and Acapulco.

By Christmas Day, December 25th, **32 million** people had left their northern latitude homes for salvation somewhere else -- with the intent to stay there until the dust literally settled. Maybe they would be gone a few months; maybe they'd be gone a few years. The settlers of the old west and the pilgrims trying to make a new life in the new world had nothing on these courageous and adventurous survivors. The enormously greater numbers of people made this migration a global problem.

Mexico was the first country which tried to stop immigrants coming across the border from the north or from the Gulf of Mexico. The irony was not lost on anyone. The big difference, however, between immigration north by Mexicans and Central Americans, and emigration south by Americans and Canadians was the level of weaponry. Americans who were flooding the Mexican borders were well armed. Tough people from Wyoming and Idaho crossed the border in four wheel drive vehicles, only to be met by Mexican border patrol and police. Thirty Mexican police and twelve Americans were killed during the first incident. Seventeen Mexican police and five Americans were killed in the second incident, during just the first day of organized resistance by Mexican authorities.

The Mexican military was called in by the President of Mexico to secure the border. One hundred and thirty Americans and Canadians were killed on day two of the confrontation. Word spread, and tens of thousands of well-armed Americans from all over the country came to the border to protect their own. President Allen called the President of Mexico and advised him that the U.S. had 230 drones "monitoring" the border and that the Pentagon was watching. On the third day of the confrontation, the sheer volume of armed civilians along the border gave the President of Mexico pause. He rationalized that the illegal immigrants would not stay in Mexico forever -- only as long as the air was dirty and the sun couldn't penetrate to the land. Or, until they ran out of money. He capitulated, and ordered the Mexican police and military to stand down.

Sixty-five percent of the tens of thousands of Americans and Canadians at the border then returned home to their dwellings in Texas, Arizona, Tennessee or Manitoba. The remaining thirty-five percent pushed on into Mexico, and the border was officially opened in both directions.

Tens of thousands of Americans, Canadians, and Europeans flew to Caracas, Venezuela; Brazilia; Bogota, Colombia; Lima, Peru; Kingston, Jamaica, and San Salvador, El Salvador. This continued until the governments of those nations were compelled to stop incoming airline flights; they were overwhelmed, there were no hotel rooms available and streets were beginning to be littered with foreigners.

The winter in the northern hemisphere had just started. The deadly cold weather had pushed the world into geo-political flux.

CHAPTER 51

CHRISTMAS EVE (ZERO+251 DAYS)

WANAKA, NEW ZEALAND – DECEMBER 24TH: Christmas Eve in the Cherokee family was a joyful experience; the presence of a five-year-old made all the difference in the world. Chef Rhino prepared a fabulous dinner, a delicious seven course spread. Around the long dining room table sat the Cherokees, Suzanne, Tank and Jolene, Jimmy and Delilah, Powers, and five off-duty *White Knights*. Ram sat dutifully behind Star. A prayer was said by Tucker and a video was presented on a wide screen TV about the real meaning of Christmas before dinner was served. Star, whose China-doll face nearly always showed happiness, said, "Will we be able to open presents tonight?" Maya and Tucker had developed a method of thinking dis-information thoughts so that Star could not accurately read their minds. They'd been practicing for days now, so that Star would not read their thoughts and know what she was getting for Christmas. This was not easy. Maya was thinking about her lab work and Tucker was thinking about the people in Antarctica, so that Star could not "pick" their brains. If they were persistent and consistent, it worked.

Star looked over at Tank. Tank was thinking intentionally about Special Agent Vinny DeLuca. Star looked at Jolene who was thinking intentionally about how to stop the infection in Tank's feet. Star, getting more frustrated, looked at Powers who was intentionally thinking about his old flame, the treasured but deceased love of his life. Star knew what everyone was doing and shrugged her shoulders.

After dinner, Tucker and Maya told Star that she could open one gift of ***their*** choosing. Tucker donned his Santa Claus hat and pulled a huge box from behind the fresh and aromatic fifteen foot Canadian spruce Christmas tree. The box was large and heavy. She quickly ripped the paper off the box, but there was no writing under it. She unfolded the box top and found a small brown unmarked box inside the larger box. Star opened the new box to find a heavy metal box. She opened the heavy metal box to find an envelope in the box. She opened the envelope to find a piece of paper. The paper had some writing on it but the photos on the paper were all she needed to see. She looked around the room to see nothing but smiling people. She was finally going to Yellowstone National Park, and Powers was going to fly her in a helicopter to give her the best possible tour. She grinned and reached for her mom with a long hug, whispering, "Can Ram go, too?"

New Zealand is on the other side of the International Date Line from America, eleven hours ahead of Special Agent Vinny DeLuca. Vinny was sitting with Agent Magnus Glass in Quantico, Virginia. He called Tank, and as soon as Tank answered the phone, Vinny said, "I have a Christmas present for you."

Tank said, "I didn't know you loved me."

Vinny said, "The name of the attorney who is the executor of Henry Li's estate is a guy named Daniel Cohen. It seems that Counselor Cohen is down on his luck. According to his estranged wife, Cohen disappeared about 45 days ago. All his accounts are stripped clean. His wife has a debt of around a hundred thousand dollars because her, and apparently also his, identities have been stolen. At first, I thought it was a marriage gone bad, and he just skipped. But the more I looked into it, the more it looked like the work of the 'ghost.' He stole the guy's identity in order to change the name on Henry Li's account. The rest of the shit he pulled on the Cohens was just for fun. My guess is that we'll never find a trace of Cohen; he's likely at the bottom of some lake that is frozen over.

"I think Maya and Suzanne will be relieved to know that their late parents were victims, and not complicit in any way with what is going on with this terrorism. Merry Christmas to you, too. What have you uncovered about the *Society for Environmental Justice*?"

"Donors to the Society are small potatoes. There is no past history of violence. Their charter is to prevent mining companies from desecrating the earth, extracting natural resources like coal, copper, silver, uranium, gold, platinum and other mining ores and leaving behind a death scene of scarred earth and acidic lakes. As best we can tell, they have no beef with the energy sector. I believe that the *Society for Environmental Justice* is a fall organization to throw us off track. It worked."

CHRISTMAS DAY – DECEMBER 25TH: Star Cherokee was definitely the *star* of the day; everyone doted on her, played with her and enjoyed the spirit of Christmas. The adults exchanged gag gifts, played cards, and otherwise relaxed and tried to put the world's problems aside. It was summer in Wanaka so the weather was not too cold to venture out (it was 45 degrees Fahrenheit). Even though the dirty air kept the sun from shining through to their faces, the men went outside and threw a football around to each other. All the players darted into the house, though, when Tank proposed that they split up into sides and play tackle football.

Tank stayed outside and threw a baseball for Ram to fetch. Tank said to Ram as they were playing, "My favorite Mark Twain quote is 'The more I learn about people, the more I like my dog.'"

Late in the afternoon, they sat around the great room and told stories on one another. Suzanne made the mistake of turning the 70" wide screen TV on to watch the news. Everyone suddenly quieted down, as, even on Christmas Day, they couldn't escape the depression that the world had fallen into. Fox News was recapping the current day's situation. After trying to keep it upbeat by talking about people visiting Jerusalem and children enjoying gifts, the anchor finally let viewers have it between the eyes. "A report was released earlier this week by the Department of Energy's Lawrence Livermore Lab entitled 'An Estimate of the Duration of the Historically Cold Weather As a Result of the Recent Volcanic Eruptions.' This report can be found on the Department of Energy web page or on a link at FoxNews.com. The report states that because of the energy released in the Mount Merapi eruption, the average size of the ash particles is ten times smaller than the particles from eruptions during all of recorded history. As a result of the very small sub-micron particles, coupled with an unusually low elevation jet stream, the particles are remaining airborne longer. The bottom line is this -- the U.S. Government estimates that this cold weather will last an additional two years."

The anchor looked out into the lens of the camera to the millions of viewers and said in a deadpan voice, "Merry Christmas. When we come back, we'll cover Japan's declaration of war on Thailand."

"Did I hear that right," asked Powers, "Japan declared war on Thailand? I sort of understood Saudi Arabia, but Thailand? I spent some interesting times in Bangkok during R&R from the Vietnam war."

"It's about rice," responded Jolene.

"I had heard that the rice paddies were freezing in Japan, that the production can't keep up with consumption, and that you can't buy rice on the open market because China is gobbling it all up." said Jimmy Ma.

Maya stood up, excused herself and said, "I have a DOE report to download and read."

Star said, "Mom, it's Christmas." Maya looked around the room and sat back down. "Tell me a story about Yellowstone."

CHAPTER 52

STRATEGIC PETROLEUM RESERVE (ZERO+253 DAYS)

NEW ORLEANS, LA – DECEMBER 26TH: The Bombay Club always had patrons, day or night. He sat at the bar sipping a Hurricane, deep in thought, pensive, and frustrated. He had no recollection of ever being stumped, of not being able to come up with a plan. He was the smartest man in the world; surely he could come up with something. He took his Hurricane in a plastic container and left the bar to wander Bourbon Street and people-watch while he continued to brew over a plan. He thought about the fact that he had hacked into the security systems at the Strategic Petroleum Reserve, studied the plethora of physical security systems, and couldn't figure how to shut down the world's largest emergency supply of oil, 727 million barrels.

The sub-forty degree weather didn't seem to bother the partying people; hell, two women lifted their sweatshirts and bared their chests at him just for the fun of watching his reaction. He was aroused, but didn't have time to think about how he felt about it. When he went down that path, it never ended well; his idea of sexual pleasure was apparently abnormal. His mind wandered to Suzanne Li – but he shook off the thought.

The people on Bourbon Street intrigued him; they were all iconoclasts, thumbing their nose at the world, telling everyone that they didn't care what anybody thought of them. "It's a good thing they don't care," the ghost thought to himself, "because I don't think much of them, either." As he walked around the French Quarter, his mind was wandering, trying to figure how he was going to disrupt the two facilities in Louisiana that consisted of 29 salt caverns.

He overheard a couple of loud drunks joking with each other, one calling out to his friend and calling him Henry. This made the ghost think of Henry Li, and his mind wandered to the day he murdered Henry. A smile crossed his face as he thought not only about the pain he caused Henry, but the emotional pain he caused the hateful psychiatrist, Ingrid Li. She damn near ruined his life; he could have been stuck in a mental hospital for the rest of his days. Then, he heard the name Henry called out again.

One never knows when an epiphany was going to strike. Why was he trying to penetrate the security of the Strategic Petroleum Reserve when he could just hit the Henry Hub in Erath, Louisiana? The Henry Hub is the interconnection of nine interstate and four intrastate pipelines that provide access to major markets throughout the country. The Henry Hub was used as the pricing point for natural gas futures trading on the New York Mercantile Exchange. If he could disrupt the operations of the Henry Hub, he could make a serious dent in the remaining U.S. energy supplies. It might be worth another 100,000 deaths.

So he left the next morning to take care of business, as he had at the LNG terminal in Lusby, Maryland. The temporary disruption of the natural gas supply to the northern states as a result of the destruction he wrought at the Henry Hub actually exceeded the 'ghost's' estimate.

"It's not my fault; I was born this way," the 'ghost' said to himself out loud, in a Motel 6 in Meridian, Mississippi, afterwards. Three percent of men and one percent of women are estimated to be sociopaths by the American Society of Psychoanalysis Physicians. Three percent of the 150 million males in the United States amounts to four and a half million male sociopaths roaming around the country. There are 3.5 billion males in the world, which means that there are 100 million male sociopaths in the world. Using the same ratio, were there 16 sociopaths in the United States Congress?

"It's not my fault; I'm just here to thin the herd. Why? What is compelling me to do this? I'm like my old cat; she used to kill voles, birds, snakes, mice -- not for food, but just because it was in her DNA, because she wanted to -- it was a sport. So why am I so different? I just like to kill humans, as many as I can. Why did God make me this way? Maybe because it is time to thin out the population; we're at 7 billion. Scientists are now claiming that the next ice age is upon us; maybe that's also God's way of thinning the herd. Maybe."

The ghost created his own algorithm that calculated the number of deaths he had compiled, based on his actions and estimates. The largest number of victims had been the elderly. Without access to heat energy in the way of natural gas, propane, electricity, oil, coal, or wood, most elderly couldn't survive this deadly cold weather. By his calculation, he had only killed 750,000 people, well below his target.

He had a lot of work yet to do.

CHAPTER 53

THE SITUATION ROOM
(ZERO+254 DAYS)

WASHINGTON, DC – DECEMBER 27TH: President Allen looked like he'd been drawn through a keyhole, washed out and hung up to dry, and he looked old. He was just 53 years old and now looked closer to 70. His eyes were swollen and his demeanor seemed halting. He convened a meeting in the situation room, and for the first time asked the vice president to join.

President Allen turned to the vice president: "I'd like you to run this meeting; it's time that you engage in the decision-making process here. With that said, I'd like the Director of the FBI to share with us his progress in identifying the perpetrator of all the energy infrastructure terrorism, and report on what group or organization is responsible for the attacks."

The Director looked around the room at the powerful people and humbly said, "It is our collective opinion based on research into the members and contributors to the *Society for Environmental Justice* that there is absolutely no truth in their culpability. They actually have applied for a name change so that the members are free from the stigma of association with the terrorist acts. The diversion wasted a lot of our time and resources, which I believe was a part of the real organization's plan."

The vice president asked, "Have you identified the real organization, yet?"

The Director said, "Not yet."

"Do you have any leads?"

The Director of the FBI said, "The Islamic State of Iraq and the Levant -- ISIL -- has claimed credit, but though we know they operate in the U.S. and Canada, we suspect that they just want to use this opportunity as a recruiting tool."

The vice president said, "So the FBI has no clue after months of investigation? Let me ask another question: who stands to gain from these attacks on our energy infrastructure. Who is on your list of potential suspects?"

Before the Director of the FBI had time to answer the question, President Allen interrupted and said, "Rather than asking the question, 'Who stands to gain,' please ask the question, 'who has gained thus far?'"

In rapid sequence, people in the room started rattling off those entities that had profited from the destruction of the energy infrastructure:

"The coal industry"

"Cruise lines"

"The manufacturer of MEGs"

"Construction companies that rebuild the infrastructure"

"Japan"

"The green energy industry"

"Russia"

"The people of North Korea"

"The funeral industry"

The last suggestion made by the President pretty much shut everyone up, after this. The list of winners was short.

"What is the status of blackouts?"

"Chicago is still without power. New York City is still operating with rolling blackouts; the TVA region is still without power; LA has power in most locations after the riots, and Caribou has power from other sources -- though there is no power from the dam. And I understand that Vancouver is still without power," said the FBI Director.

"Let me get this straight," said the vice president; "this terrorist group has been successful at creating blackouts all over the U.S.; it has branched out to successfully blackout Munich, Germany and it has stopped the production of MEGs -- and yet we don't have a single lead about who the perpetrators are. Do I have that right, director?"

Everybody at the table was looking down at their notes or their shoelaces.

CHAPTER 54

NO END IN SIGHT
(ZERO+255 DAYS)

WANAKA, NEW ZEALAND – DECEMBER 28TH:
Maya, and to a lesser extent, Tucker, were working in the laboratory, still trying to come up with an idea to help shorten the duration of the frigid cold weather. They were trying to find something that would get the suspended ash and debris out of the air, when a request to skype came in from Tucker's old boss, Stephen Sanders, CEO of ENTROPY.

"To what do we attribute the honor of this call?" asked Tucker.

"The honor is all mine," answered Sanders; "you guys did some amazing stuff with the spray which is being tested in Antarctica. If it works, you will have saved many lives. How are you coming with the other project, the one to clear the air of ash?"

"We're nowhere," Maya said as she screwed up her face with a ghoulish frown. "You know, Stephen, I'm a physicist and Tucker is an entrepreneur. We need a chemist to join this operation. Who do you have in the ENTROPY organization who can contribute to this effort? The sub-micron volcanic ash is likely to stay airborne for a very long time unless we discover some way to combine the particles and make them less aerodynamic."

"We have one of the brightest minds in the country on our staff. Our best chemist is currently on another contract, so you'll have to work remotely, using our video conferencing tools," said Stephen Sanders. "Will that work for you?"

Maya said, "It is certainly not ideal, but what I need is to pick the chemist's brain. What's his name?"

"You mean, **her** name -- Dr. Indira Gupta. I'll get the two of you linked as soon as our day starts. She's in the central time zone so it's only 4:35 a.m. where she is. But the primary reason for my call was to see if you, Tucker, could meet me somewhere; I need to speak with you in private and in person."

Tucker looked over at Maya sitting on a lab stool and made eye contact to determine if she thought it was or was not a good idea to leave the relative security of the compound. Maya cocked her head, squinted her eyes, and wrinkled her brow; synapses were arcing -- again. Finally, she asked, "Would you take Tank or Powers with you?"

"OK, Stephen, I'll bite; is there any advance information you can provide me so that I can prepare myself for the discussion? And where would you like to meet?"

"Unfortunately, I am not at liberty to provide you any information, in this format. How about Honolulu, which should be the easiest location for you? From a flight time standpoint, it is about halfway from Boston."

Tucker said, "I hear the Governor of Hawaii has temporarily shut down the airport and is not allowing anyone into the state. They are suffering from all the full flights in and empty flights out. He shut down all flights from Japan, Hong Kong, or Seoul about six weeks ago. How about Buenos Aires? It's in the southern hemisphere and is not getting overwhelmed with immigrants like other South American cities."

"Deal; meet you at the Grand Hotel in forty-eight hours."

For the last twenty-five days, Boris Slaughter had been monitoring Stephen Sanders' phone calls -- his land lines, his cell phones and even his encrypted satellite phone. Though the pay was good, it was fucking boring; listening to boring conversations and encrypted gibberish that he had to transfer to a thumb drive and send off to a PO Box in Oklahoma. Boring, boring, boring; day after day after day. Boris had to keep the van running all the time to keep from freezing, and he had to discreetly follow this guy to his home in Exeter, NH and back to his office in Boston. Twenty-five days of this damn stuff, but at $2,500 per day, he thought it was worth it. Finally, at 4:30 a.m. on the morning of the 25th day, he hit pay dirt. Sanders finally called Tucker Cherokee through the public airwaves.

Boris Slaughter called his client and said, "They are meeting in 48 hours, at the Grand Hotel, Buenos Aires, Argentina."

Through the phone, a computerized voice said in English, "You will receive a bonus when the information is validated." That was it, nothing more.

CHAPTER 55

OUT OF WITNESS PROTECTION
(ZERO+257 DAYS)

BUENOS AIRES, ARGENTINA – DECEMBER 30TH: When Tucker Cherokee and Tank Alvarez walked off the plane, they enjoyed exposure to summer weather at 55 degrees Fahrenheit, with a light breeze. Though the sun was still blocked by the ash haze, it was wonderful to feel such warm weather. They only had carry-ons, so they proceeded quickly to the immigration checkpoint. No longer was the perfunctory stamp the way of immigration. Tucker must have been asked 30 questions about why he was traveling on a U.S. Passport from New Zealand and how long he intended to stay and what he was going to do in Argentina and on and on. Tank's intimidating size and look didn't help him through customs and immigration. Fifty minutes after landing, Tucker and Tank were finally waiting at the taxi stand.

Tank was constantly surveying the crowd and identifying potential escape routes. He noticed two different people who became blips on his natural radar. Tank and Tucker got into the taxi and headed to the Grand

Hotel. Tank maintained a constant active vigilance by observing their surroundings. Tucker asked, "Something bothering you? Anything I need to know about?"

"Nothing specific, but there is an air of suspicion about -- too many people looking our way. I always get stares because of my size. But we're getting way too many observers who follow up with phone calls. Stay alert."

Tucker said, "If you know anyone in Buenos Aires who can provide us some defensive weapons and ammunition, maybe you need to call them now."

Tank said, "I did that before we left Wanaka. Someone should have left a message at the hotel check-in for us -- a contact to provide us with weapons."

"That's what makes you so special, Tank; you are always ahead of me on these things." They got to the Grand Hotel, tipped the taxi driver, and wandered into the hotel lobby. Before they got to the check-in counter, a man with a cane was aggressively honing in on Tucker. Tank stopped the man, took the cane from him and checked it for concealed firepower. It was just a cane. The man said, "You must be Tank Alvarez; I've heard good things about you, and I can see that you are thorough."

"Good to see you my friend," said Tucker; you look much better in person than over Skype. How long have you been here waiting for us? Oh, Stephen Sanders, this is Tank and Tank this is my old boss, Stephen Sanders. So, we'll check in, take 15 minutes or so to get settled, then meet you where?"

"I've been here roughly twelve hours and rented a meeting room under the name of "Parent-Teacher Conference. Down the hall, second left." See you there in 15."

Tucker checked in first and had a message from Steven Sanders. Tank checked in and had a message from Powers. It read, "3133 Siesta Street. Carlos Carlos." Tank leaned over to Tucker and said, "I'll catch up with you. Our defensive weapons are ready for us. Please, take my carry-on and stay in your hotel room until I get back, OK?" Tank turned around and went back out into the street in front of the hotel and caught a taxi. He gave the driver the address.

The driver looked at Tank, and said, "Señor, are you sure? Siesta Street is in a very rough neighborhood." Tank reaffirmed the address and told the driver that he would pay him extra to wait for him while he went inside.

It was indeed a rough neighborhood, and though it was cold and dreary by Buenos Aires standards, there were too many men hanging around outside pretending to loiter. Tank opened the taxi door and stood up. Two of the loiterers threw their cigarettes down and approached Tank. One of them said in Spanish, "You are a big one. Why does a big man like you come here?" The second man reached down and pulled a knife -- partially to intimidate the big man and partially because he was a little fearful of Tank. It was a tactical error. Tank practically ripped the man's arm off, grabbing the knife while concurrently placing his right foot into the talker's face. Both were on the pavement in less than five seconds. The man with the dislocated shoulder was screaming while the talker was out for the count.

Tank yelled out to the front door of 3133 Siesta, "Carlos, Carlos." Thirty seconds later the door opened. A man came through the door and said, "So, how do you know my friend, Powers?"

Tank said, "He trained me and now he works for me. How do *you* know Powers?"

"Not your concern. What I am giving you is a loan -- I want them back before you leave Argentina; is that understood?" Tank nodded. Suddenly, an army of twelve heavily armed men surrounded the taxi at Tank's back. He was helpless to defend himself and felt out-maneuvered by this new acquaintance. Fortunately, the taxi trunk lid opened, and the Carlos army completely filled the trunk with weapons.

Tank said, "Thank you. What kind of tools of the trade have you supplied us?"

Carlos -- or whatever his name was -- said, "What Powers told us to give you." With that last comment he backed into the building. Tank turned around and the twelve men were gone as quickly as they had arrived. He was in a hurry to return to the back seat of the taxi and head back to the hotel.

The driver said, "This is a rough neighborhood, no?"

Tank said to the driver, "I need some suitcases or something similar; I can't just walk into the hotel with all these 'tools.' Can you drive me to somewhere I can buy a container or suit case?"

"Si, señor."

In less than five minutes, the driver pulled over at a rent-a-truck place, went inside and returned with two $2 cardboard boxes big enough to hold all of the weapons.

They folded the boxes, split the weapons between the two boxes and returned them to the trunk. Powers had ordered an M16 with enough rounds to last a week, four Smith & Wesson BodyGuard 380s, 2 hand grenades, body armor, night vision goggles, three PE14-CP Pentagon Elite I knives, and several tear gas canisters. Tank thought to himself, "What the hell **was** Powers thinking?"

Once back at the hotel, Tank carried the boxes directly to the meeting room. Stephen Sanders was waiting, looking a little impatient. Tank looked at him with his cane and said, "I hear you're pretty tough. Rumor has it, you survived an episode with a People's Republic of China assassin."

"True. Though I'll never walk without a cane, I'm alive and he's not."

"Then you know how to handle these." Tank proceeded to give Stephen a Pentagon Elite I Knife, a BodyGuard 380, and a vest. "Listen, this may seem like I'm overreacting, but Tucker's cover has been blown; someone tried to ambush him and his wife, and someone tried to kidnap his daughter. This is the first time in over five years that he has escaped witness protection coverage. Call me a little paranoid, but I can't be too careful. I'm going up to his room to escort him down. Sorry we're late, but Tucker is following his security protector's orders."

The meeting room was small, roughly 25 feet by 30 feet, with a main entrance from the hotel lobby and a service entrance in the back. A table consisting of two six foot by three foot reference tables were in the middle of the room with a table cloth covering them. A pitcher of water was on the table with drinking glasses turned upside down. After Tank had escorted Tucker back down to the meeting room, Stephen and Tucker were sitting at the table. Before Tank could sit down, Stephen asked Tank to sweep the room for listening devices. Tank said, "Sorry, Mr. Sanders, but I didn't bring anything with me to sweep the room with."

"I did," Sanders said as he reached into his briefcase and brought out a portable radio-frequency scanner and handed it to Tank. Tank smiled at Sanders and proceeded to sweep the room for possible listening devices, but found none. Tank returned to the table, handed Sanders his portable sweeper and sat down at the table. Stephen Sanders stared at Tank.

Tank said, "What?"

Sanders said, "You can't listen to my conversation with Tucker. I'm sorry."

Tucker said, "Wait a minute, Stephen; there is no one in the world I would trust with whatever you are going to say, more than Tank."

"Sorry. Can you wait outside and guard the door?"

"No. I have to be inside so I can watch both the main and service entrances."

"OK. Can you wait just inside the door?" An irritated and angry Tank picked up his chair and set it just in front of the main door, about 15 feet from the table."

Sanders leaned over to Tucker and said, "Now, would you please turn off your transmitter which communicates directly into Tank's earpiece?" Tucker did as he was asked and Tank grimaced even more. Stephen Sanders did all the talking for the first twenty minutes. Tucker's lips didn't move, and he asked no questions. Tank could pick out a word or two but nothing more. Tucker leaned in and spoke for maybe thirty seconds. Sanders' reply took another five or so minutes.

Then, the service entrance door flew open; six fully armed men in combat gear surged through, while two more stayed just outside the service entrance door and protected their flank; Tank got the first shots off and drilled two of them before they could return fire -- but three rounds hit Tank square in the chest. Two of the attackers with weapons drawn went to the table Tucker and Sanders were occupying without firing; one had a stun gun in his hand when Tucker shot him between the eyes with the .38 BodyGuard which Tank had given him. Sanders shot the other attacker who got close to the table, and then rolled under the table where the boxes of weapons were hidden.

Sanders got two slugs in the back of his head. Tucker -- who also rolled under the table, to select a weapon -- came up with the M16 and started firing. The two attackers closest to the table were not returning fire. They froze, and Tucker instantly understood that their instructions were to kidnap Tucker and under no circumstances let him be killed. Their hesitation cost them their lives, as Tucker opened up and eliminated all but the two flank protectors outside the door, who escaped.

Tucker ran to Tank to check on him. Tank was the only one who had donned his vest. He was hurt, but he was going to live. Tucker ran over to Stephen Sanders and instantly knew that he had met his fate; the entire back of his head was gone. The police sirens were soon audible. Tucker wasn't anxious to explain to the police what they were doing with the firepower they had. It was going to be a long night.

Tucker promised himself that he would honor what Stephen Sanders had just asked him to do. Tucker was on a mission. But first, he had to figure out who just tried to kidnap him. There was only one reason to kidnap Tucker Cherokee; the same reason he had been in witness protection for the past five years. Someone, or more likely some nation, wants the secrets about how to make the MEGs work. So far only two nations have that secret; the United States and the People's Republic of China. Keeping this technology a secret apparently must have been as difficult as it was for the United States to keep the atomic bomb secrets after World War II. Tucker put his weapons down and his hands up waiting for the Argentina police to burst through the door.

CHAPTER 56

FIREWORKS
(ZERO+258 DAYS)

WANAKA, NEW ZEALAND – DECEMBER 31ST: For the last couple of days, Maya had been working in the lab and constantly communicating with her new partner in crime, Dr. Indira Gupta. They tried a variety of chemicals, electrical pulses, magnetic fields, changes in pH, and slight atmospheric pressure changes, but could not come up with anything practical as a solution to the problem of removing 25 cubic miles of volcanic rock pulverized into aerodynamic sub-micron particles dispersed throughout the entire stratosphere from sea level up to 75,000 feet above sea level.

Oh, they found plenty of solutions, as did competing entities at national and international laboratories. But the solutions were all totally impractical -- adding various chemicals to coagulate the ash, making them bind with each other, thereby changing the size and aerodynamic properties. The airborne volcanic ash would precipitate rapidly, fall to the ground and clear the air. The solutions worked in the lab, but the method of getting the chemicals into contact with trillions upon trillions of tiny particles made the solution impossible to implement. Maya and Indira gave up for the day; tomorrow was another day.

New Zealand was the first major country to celebrate the New Year every year because of its position just to the west side of the International Date Line -- the clock passed through midnight on December 31st there, first. The City of Wanaka celebrated the New Year by putting on a spectacular fireworks display. The haze from the volcanic ash was likely to dampen the enjoyment of the fireworks display this year, and the unusually cold summer kept many from standing outside to witness the artistry of the presentation. Star was sound asleep with her head on Maya's shoulder; Maya always enjoyed the feeling of love that came with holding Star. The first boom of the fireworks started precisely at midnight, and a broad variety of pyro techniques and designs were displayed. Star woke up and quickly recognized that this must be a special night. The fireworks only lasted seven minutes, but the variety of designs was fun to watch.

As all the pyrotechnical material dropped to the ground and the smoke cleared, Maya thought that she saw the stars for the first time in months. It lasted only a few seconds, but she was sure she saw stars. She walked hand in hand with Star back to the house -- with *White*

Knights remaining vigilant at a distance -- when Star asked, "Where's Daddy?"

Maya said, "He is in the country of Argentina, but he'll be back home soon." Maya was thinking, however, that she was surprised that she hadn't gotten a call from Tucker. Star, having previously decided that she would stop revealing that she was reading other's minds, had to keep her concern private -- and that was very hard for a five-year old.

When Maya returned to the compound, she tried to reach Tucker, but he did not answer the phone. Maya tried to reach Tank, but he did not answer his phone. So Maya called Indira, who did answer the phone. Maya said, "Are there fireworks displays anywhere near you tonight in celebration of the New Year?"

Indira said, "I have no idea; I generally find firework displays uninteresting. Why?"

"We watched fireworks here a few minutes ago, and I could have sworn that for a few seconds after the show was over, I could see the stars. You don't suppose that there is something in the fireworks that make the volcanic dust drop due to a reaction with black powder, or the potassium nitrate or the charcoal or the metal salts or even the sulfur?"

Indira said, "Interesting; I'll see if there is a display somewhere locally, and attend. If I see the stars afterwards, it will be way more exciting to me than the fireworks themselves ever could be."

CHAPTER 57

IMPRISONED
(ZERO+258 DAYS)

BUENOS AIRES - DECEMBER 31ST: Though it was past midnight in Wanaka when Powers received the call, it was still early evening on New Year's Eve in Buenos Aires. Carlos Carlos, or whatever his real name was, said: "You owe me $30,000. My tools of the trade were impounded by the police. Your friends did a poor job of handling things discreetly. They are in jail under weapons charges."

Powers said, "What jail, and who is the arresting officer?"

"How should I know such things? Until I receive my money, I will know very little. You know my routing and account numbers." He hung up.

Living conditions in an Argentine jail were slightly different from the living conditions in Tucker's Wanaka Compound, where he had gotten used to a personal chef and servants -- slightly different. Tucker was apparently not as persuasive with the Buenos Aries police as he customarily had been in the past; these folks didn't buy his story -- the truth.

WANAKA, NEW ZEALAND - JANUARY 1ST:
Maya was starting to seriously worry about Tucker. It was uncharacteristic of him not to check on her and Star -- not to call in. Maya called Jolene and asked if she'd heard from Tank. Jolene said no, but that it was not unusual for Tank to remain silent when on assignment. Maya and Star were having breakfast when Powers wandered into the kitchen where Chef Rhino was preparing his usual specialties. Powers needed sustenance and coffee. Maya asked Powers, "Have you heard from Tucker or Tank? How's it going in Argentina?"

Powers said, "No I haven't heard from Tucker or Tank." This wasn't a lie, but when Powers made eye contact with Star, he knew that he had better say something before Star said something to discredit him. "But I do have reasons to be concerned, so I am going to check it out and find out what is going on there."

Star didn't say anything, but she now knew that her dad was in trouble. She said nothing, but looked again at Powers, who was trying ***not*** to make eye contact with her. Star now understood that Powers was going to do something good for her dad, while not worrying her mom. Maya asked, "What reasons do you have to worry about Tucker?"

Powers couldn't help himself but to look at Star as he said, "A supplier of firepower to Tank wants immediate payment because he doesn't think he'll get the weapons back. I've got to check out his story."

Powers was saved by the phone. Maya received a call from Indira Gupta. Indira said, "You were right, I saw the stars for a few seconds myself. They were dim, but I saw them. I'll conduct a few bench-scale tests here and recommend some things for you to test there. This could result in a breakthrough; who knows?"

BUENOS AIRES, ARGENTINA – JANUARY 2ND: The U.S. Ambassador to Argentina made a call to the President of Argentina asking the President to intervene and release two prisoners under the names of Brinton Gray (Tucker's name under FBI witness protection) and Jorge Alvarez (Tank). The President of Argentina thanked the ambassador for the call and said he'd look into the situation; he made no promises. He proceeded to call his head of security and said, "I have a new assignment for you."

Tucker spoke loudly to Tank, who was in a separate but adjacent cell, "What do you know about due process here in Argentina? Do you think we have any rights -- like to legal counsel, or one phone call?"

"I have no idea, but I guarantee you that Powers is doing something, so I say that we just endure this until superman saves the day. I needed a couple more days to recover from being shot, and I'm still recovering from my hands and feet being nailed to the floor by that asshole. I wonder what he is up to. Damn that Vinny DeLuca for being so incompetent."

WANAKA, NEW ZEALAND – JANUARY 2ND:
Jolene was surfing the internet and trying to find any news associated with Buenos Aires. In semi-shock, she read where there was a firefight at the Grand Hotel in Buenos Aires where the police confiscated a serious cache of weapons that apparently were being sold on the black market. Seven Americans were killed in a deal gone bad, and two Americans were charged with weapons

trafficking. Two more Americans escaped, and a manhunt for them was underway.

In a separate news item out of the *Boston Globe*, it was announced that Stephen Sanders, Chief Executive Office of ENTROPY Entrepreneurs, LLC -- a major government think-tank contractor -- had died from gunshot wounds while visiting Buenos Aires, Argentina.

Jolene immediately called Powers and asked, "Do you know anything about Tank and Tucker? I just learned of the death of Sanders and the death of a bunch of Americans in Argentina. What the hell is going on, and why are you not sharing information and doing something about it? I know you have tentacles everywhere. What is going on and have you told Maya?"

"Calm down, Jolene. Both Tank and Tucker are alive and an operation is being planned."

Jolene asked, "Why are you keeping this from me, and why am I not a part of the operation?"

"Jolene, it is not a *White Knight* operation."

"Well you damn well better tell Maya what's going on before I do."

BUENOS AIRES, ARGENTINA – JANUARY 2ND: The head of security informed the President of Argentina that he was ready to give him a report on his new assignment. The head of security was immediately summoned to the president's office. The president said with a wry smile, "I love same-day delivery of information; you should offer that service more often. So what have you learned about our incarcerated guests?"

"One of our guests, Jorge Alvarez, is a famous bodyguard. He was the guy who stopped the terrorist attack in Kyoto this year -- or rather, last year. He was protecting the president of New Zealand at the time. He is legitimate and very unlikely to be trafficking weapons. He is more likely to be using the weapons to protect his customers."

"So, who is his customer here in Buenos Aires?"

"One of the Americans who were killed was Stephen Sanders, the CEO of ENTROPY. I did a little digging and discovered that ENTROPY is a big U.S. Government contractor. I have no idea what he was doing in Buenos Aires unless he was here just to meet the other guy in custody. The two guys from New Zealand flew in the same day the firefight occurred. Stephen Sanders flew in the night before. They weren't here as tourists. The third guy in question is Brinton Gray, or so his American passport claims. I did some checking with our own State Investigative Services and they did a facial recognition check on this guy. His real name is Tucker Cherokee. Do you know that name?" The president shook his head no. "He used to be employed by ENTROPY; he is the inventor of the Magnetic Electricity Generator (MEG). People have been looking for him for years."

"Then we have some*one* of value to trade for some*thing* from the Americans. What do you think his value is to them? How far can I push the Americans?"

The head of security squinted his eyes, gave the president his most evil look, and said, "Sir, would it not be more valuable to learn how to make the MEG work? Or possibly he is worth more to the people they were having the shoot-out with."

"And who would that be?"

"Some organization was trying to kidnap Tucker Cherokee. I figure with eight attackers, fully armed and dressed in tactical gear, the only reason that Mr. Cherokee is alive is because they didn't want to kill him. They didn't expect him to be sitting there with an M16. Someone wants him real bad. The other dead Americans in the operation were part of a group of mercenaries. They could have been hired by anyone. We'll follow the thread and see what turns up. In the meantime, before we sell him to whichever organization wants him, you might want me to ask him nicely how the MEG technology works."

Later during the same day, Tucker was picking at what the prison kitchen referred to as food. The hunger he felt was too much, so he tried to eat it without tasting it; mind over matter. It didn't work; it was awful and he damn near vomited. He persevered, because he needed his strength for the time when Powers and the cavalry might arrive. Tank, on the other hand, just ate the food, didn't feel sick, and would have eaten more if there had been more available. Tank said he'd eaten much worse food than this, to stay alive.

A door to the prison hallway was unlocked and opened. Four people walked through the door -- the arresting officer with his pistol in its holster, the prison warden, a big security guard with a shotgun in his hand and a pistol in a shoulder holster, and a small but impeccably dressed man who gave off the air of being in charge. He stared at Tucker for a few seconds, and then walked to the next cell (his entourage following him step by step) and stared at Tank. The head of security said, "Well, big man, you failed to protect your client." The head of security walked back to Tucker's cell (his entourage comically following him, step by step) and said to the warden, "Open this cell; I want to take this one with me."

The security guard pulled out the keys, lowered the shotgun to open the cell door and unlocked the door. Tucker immediately kicked the security guard in the face while he grabbed the guard's shotgun. The 12 gauge shotgun discharged harmlessly in the scuffle, but Tucker was able to use the butt of the shotgun to smash the face of the arresting officer. The two armed guys were down when the little guy in charge pulled a .38 Beretta and shot Tucker in the right leg. He said, "Stop, or I'll shoot you in the knee." The downed security guard was back on his feet. Tucker didn't have a chance. The head of security said, "You don't act like a scientist. Where'd you learn to fight like that?"

Tucker was taken to an interrogation room. The head of security said to a handcuffed Tucker, "You know that you have been abandoned by your country, the big bad United States. You know that you have no right to a lawyer in our country, as a foreign terrorist. So, if you want your freedom, you'll need to answer my questions. Do you understand?"

Tucker said, "Yes, I understand. Do you understand that if I bleed to death, I won't be able to answer your questions? Would you please first get me medical attention and stop this bleeding, or did you forget that you shot me in the leg?"

The head of security thought about the request. Should he use the bleeding as a death threat to get answers, or was Tucker going to pass out before he gave him all the answers his country needed? The head of security had no idea how complicated the answers were, so he decided to call the prison infirmary doctor to treat Tucker's leg wound.

Fifteen minutes later, after Tucker got permission to lie down and raise his leg up to reduce the bleeding, the doctor arrived. He put a tourniquet on Tucker's leg, extracted the lodged bullet without anesthesia, applied topical disinfectant, gave him a shot of antibiotic medicine, and left. The Argentine head of security sat down and said, "I want to know how to make the MEG work so that our country has the same energy advantages that your country selfishly keeps to itself."

Tucker said, "Sure; what do you want to know?"

The head of security had no idea how to start asking questions so he said to Tucker, "Write it down on this pad and paper." Tucker nodded affirmatively and started writing.

One hour and twenty two pages later, he said to the interrogator, "I need more paper and a few more sharpened pencils." Another 45 minutes passed by, and Tucker was still writing ... when he noticed a red dot on the forehead of the Argentine head of security. Tucker intentionally dropped his pencil and reached under the table to pick it up. He took his time finding the pencil and lifting his body off the floor. By the time he was sitting up, back in the chair, everyone else in the room was dead. It was incredibly quick and quiet. He looked in the direction of the door to the interrogation room to see three black ops fighters standing there, encouraging him to follow them. Tucker knew that his feet had been shackled and tied to the desk. What he couldn't figure out was how these special ops guys broke the chain of his shackles without him knowing it. It didn't matter; he followed them.

Tank had already been freed. The escort took them to a waiting Hummer which transported them to a waiting Apache helicopter. The helicopter was idling and waiting to fly them to the British Falkland Islands where there they were to be met by no less than the Chairman of the Joint Chiefs of Staff, Admiral Maxx Longstaff.

Tucker had time during the trip between Buenos Aires and the Falkland Islands to make sure that someone notified Powers and his loved ones in Wanaka that he and Tank were safe. He also had time to individually thank his and Tank's rescuers. Tucker asked them, "Are you guys a part of the famous Seal Team Six?" No one answered his question, which was answer enough for Tucker.

CHAPTER 58

PALO VERDE NUCLEAR PLANT (ZERO+260 DAYS)

PALO VERDE, ARIZONA – JANUARY 2ND:
The ghost researched the nuclear power industry, and figured it to be the hardest to penetrate. The Palo Verde site west of Phoenix was not too distant from the border of California, where the bulk of its electrical energy was used. The anti-nuclear-power crowd in California didn't seem to mind using the electricity generated right across the border. Palo Verde had three large nuclear reactors which together made Palo Verde the largest nuclear power plant site in the United States, in terms of total megawatt production.

It was impenetrable from a force-protection standpoint. The ghost wasn't going to try to damage the reactors, or try to shut the plant down by damaging the reactor cooling water systems, or even by using his cyber skills. He did not believe that he could succeed with any of those tactics. He settled on trying to do something to the transmission lines. After the electricity left the plants, there were plenty of opportunities to shut the plant down by collapsing transmission towers or ruining power transformers, because there would then be nowhere for the power to go. The transmission towers were huge and there were many of them; they left the plant in the direction of Phoenix and in the direction of Los Angeles. The North America Electric Reliability Corporation knew that transformers were the key, the vulnerable underbelly of the electric industry. There are 55,000 vulnerable transformers in the country. A half million Americans on average each day experience a power outage of an hour or more, three percent caused by sabotage -- amounting to 15,000 victims a day. He identified eighteen different transformers which needed to be taken out. He hired, through the auspices of the *Society for Environmental Justice*, seventeen radical environmentalists aged 17 through 21. He gave them bolt-cutters to break through chain-link fences, and instructions about how to maximize damage by turning a valve and draining transformer coolant. At a pre-determined peak demand time, all eighteen transformers were taken out.

The shock to the power grid was too great for the people who re-route electricity to be able to prevent a blackout. Five large population counties in California and two large population counties in Arizona were left without power. The blackouts stimulated ***more*** riots in

Los Angeles. It took 37 days to bring power back up to the pre-attack level.

Nine of the seventeen young radical anti-nuclear-power environmentalists were caught by the FBI and local police, since the transformers and substations had surveillance cameras. They were all harshly (according to their lawyers) interrogated to determine who recruited them, provided them tools and paid them. Not one of them knew who the mastermind was. However, there was no doubt in the mind of the chief interrogator, Special Agent Vinny DeLuca, who the terrorist leader was.

CHAPTER 59

FALKLAND ISLANDS (ZERO+261 DAYS)

FALKLAND ISLANDS – JANUARY 3RD: As soon as he was told that the Chairman of the Joint Chiefs of Staff was on-site, Tucker knew what he wanted. It was the Chairman who had hired ENTROPY, and who had imparted to Stephen Sanders what he wanted an extremely black project to accomplish. After they landed, Tucker was taken to a medical center where paramedics cleaned and re-dressed his leg wound.

The Chairman walked into the medical center and everything stopped; all military personnel stood at attention and saluted Admiral Maxx Longstaff, second in command only to the Commander in Chief. He saluted back and said "At ease, everyone." He walked up to Tucker and said, "Mr. Cherokee, were you and Mr. Sanders able to meet prior to the attack?"

Tucker said, "Yes." He remained silent, awaiting further information from the number two guy.

As if appreciating Tucker's laconic demeanor, he asked, "Did you and Mr. Sanders complete the discussion prior to the attack?"

Tucker said, "Yes."

"And your answer to Sanders?"

"It was yes."

"Are you well enough to travel?" The Chairman was looking at the paramedic when he asked Tucker the question.

Both the paramedic and Tucker in unison said, "Yes," but the medic added, "Sir." "However," Tucker added, "not without my personal protection team, nor without additional security for the Wanaka Compound. And, sir, would you consider adding resources to help discover who just tried to kidnap me?"

"Yes, Yes and Yes." Nothing else was said. The Chairman of the Joint Chiefs of Staff and his entourage turned and left. The Special Ops guys did not leave with the others.

The leader of the Special Operations unit came over to Tucker and said, "We are your new Wanaka Compound security team until your operation is over. Tucker's mouth nearly hit the floor. The unit leader also handed Tucker some papers. Tucker asked Tank to come over and join the conversation.

Tucker said to Tank, "Meet your new security unit to help us in Wanaka."

Tank's eyes were as big as saucers when he said to the unit leader, "You have no idea how good this makes us feel." Tank and the leader of the Special Operations Team talked about the layout, the threat, the firepower, and about the people whom they were protecting.

Tucker finally looked down at the papers he was handed to see that the papers were in *his* handwriting; it was the manuscript he had been writing to explain to the head of security for Argentina how an MEG worked. It was all bullshit, so he tossed it into the trash. Tucker asked the unit leader how he and Tank were going to get from the Falkland Islands to rendezvous with his operations leader in Fort Meade, Maryland. A man whom Tucker had not noticed before, said with a British accent, "Allow me to be your escort. Her Majesty would be honored to support the United States in your very important operation."

"Well, thank you, but who are you, and what do you know about my operation?"

"I know nothing of your operation, only that the Director of MI6 ordered me to support you with every possible tool at my disposal, which is quite impressive, I might add."

"Do you have a tool to get me to Andrews Air Force Base?"

"No need, my dear friend; Baltimore-Washington International is closer to Ft. Meade than Andrews Air Force Base. We have a Lear jet with a crew waiting for you and Tank when you are ready to leave."

"There probably is a secure phone in your toolbox; might I use it to make a call before we leave?"

"But of course."

Tucker made a call to the operations leader and asked if this British connection was legitimate. The answer should have been intuitive. "You realize that you are standing in British territory, right?"

Tucker looked over at the British agent and said, "Is there a decent meal in that toolbox? We've been eating the equivalent of cardboard for three days."

CHAPTER 60

MASS PRODUCTION
(ZERO+263 DAYS)

WASHINGTON, DC – JANUARY 5TH: The Secretary of Health and Human Services (HHS), the Secretary of Commerce, the Chief of Staff, Rocky Bishop, and the Press Secretary, Andy Snow, sat in the Oval Office with the President of the United States, Winston Allen. The president asked, "Have you read the Northamer-Wong Report to the New Zealand Department of Health?" The HHS Secretary shook his head affirmatively but the others shook their heads no. "It works; the damn spray works. Thirty-six days ago, I promised the people that we would make this available to them as soon as possible. Lives are at stake here. Comments?"

The HHS Secretary said, "The standards and protocols for testing have not been met. Side effects, long term effects, or co-mingling with prescription medications have not been determined. Rushing it to market is unacceptable. I strongly urge that we test it further. The same people you are trying to save may have adverse reactions and die from its use or overuse. We don't know at what age we can apply the spray. Would you spray it on a newborn? Would you spray it on your 92 year old mother? How much would you spray? Should a pregnant woman use it? Sir, release it at your peril."

The president said, "Maybe five to ten million people will freeze to death while you're following protocol. Let me guess … you'll have a report to me right after the cold weather crisis is over -- in two years or so?"

The Chief of Staff said, "Sir, you are damned if you do and damned if you don't … make the spray available to people freezing to death. Is there a way that you can release it with some sort of a disclaimer, or put a warning on it like we do cigarettes?"

President Allen turned to the Secretary of Commerce and asked, "How much inventory did we prepare?"

"We awarded multiple contracts to companies like DuPont, DOW, and BASF. We have enough raw stockpile to treat 200 million people for six months."

"Is there any way we can share the technology with the rest of the world? Every country should be able to supply their people with the Heat Application Protection Innovation (HAPI) spray."

The chief of staff, Rocky Bishop said, "We would get a lot of positive press if we shared the formula for the production of the spray with our friends -- both of them -- and the poorer nations in the higher latitudes."

The president asked, "What is the downside to making an announcement today?"

The Secretary of HHS said, "The United Nations will try you in International Court for 'Crimes-Against-Humanity' when the side effects manifest themselves and hundreds of thousands of people die."

President Allen said, "Gee, let me think, do I want to worry about the potential of killing a hundred thousand people or the certainty of millions freezing to death? That's a really hard decision. And isn't the Hague gang still trying Milosevic?

"Andy, set up a press conference."

WASHINGTON, D.C., JANUARY 6TH: The camera zoomed in on the United States President, Winston Allen, as he addressed the nation during prime time. He looked straight into the camera and said, "Finally, I have little bit of good news to present with a little bit of bad news.

The good news is that the testing of the Heat Application Protection Innovation -- HAPI -- spray in Antarctica went very well. I told you back on November 30th that we would try to make this spray available as soon as possible, to keep you warmer in this deadly cold weather. The United Sates has a backlog of enough spray to treat over 200 million people, while continuing production of more HAPI spray.

"Further, we will make this technology available to any nation which wants to produce the HAPI spray for its own people."

President Allen suddenly turned solemn. He said, "Sadly, one of the significant contributors to the development of this technology died before he could see the manifestations of this discovery, his brainchild. The Chief Executive Officer of ENTROPY, Stephen Sanders, died on December 30th, the same day the Antarctica report was released. God Bless his soul."

The first two million 5 oz. cans of HAPI spray were prioritized to the Department of Defense. The next 50,000 cans were airlifted and dropped in remote artic locations like Prudhoe Bay, Alaska. The next 20 million cans were shipped to various commercial drug stores throughout the north from Nome, Alaska to Caribou, Maine. Another 20 million cans were sold to the U.S.'s northern neighbor, Canada. Within three weeks, the death rate from freezing to death dropped by 35%. Thousands and thousands of people returned to their homes from their adventures south of various borders.

CHAPTER 61

PERSEVERANCE
(ZERO+266 DAYS)

WANAKA, NEW ZEALAND – JANUARY 8TH: Dr. Indira Gupta and Maya Cherokee were comparing notes, modifying test plans, and discussing scenarios. The brain power between the physicist and chemist was enormous, but they were unable to develop a breakthrough result.

"Let's revisit our premise for our current path forward," said Indira; "We saw stars after fireworks and immediately thought that the chemical and physical impact of the fireworks in direct contact with the ash and debris somehow precipitated the ash and cleared the air. But for the stars to be seen, the air between the fireworks -- which topped off at maybe 3,000 feet -- and the top of the atmospheric dust at 60,000 feet would have to be clear. How could that happen? The only way is that somehow a vacuum hole or column of pressure or light pushed everything up through the troposphere due to something caused by the fireworks. What could that be?"

Maya was pensively thinking about Indira's observation when she said, "The list is short; it could be heat from the energetics; it could be sound waves; it could be a unique light wavelength; it could be a pressure shock, and maybe the chemicals in the fireworks are acting as catalysts rather than reactive chemicals."

Indira said, "I think we can discount the light wavelengths, but for the remainder of the options we need to develop a new test plan. I'll prepare the plan and, as usual, you can perform the tests.

"On another subject, when will Tucker return home? I understand that Tank is with him. Do you feel safe and well-protected?"

Maya said, "As far as Tucker is concerned, he is on an assignment which he refuses to discuss with me. I don't know when he'll be back. After over five years of being together constantly, with almost no separation due to his or my travel, this is difficult to get used to. As far as being safe, maybe you haven't heard, but we're now protected by a Department of Defense Special Operations Unit like Seal Team Six types."

Indira said, "Good. With you feeling secure and not worried, I know you'll be able to concentrate on your work."

CHAPTER 62

DETAILS OF THE OPERATION
(ZERO+267 DAYS)

FORT MEADE, MARYLAND – JANUARY 9TH: The Global 8000 Lear jet landed at BWI from the Falkland Islands without a bump -- the perfect landing. It didn't wake either Tucker or Tank. When the stewardess attempted to gently wake Tucker, he reacted as if someone was attacking him and damn near cold-cocked the innocent lady. She decided against waking Tank up; she'd leave that task to someone else.

The Brit walked down the aisle to Tank and Tucker and said, "This is where we part ways. You'll have to find your own way to Fort Meade from BWI. For some reason, I suspect that won't be very difficult for you. You will be going places that even the United States' best friend, the British can't go. But I suspect that I will see you again soon."

Tucker thanked the MI6 agent profusely, with genuine appreciation for his help, saying "As a civilian and on behalf of the people United States, I thank you and the United Kingdom for your support and friendship."

Tucker and Tank were without possessions or passports. They had no identification, as it was confiscated by the Buenos Aires police. The Brit gave them some cash for a taxi. Tank and Tucker both needed a shower, a change of clothes, a shave, and a chance to clean up. As they both limped on the tarmac (Tucker with a crutch) in the direction of the nearest concourse, three uniformed Army soldiers approached them. One of the soldiers was a full colonel; the other two were enlisted. The colonel said, "Mr. Cherokee and Mr. Alvarez, would you please follow me? We are your transportation to Fort Meade."

The colonel crawled into the front passenger seat of the running government-issued Suburban; the driver was waiting for them. Tucker and Tank got into the back seat. They drove off, leaving the two other soldiers behind. The colonel opened an envelope and handed Tucker an identification badge to allow him access into most areas in Fort Meade, plus a new United States passport and a Virginia driver's license, all under his real name, Tucker Cherokee -- Tucker was officially out from under witness protection.

The colonel handed Tank a Fort Meade access badge with different colors and codes than Tucker's, along with a new passport and a driver's license. The colonel said, "You will not have the same access as Mr. Cherokee. I do not know why you two civilians are being granted this access, or what your operation is, but as long as you are at Fort Meade, I will ensure your safety."

"Colonel," said Tucker, "I know it is not in your job description, but is it possible for us to get cleaned up before we enter Fort Meade? We can't look or smell very good."

"Roger that. We have a recreational center where you can clean up. We probably can get some greens for you to wear, but I'm not sure we have any in the big guy's size."

Getting into Fort Meade was not as easy as expected, after getting the badges from the colonel. The guards at the gate gave the access badges great scrutiny, made a couple of phone calls, confirmed entrance access, and finally waved them in. Just on the other side of the gate, the military police pulled them over. The driver of the Suburban was excused from his responsibilities and an MP sat in the driver's seat. The colonel didn't say one word. The MP put it in gear, passed the recreational center and drove to a windowless, nameless block building only 40 feet by 40 feet square. Tank spotted seven guards around the building. It looked like a prison. Tank was getting nervous and started showing some anxiety. The observant MP said, "We're going to escort Mr. Cherokee into this building and take you, Mr. Alvarez, and the Colonel back to the recreation center.

Tucker thought, "Even the colonel can't go into this building." Tucker got out with his crutch, and moved in the direction of the block building when the front door opened. General Ray La Salle greeted Tucker warmly and said, "You've had quite an exciting few days, Mr. Cherokee; please come in and tell me the whole story."

Once inside the building, Tucker looked around and was surprised that the building wasn't covered with wall-to-wall monitors and people walking around busily carrying messages from point to point. Instead there were two desks, a laptop on each desk mounted to the table so they couldn't be removed. No other hardware, no printer, no phones -- no anything else. The door closed, and only LaSalle and Tucker were in the room.

LaSalle said, "I'm sorry for your loss. Stephen Sanders was a good man. He was quite a fan of yours. He said that if there was anyone who could help me strategize and come up with ideas, you were the guy, and that you could be trusted above all others. That's a pretty impressive recommendation. Obviously, I still checked you out. You may not know this, but when you were on the run after discovering NEUREM or --- what do they call it now,

MEG --- I was at the Pentagon recommending that they protect you. Anyway, you checked out. Now that Sanders is dead, only three of us know what the operation is all about, the two of us and the Chairman of the Joint Chiefs of Staff; that's a small group. You can't tell Tank, and you can't tell Maya about our operation. Are we clear?"

"Yes."

"Good." The General paused.

"Russia and Japan have thumbed their noses at us, and basically told us that they no longer fear a reprisal from the United States. Our past example of *not* defending friends which we signed treaties *to* defend pretty much told Japan that they were on their own. I'm sure that Taiwan, Israel, and Ukraine feel the same way. Russia read the tea leaves and decided that we wouldn't make them pay for their aggression in acquiring Angola as Russian territory. We expect more of the same, and so does the president. He asked the Secretary of Defense and the Chairman of the Joint Chiefs of Staff to come up with a counterplan to make Russia and Japan pay for their aggression. That's where you come in, my friend; you and I are supposed to have the best minds for coming up with strategies like this. Whether that is true is another story, but let's come up with our best college try."

Tucker asked, "Why is the Secretary of Defense not in the need-to-know loop?"

"I already like the way you your mind works, Tucker. The reason the need-to-know loop is so small is because there is someone in the administration conspiring with the Russians and Japanese. The reason I have an office here in Fort Meade, famous for its National Security Agency presence, is because the NSA and the Defense Intelligence Agency have uncovered correspondence … between someone in the White House and Russia. Part of our assignment is to discover who that is and come up with a plan to stop it. You and I will have unprecedented access to NSA surveillance information, the National Geospatial Intelligence Agency satellite information and the Department of Energy's Office of Intelligence and Counterintelligence. We have thirty days to have counterplans for the chairman to present to the president.

"By the way," continued LaSalle, "the Chairman asked me to tell you that your request has been fulfilled; we know who tried to kidnap you in Argentina. Not that you need additional incentive, but we picked up a man named Boris Slaughter who was intercepting Stephen Sanders' calls and sending recordings requiring de-cryption to a post office box in Oklahoma. After a persuasive interview, he admitted that he was responsible for telling his customer that Sanders was going to meet with you in Buenos Aires. The post office box confirmed Slaughter's response, that it is someone high up in the Russian Politburo who hired American mercenaries to kidnap you."

CHAPTER 63

THE DEADLY COLD WINTER (ZERO+270 DAYS)

BUFFALO, NEW YORK – JANUARY 12TH: Hypothermia occurs when a person's normal body temperature drops below 95 degrees Fahrenheit. Seniors are the most susceptible to hypothermia because their metabolism is slower than that of younger people. There are over 40 million seniors in the United States alone, over the age of 65 years. Extrapolate that to the world at the same ratio, and there are 903 million seniors at risk from the deadly cold weather, nearly three times the population of the United States.

When the body temperature drops, the person begins to shiver uncontrollably. After a while, the shivering stops and a person's ability to take in oxygen slows down. At the end, the person will experience extreme heat as their bodies shut down. By then, the person is usually unconscious.

The assisted-living establishments, senior living homes, and nursing homes had been doing their best for months now to keep their heat on, and to keep their inventory of fuel high enough to protect their patrons continuously. The U.S. Government recommended that people turn their thermostats down to 50 degrees Fahrenheit in the northern latitudes, and dress warmly -- especially where the temperatures outside averaged less than 10 degrees.

Access to the HAPI spray was limited, and the Buffalo senior centers had only been able to apply the spray to 20 percent of their residents. Harvey Stringmaster was a stubborn 91 year old former newspaper editor. Harvey was 5'4" tall, weighed 115 pounds, and still wore a bow tie every day during his walks. The people in his senior living home issued a bulletin to all residents and responsible parties that the outdoor wind chill temperature was minus 11 degrees Fahrenheit, and that they were not to go outside. Harvey was not going to be told what to do. He needed his daily walk as much as he needed a daily meal. He slipped out and walked two blocks before he started to shiver uncontrollably. Harvey recognized that he needed to return to the senior center. He was only 50 yards from the front door before he couldn't take another step. He was found dead, fingers blue, and eyes still open. Harvey was one of three million similar stories during the deadly cold winter.

"Thank God for our Riteway Model 37 wood burning stove," said Thurman Lynwood. Thurman was proud of his ability to keep his family warm. His small home was fairly easy to keep heated; he was able to maintain a household temperature of 68 degrees Fahrenheit. But it took a lot of wood. The wood added more fine ash to the atmosphere, exacerbating an already ash-laden sky. Keeping the stockpile of wood high enough to ensure that he wouldn't run out of wood was tedious. Thurman would drive his four wheel drive truck through the snow to locations where forests were not protected by authorities. He'd down a tree, cut it in twenty inch long pieces and load them onto the truck. He'd have to haul it back, split the wood, and cover it from the elements. Thurman and 45 million others in similar situations in North America had depleted the forests by five percent in six months.

Bruce Williamson used to be an editor for the county newspaper. Print-only newspapers had fallen into bankruptcy at an alarming rate and Bruce was a victim of the times. Bruce started blogging, both to kill time while he looked for a job and to vent his pent up need to write. He aspired to be another Matt Drudge; he liked the sound of the "Williamson Report." He posted the following articles on his report.

Anchorage, Alaska -- Polar Bears are seen hundreds of miles further south than ever before, compared with their previous natural habitat.

Knoxville, Tennessee -- Botanists at the University of Tennessee predict that the deadly cold weather is likely to kill Camellias, Dogwoods, and Azaleas in the region, and that their ability to survive has moved 300 miles south.

Bluefield, West Virginia -- The Executive Order issued by President Allen has created a renaissance for the coal industry. Unemployment in the state of West Virginia has hit an all-time low of 2.4 percent. Many hundreds have moved there, making it a boom area like the Dakotas.

Miami, Florida -- The Governor of Florida requested that the National Guard protect the residents of Dade County from violent New England immigrant protestors who are demanding food and shelter from the State of Florida.

Richmond, Kentucky -- Charles Washington, CEO of Charleston Energy Group, announced an exclusive long- term supply agreement with the Saskatchewan Rare Earth Mining Company. "This supply agreement allows us to maintain our current production rate of MEGs and draw down our three year backlog."

The Hague, Netherlands -- An apparent terrorist act blacked out the city yesterday, leaving 150,000 without power at a time when the lowest temperature of the winter hit the city. The mode of attack resembled the attacks on the energy infrastructure in the United States and Canada.

Chicago, Illinois -- The Mayor of Chicago had been hung in effigy in downtown Chicago yesterday while hundreds of thousands of people endured the frigid subzero temperatures. The power had been out in most of Chicago for 55 days with no forecast date for restoration of power. The Chicago mayor had refused to lift martial law since it was imposed on November 26th.

Los Angeles, California -- Unemployment rose to 18.3 percent in Los Angeles County and 39.1 percent for ages 18 through 25. The unemployed began rioting in front of the Mayor's office, demanding unemployment compensation extension for another two years.

Havana, Cuba -- An unprecedented number of Cuban Americans have attempted to migrate to Cuba. The ruined citrus crop in Florida created a gap in available citrus worker jobs, and this combined with an influx of low wage workers from the northern latitudes has driven some Cuban Americans to attempt to return to their estranged families. Unfortunately, approximately 320 have failed to reach Cuba, and those who have reached the shores have been turned away. Nineteen are said to have died from shark attacks.

St. Johns, Newfoundland -- A plea for help has been issued by the mayor of St. Johns, today, for heating fuel and food. The frigid weather has left Newfoundland ice-bound, where fishing vessels and ferries cannot negotiate the tempestuous northern Atlantic Ocean. Ottawa air-dropped food but has not been able to provide the needed heating fuel. Newfoundland is at serious risk of being completely deforested by the beginning of spring, as trees are felled for fuel.

Washington, DC -- The Federal Bureau of Investigation (FBI) announced today another run on ammunition by gun owners. Violent crime has increased by 42 percent over violent crime statistics for last year. The FBI announced that they forecast an additional increase in violent crimes this year, based on the run on ammunition. Both private and government buyers are showing signs of urgent purchasing, with the government getting the lion's share. The FBI stated that the extremely cold weather, coupled with high unemployment, has created desperation for food and shelter, and is the genesis of the increase in crime rates. There is some clear evidence of public reaction to aggressive government purchasing of ammunition. Long lines forming at Wal-Marts have received recent press attention, when infrequent ammunition deliveries occur.

Ames, Iowa -- Researchers at the University of Iowa, in cooperation with the Department of Agriculture's Ames Laboratory, have announced today a potential breakthrough in cold weather crop production. Crop production is down and food prices are up, due to the deadly cold weather.

CHAPTER 64

COUNTERMOVES
(ZERO+297 DAYS)

WASHINGTON, DC – FEBRUARY 8TH: The President of the United States, Winston Allen, had summoned Chairman Maxx Longstaff to the West Wing of the White House. The Commander-in-Chief had never before summoned the Chairman like this. It was the first time the Chairman had ever sat in the Oval Office, one-on-one with the president. "At ease," Allen said jokingly, "You're not being fired."

The Chairman never cracked a smile and never relaxed. His eyes didn't seem to be emitting too much light today.

"Do you recall the conversation we had back when Russia was declaring war on Angola? You said, in so many words, that we would either have to push back on Russia that day or push back on Russia later. My response to you was to come back to me with a countermove, a duplicitous strategy and push back plan. Well, what did you come up with? I'm ready to push back. What have you got?"

Light started to show from the Chairman's brilliant eyes; a smile spread across his face; he was actually beaming. The Commander-In-Chief could not help but beam back at the contagious lift in spirit and said, "Well that's a very encouraging reaction. I'm actually getting optimistic; what have you got?"

"Sir," started the Chairman, "I was hoping that when you summoned me here, that I might get the opportunity to bring up the same subject. With your permission, I'd like to invite two men to join us who have prepared potential countermoves for your consideration. One of them is well known to you -- General Ray LaSalle. The other, sir, is a civilian who has been instrumental in supporting the United States' national security in numerous ways. His name is Tucker Cherokee."

The President said, "I know who Tucker Cherokee is, and I'd love to thank him for his service to our country, even though he is a civilian. Please invite them both in."

As General La Salle and Tucker Cherokee entered the Oval Office, President Allen said, "It's good to see you again, General, and I know that I will be pleased with your analysis. And welcome to the Oval Office, Mr. Cherokee; thank you for all that you have done. The discovery of NEUREM generators -- or MEGs -- is enough, but the

development of the HAPI spray may well save millions."
Tucker nodded and smiled with appreciation.

"OK, please sit down. What do you gents have for me?
It's time for the United States to knock Russia and Japan
down a peg or two before their aggression manifests itself
again. But first, Maxx, I'd like to know how and why
you recruited Mr. Cherokee on a highly classified strictly
Pentagon and Intelligence Agency matter. It's not like
you, Chairman, to break protocol."

"It saddens me to tell you that it was a matter of trust.
Someone in the Federal Government was complicit with
the attacks on our energy infrastructure. The only person
I fully trusted, even in the Pentagon, was General LaSalle.
I thought about who -- outside the Government -- I
could trust to involve in the blackest of projects, and
that was Steven Sanders, CEO of ENTROPY. Tucker,
here, developed the HAPI spray under the ENTROPY
umbrella. Sanders convinced me to involve him because
of his impeccable reputation, his brilliant mind, and the
fact that no one -- considering his wealth -- could bribe
him to betray his country."

"Let's continue; I have a video conference with the
Prime Minister of Canada in 45 minutes."

The Chairman of the Joint Chiefs of Staff nodded, with a smile, to Ray. Ray stood up and said, "Mr. President, we have four separate countermoves or operations. The first countermove is dubbed "Operation MEG." The second countermove is dubbed "Operation Duplicitous." We refer to the third countermove as "Operation Outage," and we call the final countermove "Operation Traitor."

CHAPTER 65

CHEROKEE/LASALLE COUNTERMOVE #1 - OPERATION MEG (ZERO+301 DAYS)

WASHINGTON, DC -- FEBRUARY 12TH: The Press Room was filled to capacity; several of the White House correspondents were still wearing painters' or surgical masks to keep the ash out of their noses and mouths when outside. Others still had their earmuffs on; it was three degrees Fahrenheit out there. It was 50 degrees in the Press Room. The president walked up to the podium with network cameras running and said, "Good afternoon. I have one short announcement to make, and then I'd like to entertain questions.

"In view of the extended period of deadly cold weather and the inadequate amount of heating fuel available around the world, the United States has elected to make the technology for the production of the neutrino-based electricity generators, recently renamed Magnetic Electricity Generators or MEGs, available to all nations of the world. Electricity without fuel in view of these extended incredibly cold temperatures is too valuable to the lives of the citizens of the world to keep secret. We will open our books to all nations, friend or foe, for the technology. The Charleston Energy Group, the United States' current supplier of MEGs, has agreed to work with any nation interested in the technology. For more information, please go to energy.gov website for a link to MEG production.

"It is our hope that millions of lives may be saved by making this extremely valuable technology available to all. Now, I would like to do my best to answer your questions."

Associated Press: "The MEG technology gave the United States a competitive edge over other nations, in the manufacturing industry. Did we just give away that advantage; will the U.S. lose jobs over this generous offer?"

President Allen: "The more MEGs there are in use, the greater the chance that they will drive the cost of energy down, everywhere. Lower oil and natural gas prices worldwide will stimulate the world economy, and help all nations pull out of a low point by increasing the number of jobs available."

Wall Street Journal: "It seems to me that shareholders of Charleston Energy Group will be the biggest losers. How do you reconcile this policy change to the shareholders?"

President Allen: "CEH is producing MEGs at full capacity but they haven't even made a dent in even the domestic demand. Making the technology available to all nations does not mean the technology is free or without a license fee. Last question."

Fox News: "We are also making the technology available to our enemies, according to your statement. Russia and Japan, in the opinion of some, have not earned the right to this technology. How would you answer that criticism?"

President Allen: "It would be impossible to keep it a secret from them, with every other nation on earth having the knowledge. This could not be avoided. Thank you, ladies and gentlemen of the press."

The president went backstage; the secret service escorted him to a briefing room, and the president convened a meeting with a grim-faced vice president and concerned cabinet members. The vice president's face was red when he spoke to the president, "You should have consulted with us before making an announcement of this importance. Congress is going to have a hissy fit and is likely to initiate impeachment hearings. What were you thinking?"

"Is there something about the announcement that troubles you, Mr. Vice President?"

The vice president's survival instincts went on high alert. There was something about the president's demeanor and tone of voice that shut him up. He had never been called "Mr. Vice President" by the president before. Something was wrong. The vice president backed off and said, "I am just a little concerned about further destabilizing our relationship with oil- and natural gas-producing nations. It would have been nice for them to have been included in the decision making."

"Do you think that driving the price of oil down is a bad thing?"

"No, but I do think that the unintended consequences of making this technology -- energy without fuel -- available to all had not been fully vetted before you made the decision."

"You underestimate me, much like the Secretary of Health and Human Services underestimated me. It's good to be risk-averse, but not at the detriment of so **many** lives."

The vice president's phone was in his shirt pocket and vibrated three times while in conversation with the president. He never let on that it was vibrating, and he never answered the phone.

CHAPTER 66

CHEROKEE/LASALLE COUNTERMOVE #2 - OPERATION DUPLICITOUS (STARTED ZERO+351 DAYS)

ASTANA, REPUBLIC OF KAZAKHSTAN – APRIL 3RD: The stated mission of ISIL -- the Islamic State of Iraq and the Levant -- is to achieve the caliphate, the political union of the world under Muslim rule. The leaders and soldiers of the movement have devotion, passion, faith, youth, and commitment to their cause. What they don't have is firepower. To accomplish the caliphate, the Islamic leaders need to be able to conquer regions of the world which have superior firepower.

Tremendous progress was achieved in Syria and Iraq, because the nations with superior militaries chose not to engage in a civil war. And, the U.S. left a lot of equipment behind.

The Republic of Kazakhstan is a former Soviet state which borders Russia. The U.S. Ambassador to Kazakhstan met with Mr. Smith, a U.S. Government employee. Mr. Smith had flown in from Washington,

DC to Astana yesterday with words of wisdom from the Department of State, and an assignment that required him to meet with the spiritual leader of the Sunni tribe in Kazakhstan.

Mr. Smith arrived at the Nur-Astana Mosque in the capital Astana, the largest mosque in Kazakhstan. The spiritual leader did not welcome the infidel, but accepted his presence. Mr. Smith spoke with the Sunni leader in Russian and asked him if he thought that now was the time to achieve the caliphate. The Kazakh pretended not to understand Russian but his eyes belied this. The Sunni leader spoke in Kazakh to a standing subordinate to translate his answer to Mr. Smith: "It is always time for the caliphate."

Mr. Smith said in Russian again, "You are no doubt aware that the caliphate is underway in Iraq and Syria, and that it is spreading. I speak to you today, on behalf of the leaders of the caliphate, to say that they would like your support to spread the caliphate into Russian territory, predominantly by people of the Islamic faith."

The Sunni leader said -- in Russian, "Who are you? You are not from ISIL. You are not Sunni. You are not Muslim. You are not Russian."

Mr. Smith said, "I am your friend. I represent power, the kind of power that you will need to make the caliphate successful in several regions in Russia. It is your destiny to participate in the caliphate, and I represent a tool that you need to make it happen. I will provide safe passage for thousands of ISIL operatives to serve under your leadership. I will make sure that you have the tools you currently only dream of, to conquer territory that currently belongs to the Big Bear. I can provide training to your soldiers about how to use the tools you are blessed to receive."

"You are American, no? You are famous for talking big but not having the stomach or integrity to deliver, after your big talk. Why should I trust you?"

Mr. Smith said, "Let us be honest with each other; we will never trust each other, but we have a common enemy. How is it said, 'An enemy of my enemy is my friend?' Let me demonstrate power so that you know that I am legitimate. Please, follow me to the entrance of this spectacular mosque." The three of them walked casually through the doors to the dreary, smoggy, snowy and very cold outside. "In the distance, looking north, you see that boulder on the mountainside? Here -- use my pocket binoculars." He could actually see that far, despite the fine dust in the air. The Sunni spiritual leader of the Kazakhs focused the binoculars. Mr. Smith reached into his suitcase and pulled out a satellite phone and said, "Now."

Seconds later the boulder roughly two miles away was struck by a guided rocket and blown to a million pieces in dramatic fashion, with incredible force, noise and smoke. "Our armed unmanned air assets are the most powerful, accurate, and reliable in the world -- bar none. Though we will not allow you to use them -- nor will we use them -- in Russian territory, we will protect the sovereignty of the Republic of Kazakhstan; your soldiers will be able to have a home base that is a safe refuge."

"Will our jihadists have access to the HAPI spray? We are very cold here all the time. Our fighters are loyal and passionate in their love of Allah but they are ineffective if they are nearly frozen to death in this deadly cold weather."

Mr. Smith replied, "Yes."

Mr. Smith repeated the process of encouraging spiritual leaders of Islam to follow the ISIL movement of achieving the caliphate in every nation bordering with Russia. Even Poland and the Balkan states had an

Islamic contingent which was anxious to participate in the caliphate; it was their destiny. Russia had a 13,748 mile border with 13 countries: Norway, Finland, Estonia, Latvia, Lithuania, Belarus, Georgia, Ukraine, Azerbaijan, Kazakhstan, Mongolia, the People's Republic of China, and North Korea. Mr. Smith introduced himself to the spiritual leader of each country. ISIL operatives were infiltrated into each. A strategy was suggested by Mr. Smith to the ISIL leaders.

Mr. Smith then visited the spiritual leader of Angola and each of the countries which border Angola. The support for the caliphate was universal; every Islamic spiritual leader was willing to work with ISIL warriors to initiate a global caliphate movement.

The strategy was fixed; training was completed; tactics were established; low tech weaponry (mostly Russian) was provided, and a timeline developed. On the same day at exactly the same time from 17 different launch points, ISIL penetrated Russian territory. On the first day of cross-border actions, ISIL only penetrated an average of a half mile. There were a couple of clashes and confrontations, but very few serious battles. On the second day, the ISIL army penetrated 1.5 miles into Russian territory from all 17 launch points. This time, the Russian army was more prepared, and there were casualties of war. The Russian army deployed along the border at these 17 launch points and announced through Al Jazeera TV that they would not tolerate further ISIL aggression. This, of course, aggravated the problem. On the third day, ISIL launched an attack from 17 ***different*** launch points, catching the Russian army off guard.

Russia was reluctant to penetrate the sovereign nations harboring the ISIL fighters, fearing worldwide retribution. Each of the neighboring nations was strongly declaring innocence, stating that their governments were unwilling victims of the caliphate. For the next six months, Russia would fight back the ISIL caliphate movement along this 13,748 mile border. The resources expended to conduct counterinsurgency warfare, the soldiers lost, the time the Kremlin focused on maintaining its border integrity, all resulted in the inability to deal with domestic instability in Angola, thousands of miles away. The decision to protect its own borders had precedence over maintaining territorial control of Angola.

Russia knew that the Angolan rebels were well armed, but never could secure "smoking gun" evidence that the Americans were providing the weapons.

CHAPTER 67

BINGO
(ZERO+353 DAYS)

WANAKA, NEW ZEALAND - APRIL 5th: Maya was no longer herself; she was possessed by the demon that researchers around the world all know well -- single-mindedness. Nothing else matters when a researcher thinks that he -- or she -- is close to a discovery. Maya and Indira knew that they were close. The video conferencing was constant now; it hadn't been turned off in days. The beautiful Maya looked ragged, needing sleep, eyes puffy, dehydrated, and unwashed. Mammy, Chef Rhino, Suzanne, and Jolene were taking care of Star, so Maya wasn't worried about her baby's well-being; she didn't even take calls from Tucker. Suzanne tried to get Maya to eat and rest, but to no avail. Star was brought down to the lab to say goodnight to her mother. Star concentrated hard on her mother's thoughts but didn't understand any of them. Except her love.

Indira said over the video-conference monitor, "Maya, I'm suffering from sleep deprivation; I'm beginning to lose concentration and the ability to think logically.

My creativity is gone. I need to recharge my batteries. I recommend that you do the same. I'll call you tomorrow, and we can review the progress we made today." Maya did not respond, as though she had heard nothing Indira had said. "Maya, you look awful; you need some rest."

Maya said, "OK," still not acknowledging what Indira had said. Indira signed off, and Maya kept concentrating on the task at hand. "Shock," she said to herself, "Maybe a pressure shock or pulse in the presence of a catalyst of some sort. She filled a Plexiglas 55 gallon drum with volcanic ash ground to a sub-micron size and concentration similar to what was in the atmosphere. Maya had, weeks before, ordered a Department of Transportation (DOT) shaker from ENTROPY, used to test containers for compliance with integrity tests. She energized the shaker for 30 seconds to the point where the suspended ash was uniform throughout the Plexiglas drum.

She had run the test 63 previous times with different chemicals to act as catalysts. She had a spark plug inserted into the drum to create a spark and shock the air space. There also was a fiber-optic cable inserted into the drum to test various light inputs, plus there was an ultrasonic probe. She dialed in the light and sound frequencies she wanted to test, and pushed the spark plug starter.

The Plexiglas drum made a sound similar to the thunder that accompanies a lightning strike overhead. "Damn," Maya said, "it cracked. I'll have to get a new one. I'm glad I ordered a spare." Then it hit her: the volcanic dust was gone; the container was clear. At about that same moment, the *White Knight* and Special Forces Unit security guards burst into the lab in force, guns out, safeties off, and ready for battle. The sharp thunder sound had scared the hell out of the civilians and activated the protection reflexes of the military security team.

Maya explained what happened, and everyone relaxed -- and started back up to the main level. But Maya stopped them and asked them to stay and observe a re-test, to see if it happened again. While *White Knights* removed the cracked Plexiglas drum, Maya observed the talcum-powder-like residue on the inside of the cracked drum. She asked them to place it on white paper near her, for sampling. Then, she prepared another drum with her calculated recipe that simulated the conditions outside, worldwide -- a specific concentration of tiny volcanic dust. She attached a new spark plug, a new fiber optic cable, and a new ultrasonic probe. Maya and her security army were ready to repeat the experiment.

The crack like thunder was just as intense on experiment number 65 as it was on experiment 64. The last Plexiglas drum was cracked and the container was coated inside, at the bottom, with talcum-like powder again. The security team in the basement lab did not know what it meant, but they knew that it was a good thing, because Maya was beaming with a smile from ear to ear.

CHAPTER 68

CHEROKEE/LASALLE COUNTERMOVE #3 - OPERATION OUTAGE (STARTED ZERO + 376 DAYS)

ROKKASHO-MURA, JAPAN – APRIL 28TH: Today, information on the basic technology for making nuclear weapons is more widespread in the scientific community than in past decades. Back in the day when Klaus Fuchs and the Rosenbergs provided the knowledge to the Soviet Union, it was a well-guarded secret. Today, through the internet and a Pakistani activist, even the most pathetic of countries (North Korea) and terrorist groups have access to the basic knowledge about manufacturing a nuclear weapon. There remain many top secret tricks of the trade, but the most difficult part of creating a nuclear bomb is the acquisition of the enriched nuclear materials such as weapons grade uranium or plutonium.

Japan's robust nuclear power program embraced the entire cradle-to-grave nuclear fuel cycle. The United States did not reprocess spent nuclear fuel -- it became "waste." The original architects of the nuclear power industry conceptually minimized nuclear waste by chemically "reprocessing" the spent or used fuel for reuse. The Carter administration put an end to "reprocessing" in the United States, thereby creating an endless debate about what to do with this "nuclear waste."

But Japan *did* reprocess its spent nuclear fuel. A byproduct of reprocessing was the production of materials suitable for weapons production. Hence, Japan was able to produce the nuclear weapons which were used to threaten Saudi Arabia. The $27 billion Rokkasho-Mura reprocessing plant required outages when the plant was shut down for maintenance. During a typical outage, hundreds of temporary workers were used to perform scheduled maintenance. Tadeshi Nakajima was an outage health physicist who went from nuclear power plant to nuclear power plant to provide outage maintenance. This was his first maintenance experience at the reprocessing plant, and he was excited about the opportunity. As a health physicist, his job was to make sure that workers in this narrow field followed strict protocols and limited their exposure to radiation. Nakajima was in the process of dressing out, with radiation protective clothing, when a man sat just a little too close to him on the bench where he was putting his nylon-reinforced-paper shoe coverings -- or booties -- on.

Nakajima didn't recognize the guy who had invaded his space, so he just simply scooted his butt down, getting a bit further away. The stranger moved fast -- a syringe was jammed into Nakajima's neck and he was unconscious within seconds. The stranger removed Nakajima's "Thermo-Luminescent Dosimeter" -- TLD -- and access badge, and hid him in a janitorial closet -- he'd be out for 45 minutes or more.

The stranger used Nakajima's badge to access several low radiation areas which contained electronic devices important to nuclear reprocessing. Using a Magnastroyer single pass slot degausser, a hand-held source of extremely strong magnetism, he brushed the powerful permanent magnet against control room computers, electronic instruments, data recorders, timers, and gauges. These computers, instruments, and electronic devices would have to be replaced or reprogrammed. The plant's control systems were shut down.

Rokkasho-Mura would not be producing enriched uranium or plutonium for some time. Nor would Japan be able to benefit financially from reprocessing fuel for nuclear power plants around the world.

A note was left in kanji, addressed to Akio Yamada, notifying him that there was much more degaussing to come, all across the nation. The magnetic field generator would render computers and electronic equipment useless

in all Japanese industries. Japan Inc., would be hurt badly
if the control of their Japanese manufacturing industries
were rendered useless. Unless, of course, Japan permitted
free elections in Thailand about whether or not Thailand's
citizens preferred to remain a territory of Japan.

CHAPTER 69

CHEROKEE/LASALLE COUNTERMOVE #4 - OPERATION TRAITOR (ZERO+377 DAYS)

WASHINGTON, DC – APRIL 29TH: The vice president was furious with President Allen: "How could he be so ignorant and altruistic, to think that giving away a superior technological advantage was in the United States' best interest?" His smart phone vibrated again. He looked down and reviewed a text message, "urgent that you contact me ASAP." The vice president didn't recognize the phone number.

The vice president's phone vibrated two more times from two separate phone numbers within minutes of each other. The text messages were not respectful of a man in his position, of his stature, or of his power. That was information enough about the origin of the texts.

The nation states and organizations most hurt by the Allen decision were the oil, natural gas, and coal producing nations which depend on the sale of their natural energy resources to survive. The cabal's clever oil-rich-nation takeover plan was jeopardized by Allen's unilateral move; it made the vice president look powerless. The phone vibrated again. It was the Director of the FBI. "Holy Shit; they're closing in."

The phone hysterically vibrated and the vice president finally acquiesced and answered it. With a deep breath he answered, "What do you want?"

A mechanical-sounding artificial voice said, "I want you to meet me at Tyson's Corner II, in the east garage, second level, row C, space C23; 2230 tonight." Then, the call was disconnected.

The Vice President thought about whether or not to show up. "What were the consequences of not showing up?" He decided to show.

The parking lot was fairly empty at 10:30 p.m. C23 was a good distance from the elevator, and remote. The vice president heard the sound of footfalls echoing off the parking lot concrete walls. He watched as a man a little over six feet tall approached. Something about the man's gait and the way he carried himself made the approaching man seem less threatening. When the man was within thirty feet, he said, "Good job on your disguise; if I hadn't selected the rendezvous point myself, I would not have recognized you. But I have to say, the wig is low quality; you can do better."

The vice president said nothing.

The man said, "You understand, of course, that we were bound to uncover your wrongdoings, right? It's hard to maintain privacy when you communicate with the enemy on your personal land line. What the hell were you thinking? We have solid, indisputable evidence that you have been directly communicating with President Karloff of Russia and the Prime Minister of Japan, during the period of time when the two countries were "conquering" independent nations. Did you really think that you wouldn't get caught performing your treasonous and traitorous assistance?"

The vice president reminded Tucker of "a deer in the headlights." The vice president said, "You think that I've been in contact with and I'm in cahoots with Russia and Japan? You are way off base, son. Whoever you are, you have been fed some bad shit."

Tucker smiled and asked, "Why did you agree to meet with me without your Secret Service protection on short notice, without question, unless you are guilty of something?"

The vice president took a deep breath, paused for a minute, and then said, "I'm trying to cover up the fact that my son was picked up back home in Nebraska for possession of a couple of ounces of marijuana. I just didn't need the publicity -- it might prevent me from succeeding the president."

Tucker already knew this but didn't let on. He asked, "So who is trying to set you up?"

"I'm in politics; enemies are part of the job. Our administration represents 52% of the population. That leaves me with more than 150 million enemies domestically and who knows how many enemies internationally. How difficult is it to make calls to Russia and Japan and make it look like someone else made the call?"

Tucker said with a smile, "It can be done, and yet we can still trace the origin of the call. Okay. I'm authorized by your boss to recruit you into a sting."

CHEVY CHASE, MARYLAND – APRIL 30TH:
It was almost May, yet here he was wearing ear muffs, a Kazakh hat, thermal underwear, a ski jacket and a surgical mask. "Was the weather ever going to break?" He looked left to right, turned 90 degrees and repeated the survey.

He didn't know what direction the vice president was going to approach him from in this cavernous parking garage. He was conflicted with emotion. On one hand, he was glad that the whole ordeal was going to be over and disclosed. On the other hand, he was paralyzed with fear that this meeting with the vice president would end with the death of his granddaughter. He'd seen the video of her bedroom; he'd been sent articles of clothing that belonged to his granddaughter, and he'd been warned that any search of her room would result in immediate detonation of a planted bomb.

The vice president surprised the man from behind. The vice president said, "I never would have suspected you to be a traitor."

"I am being blackmailed. There is a bomb in my granddaughter's bedroom. I didn't feel that I had a choice. What would you do?"

"Our conversation is being recorded. This is an opportunity for you to confess all of your sins. Let's hear it."

"The prime minister of Japan and the president of Russia have agents in the United States who are keeping us pre-occupied with the terrorist organization which is destroying energy infrastructure -- in America, Canada, and Europe -- with the purpose of distracting us, to provide them with an opportunity to expand their empires. Their goal, of course, was to secure natural energy resources and farmable land."

The vice president said with extreme hate in his voice, "Tell me something I don't know. What was your role in the murder of hundreds of thousands of American citizens by freezing to death, to save your granddaughter?"

"Primarily to provide inside information about the will of the United States to react to their aggression … and to secure a vial of FLPC3 stored at the Centers for Disease Control in Atlanta. As Secretary of Health and Human Services, I had unlimited access."

"You son-of-a-bitch, we had that ass-hole 'ghost' in custody. That vial allowed him to escape. Your treasonous acts……" An Improvised Explosive Device (IED) buried in a tamper-proof trash receptacle about twenty feet from their rendezvous point exploded with enough force to decapitate the Secretary of HHS and shred the vice president's body. Nearby FBI and Secret Service agents in full battle gear listening to the exchange rapidly searched the area in an attempt to find the person who had detonated the bomb. Simultaneously with the IED explosion, a bomb was detonated in the bedroom of the HHS Secretary's granddaughter.

Later, reviewing the results of the operation, Tucker said to General LaSalle, "Well we succeeded at bringing out the 'ghost,' but the motherfucker outsmarted us again."

CHAPTER 70

OPERATION INTIMIDATION (ZERO+378 DAYS)

SEA OF JAPAN – APRIL 30TH: The *Nimitz* class supercarrier *USS George H.W. Bush* was cruising at 27 knots, displacing 114,000 tons, on a cold and choppy Sea of Japan. There were 48 other surface ships and six submarines involved in the military exercise in the waters between Russia and Japan. Five other nations joined the U.S. Pacific Fleet Commander in the military exercise "Operation Intimidation" as a demonstration of solidarity, and to send a message to both Japan and Russia that further aggression would not be tolerated. Canada contributed a submarine and the *HMCS Calgary*. New Zealand participated with its Mine Countermeasure Detachment unit and the *HMNZS Canterbury*. Australia sent the *HMAS Success*, a submarine and an AP-3C Orion. The People's Republic of China contributed six destroyers to the effort, and the Republic of Korea fielded a submarine, along with the *ROK Wang Geon*. The entire operation included 25,000 warfighters including pilots of F-22 Raptors and 190 other aircraft.

Thousands of targets consisting of drones and balloons were released over the remote sea to demonstrate the accuracy of Tomahawk and RIM-162 Missiles. The sub-zero weather, 15 foot swells, and 25 knot winds made the exercise environment hazardous duty, but the message was obviously effective. The Prime Minister of Japan mobilized 32 of the Japanese Navy's 114 vessels to the Sea of Japan, off the shores of Kanazawa from the Yokosuka Naval Base.

Russian President Karloff placed the Naval Base at Vladivostok on high alert and deployed four attack submarines out into the Sea of Japan as a precaution. As "Operation Intimidation" got underway and hundreds of missiles were launched to down drones and balloons, tension reached a head-splitting crisis point as satellite images viewed in Moscow, Tokyo and Washington, D.C. were viewed. The firepower on display was frightening, and the tons of ordnance dissipated into the atmosphere rivaled the "Shock and Awe" effort during Operation Iraqi Freedom. The F-22 Raptors flew dangerously close to Russian and Japanese air space.

President Winston Allen picked up the red phone; he was expecting the call. Russian President Karloff said,

"Why are you provoking Russia? What is your point? This is not going to end well if you continue to conduct military operations adjacent to our submarine base. In fact, it seems foolish on your part."

President Allen asked, "Did I just detect a threat, President Karloff? We know exactly where your four submarines are, and we'll take them out if you act aggressively. It is not our intent to 'provoke' Russia. If we wanted to provoke Russia, we would strike first without warning; Vladivostok would be the site of the next 'Peace Museum.' If you feel provoked, then I suggest that you seek medical help for your condition. The point of our military exercise is to remind the nations of the world, including Russia, that -- if we choose to -- the largest, most sophisticated, and most powerful navy in the world can put an end to hegemony. Have I made myself clear?"

"Words. I hear words, nothing more."

"You called me because you were observing more than words. We have an American expression that you may have heard, 'shit happens.' Make sure it doesn't happen to you. I'd like to remind you that the People's Republic of China is participating in this military exercise. They're just waiting for you to do something stupid, so that they can share with South Korea the territory of North Korea which you recently seized."

The Prime Minister of Japan called President Allen while Allen was on the phone with the Russian president. President Allen told his chief of staff to keep the Prime Minister of Japan on hold. Winston Allen continued, "President Karloff, stop your territorial conquest. Be grateful that America was preoccupied with terrorists when you made your land grab. We actually were ambivalent about Russia grabbing North Korean territory. Angola was another story; your greed is appalling. Just stop." President Allen hung up.

"Please put the Prime Minister of Japan on the line," President Allen said to his Chief of Staff.

"Hello, Mr. Prime Minister; this is quite exciting, hearing from you."

The Prime Minister of Japan hesitated, and finally said, "President Allen, you insult me by putting me on hold."

"I was on the phone with your brother, Russian President Karloff. I had a choice, insult him or insult you, and his call was first. What is it that you want?"

"I demand that you stop your provocative military exercises with our regional competitors, on our doorstep. You have come close to entering our territorial waters and our air space. We have been at peace for almost 70 years; you are threatening that peace. What is your motive for such careless conduct?"

"You have a short memory, Mr. Prime Minister; it is Japan which broke the 1945 Amnesty Agreement."

"We could no longer trust the United States to defend us; we observed the way you abandoned Ukraine, despite an agreement to defend them. How could we trust you?"

"Are you telling me that you did not notice that we had a change in administration?"

"As did we."

"Yes; I haven't yet explained to you why I was so excited to hear from you, Mr. Prime Minister. Yours is the first call I have ever received from the other side."

Silence. Finally, "I don't understand your statement."

"Sure you do, whoever you really are. My intelligence says that the Prime Minister committed suicide. You can imagine how excited I am to get a call from him."

"You are mistaken; your intelligence is false. As your famous American author said, 'the rumor of my death is greatly exaggerated'."

"Allow me to guess who you really are -- AkioYamada. How good do you think my intelligence is now?"

Silence.

"I thought so. Let me be clear. You make one wrong move relative to the operation we are conducting in the Sea of Japan, and we will declare that Okinawa is American territory. Good luck getting it back. You make a serious mistake like sinking an American vessel and we will confiscate Saudi Arabia from you. You don't have the air superiority to stop us, and your pathetic excuse for a nuclear threat is not in the least intimidating to us. Are we clear, Mr. Yamada? You sink an American aircraft carrier and we will declare the island of Hokkaido to be American territory. That might prove to be a problem for your political ambitions.

"Now that we are having our first candid conversation, Mr. Yamada, I am going to ask you a question. You will have 30 seconds to answer my question. Who in my administration is supporting you and contributing to your plans? I already know the answer; I'm just testing your honesty."

Mr. Yamada answered President Allen's question, and confirmed what he already knew.

Operation Intimidation continued through the night and into the morning, as planned, until 0800 local time. Despite the frigid cold weather, thousands of troops from all six nations mustered on-deck to observe the success or failure of their secondary mission. Though brief, all personnel felt direct sunshine for the first time in months. The smiles on the faces of sailors and soldiers of the participating nations were accompanied with private tears. The mission was a success.

President Allen, the Chairman of the Joint Chiefs of Staff, General LaSalle and Tucker Cherokee jumped with excitement and hi-fived each other when the satellite view of the Pacific Fleet sparkled with reflected sunlight for a brief moment. The hole created in the dusty atmosphere, as a result of the full scale experiment, filled itself in with more ash and airborne debris -- but it was obvious that a large amount of ash and debris agglomerated and fell to the surface of the earth. Later calculations concluded that a full one percent of the atmospheric ash was removed from the air.

The ordnance prepared for Operation Intimidation was formulated by Maya Cherokee. The 200 aircraft engaged in the exercise were "armed" with powerful ultrasonic generators to create the exact frequency used by Maya and Indira's bench tests. No one was sure exactly why it worked, just that it did. The most popular theory adopted by scientists was that the tiny submicron ash particles exhibited resonance frequencies which, coupled with the ordnance catalyst formula, caused the particles to bond and precipitate -- changing their aerodynamic properties.

CHAPTER 71

FBI'S MOST WANTED
(ZERO+379 DAYS)

CHICAGO, ILLINOIS – MAY 1ST: Richard opened his eyes. He was groggy, nauseas, and anxious. He tried to sit up, but felt too weak, so he just lay there trying to recall what had happened to him. The last thing he remembered was falling asleep while watching David Letterman. He struggled again to get up to use the rest room; it was not easy. His stomach muscles failed him; he had to roll to one side before he could sit up straight; then he looked around. He thought to himself, "This is not my home; where the hell am I?" He was in a hot windowless room. Richard remembered how cold he was when he went to bed last night. "Why is this room so hot?" Richard shuffled around the room looking for a door to a bathroom. His nose itched. He started to scratch it but discovered that his nose and the rest of his face was covered with a gauze-like material. He started to panic. Adrenaline started to surge through his veins, and the energy stimulated him to be more aggressive in his search for a way out of the hot room. What he found was a boiler; he was obviously in the basement of a large facility. "What am I doing in a boiler room? How did I get here? Why do I have bandages on my face?" Nothing made sense to him.

He found a door to a stairway up to the upper floors. He was relieved, but only temporarily. He reached the first floor and opened a door to the facility lobby. He recognized nothing except the expression on the faces of the other people in the lobby -- expressions of shock, fear, and apprehension. The security guards immediately pulled their Tasers as if they were going to need them. Each of the three guards in white medical coats was intimidatingly large and mean-looking. One of them approached Richard and said, "What is your name and how did you get into the basement?"

"My name is Richard Holder. Where am I?"

The lead security guard looked at the lobby administrator and nodded his head. She looked at the facility patient list and said, "We do not have anyone registered here by that name." The guard said, "What's your real name, Richard?"

"That *is* my real name." Richard started to look for his wallet in his back pocket but found nothing.

The security guard said condescendingly, as if speaking to a child, "OK, Mr. Holder, let's get you back to our medical center and get a look at you, to make sure that you are healthy enough to leave here."

Sensing that he was as close as he was going to get to the front door, Richard bolted to get past the guards. He had no idea how painful getting tasered was; he screamed.

When he awoke again, he was strapped to a rolling table. Nurses were removing the bandages from his face. When the bandages were finally removed, one of the nurses said, "It's him; it's the guy the FBI has been looking for; the guy who escaped from here."

Special Agent Vinny DeLuca was escorted into the padded room at the Elgin Mental Health Center to interrogate a shackled Richard Holder. Vinny smiled at Richard and said, "Your parents must have hated you to call you Dick Holder. I knew a guy whose parents named him Richard Head. It wasn't until he became a Navy Seal that people quit calling him 'Dick Head'. Are you related to Eric?"

"Do I look like I'm related to Eric Holder?"

"No, you look like a ghost. Let me take your picture here and send it to a friend of mine." Vinny used his iPhone to take Holder's digital photograph, and forwarded the photo to Tank Alvarez with a note that said, "Please, confirm."

"What the hell are you talking about, do I look like a ghost?"

"Not **a** ghost, **the** 'ghost'. You see, there was a sociopath patient here who escaped and became a terrorist. I think you are him. We call him the 'ghost' because he has been able to disappear as if he never existed, from every scene of carnage he has created. He is transparent, a chameleon, and an artist at disguise."

"Well I'm not him; check my fingerprints, DNA, or give me a polygraph. Call my parents; check me out. I'm not him. Check my face out, it's recently been operated on; someone operated on me and performed plastic surgery without my knowledge."

Vinny was thinking about it when he got a response from Tank. "Confirmed." Vinny turned, spoke into his microphone and said, "Arrest him, and take him to Quantico for interrogation. We got him."

CHAPTER 72

WHO IS THE GHOST?
(ZERO+387 DAYS)

QUANTICO, VIRGINIA – MAY 9TH: Richard Holder was escorted into the interview room for the 8th straight day. He had been Mirandized, provided an attorney, and held without bail. Holder's attorney was a young arrogant pretentious jerk who offended DeLuca just by being in the same universe. The attorney wore a $1,200 suit, shoes that looked like they had never been worn, and an obnoxiously loud Mickey Mouse tie. This 135 pound attorney looked as if he was ready to do battle *again* with Vinny DeLuca. In the attorney's mind, Special Agent Deluca was a clown. To Vinny, the attorney was a subhuman piece of shit.

But Vinny wasn't the one to enter the interview room this time; Vinny stayed behind the one-way observation glass. One of the largest and most powerful looking people the attorney and Holder had ever met walked in, and stood at the table. Tank did not sit down. He just stared at Holder for a full two minutes. Finally, the lawyer said, "Who are you and what do you want with my client?"

"Shut up!"

The attorney stood up and said, "I.." Before the attorney got the next word out, Tank had picked up the six foot long interview table with one hand and thrown it against the wall of the interview room, while in one fluid motion his other hand had pulled a nail gun from behind his back. He put the gun on the left foot of Richard Holder but did not pull the trigger. Instead, Tank said, "You have 30 seconds to remove the shoe and sock from your right foot. 29, 28."

The lawyer was yelling and babbling but Tank ignored him and so did Richard Holder, who couldn't get his right shoe off fast enough. Tank said, "Talk to me while you are removing your shoe. Who gave you the DARPA chemical you used on me in Chicago? Why did you kill Dr. Ingrid Li?"

Richard Holder answered, "I did not kill anyone. I will take a polygraph. I have no fucking idea what you are talking about. Are you nuts? What is a DARPA chemical?" By this time, his shoe was off. The attorney was still yelling and screaming at Tank. Tank completely tuned out the kid, which infuriated him even more. The lawyer made a youthful mistake; he touched Tank in an attempt to get his attention. Tank very casually and with little effort swatted him with an open hand. With the lawyer unconscious, Tank could complete the interview. Tank lifted Richard's foot off the ground to inspect it with an LED flashlight. This, of course, put Richard on the ground with his back on the floor. Tank was thorough, checking not only for the scar that he would have to have, if a nail had been driven through his foot, but also evidence to determine if plastic surgery was performed on his foot to successfully hide the scar. Tank let Richard's foot go and said, "Stand up and look into my eyes." The eyes had the same coloring as the guy he had interviewed in Chicago, but not the same intelligence or evilness. Tank said, "Vinny, it's time for you to come on in; we need to interview this guy together before the unconscious mouth wakes up."

Tank put the nail gun down and said to Richard, "The nail gun was loaded. I would have used it on you if I had confirmed that you were the same guy who put nails in my hands and feet." Tank showed Richard the palms of his hands. Richard remained quiet. Tank picked up the table, set it on all four legs and said, "You can sit down now. I'd suggest that you fire that twit when he wakes up. He's worthless to you."

"I take it that you have no memory about what happened to you," Tank continued. "I've had that experience myself. He looked over at Vinny and asked, "What was the name of that drug?"

Vinny said, "It is unpronounceable."

"OK. Richard, did you notice anyone stalking you or following you? Anyone staring at you? Do you have a twin?"

Richard said, "No, to all three questions."

"OK. You are exactly the same body shape, height, weight, eye color, and hair style and hair color as the 'ghost.' The only thing different is your voice and the obvious lack of a nail gun scar. I could see in your eyes when I walked in the room that you didn't recognize me. If you had been the other guy, you would have looked at me as if I was your worst nightmare."

Tank continued, "Where do you work?"

Richard said, "I work for an IT company."

"Have you ever noticed anyone who looks like you do now?"

"No."

"Do you have a photo of yourself, before the surgery?"

"Back home. If you let me use a computer, you can see my face on Facebook."

Vinny and Tank looked at each other and shook their heads in unison. Vinny said, "Let me guess. You have revealed your height, weight, eye coloring, birthdate, hair color and everything a bad guy would need to identify his double." Richard didn't deny it.

The lawyer woke up with his mouth running, saying something about lawsuits, assault and battery, and jail time -- when Richard told him that he was fired. Richard told the attorney that this big guy had already exonerated him in the short time that he was taking a nap.

CHICAGO, ILLINOIS – MAY 9TH: It was a burden, being the smartest person in the world. Too bad he was criminally insane. He was too smart to be caught again. He couldn't allow himself to be interned in a mental hospital; there were too many people to kill.

There was only one person in the world who knew who he really was, his father. His father gave him assignments that he knew his son would enjoy. The 'ghost' knew that he was being manipulated by his father for some nefarious scheme, but he didn't care; it gave him purpose. He thought to himself, "I know I'm different; different like Jeffrey Dahmer; different like Hannibal Lector; different like Joseph Stalin. I know that I derive enjoyment from things totally unacceptable to others." The 'ghost' knew that he was a mentally ill man. He talked to himself; he talked to others as little as possible. He was never sure if he had said something telegraphing his socially maladjusted behavior. Fortunately, he was non-descript in his appearance at 5 feet 7 inches tall; 160 pounds, Caucasian, brown hair, brown eyes, and with no distinguishing features. He was neither handsome nor ugly. He had no accent when he did speak, and he dressed in inconspicuous jeans, running shoes, sweatshirts, and inexpensive jackets. He drew no one's attention.

The 'ghost' was pleased to receive a call from his father on the satellite phone; he hadn't heard from him in over two weeks and he was beginning to fear that his father did not have another assignment for him.

His father said, "You did very well, my son; no one else in the world could have been as successful and accomplished as much as you have, over this past year. I am very proud of you -- and once again, you have demonstrated that you are the smartest person in the world. And, I might add, you are amazingly capable.

"You single-handedly kept the United States, and to a lesser extent the European Union, fully occupied to the point that their preoccupation with trying to capture you -- and your cleverly 'uninvolved' *Society for Environmental Justice* -- kept them from interfering with the rest of the world. Our cabal is eternally grateful to you. Japan was able to secure all the food and energy they will need to sustain their culture. Russia has been able to expand its boundaries to include badly needed warm weather ports. North Korea is a shadow of itself to the benefit of everyone, including the poor North Korean people. Russia and South Korea are grateful.

"All this happened because of you, my son. By my count, you created havoc in Vancouver, Maine, Chicago, New York, Alaska, Tennessee, Alabama, Kentucky, Louisiana, Maryland, Arizona, California, Washington, D.C. and Germany.

"But I have one more assignment for you," said Alexander Sversk. "It is time for you to come to Russia and help me rise to power, to be Prime Minister and President of Russia. After all, you're still behind Stalin and Mao as the most prolific mass murderer in history."

EPILOGUE

CHAPTER 73

BLUE SKY
(ZERO+511 DAYS)

BALI, INDONESIA – (FOUR MONTHS AFTER OPERATION INTIMIDATION) SEPTEMBER 10TH: Star Li Cherokee was playing in the sand on the Bali beach, enjoying the warmth of the sun and the sound of the waves. She was chasing a sand crab and watching the seagulls. Maya was lying on a lounge chair, under a Jacaranda tree, reading a novel, and otherwise enjoying her newfound life outside of witness protection. A gentle breeze wafted her luscious hair; a straw Panama hat kept the sun from directly shining on her electronic book reader. She was wearing sunglasses and breathing air without a mask -- what a concept: freedom. She was reminiscing about the past four months and how their discoveries were used to help so many people. The HAPI spray allowed millions of people to live at home in the high latitudes without freezing to death. Alleged side effects were kept to a manageable level. Some people were dumb enough to intentionally inject it, despite warnings and caveats.

It took only a couple of weeks for the scientific world to find ways to accelerate the process Maya and Indira developed. Tucker, Maya, and Indira had an acronym party and came up with the acronym 'APE' for "Ash Precipitation Experiment." The APE process was perfected and continuously used all around the world until the air was clear enough for the sun to re-heat the earth.

Tucker was asleep on a lounge chair under an umbrella next to a beautiful bougainvillea. This was a great and relaxing vacation. Next week, however, Tucker was expected to attend a meeting in Boston to accept the position of Chairman of the Board of ENTROPY Entrepreneurs, LLC. Who knew what kind of projects he and Maya would get into after he assumed his new role?

Tucker was expected to meet with Chairman Maxx Longstaff and General Ray LaSalle to review a wish-list of Department of Defense research priorities. Tucker also secured a new contract with the Department of Energy to develop improvements in the production and manufacturing methods for MEGs, in order to fill a world-wide backlog.

Maya's cell phone rang; she looked down at the window to view "Unknown Number." Maya thought to herself, "Please don't let this ruin our vacation!"

Maya answered. "Hello."

Silence for a few seconds preceded the sound of a little girl's voice, "Hello, Mrs. Cherokee; may I speak to Star?"

Maya smiled and said, "Sure, Melissa; Star would love to talk to you." Maya called Star and handed her the cell phone.

Tucker said to Maya, "It sounds like Star and Melissa have become very good friends."

"I thought you were asleep. Yes, thanks to you they're friends. If the NSA had not picked up all of the phone calls between the Secretary of HHS and the 'ghost,' you wouldn't have been able to save her. If you hadn't insisted that the Secretary's daughter take his granddaughter, the night of the bombing, to an animated 3-D movie, *The Wizard of Oz*, she wouldn't be around to befriend Star. I thought it was cute when Melissa's parents arranged for her to skype with you and thank you for saving her life. It was great that Star was in the room when they called. Star needed a friend around her age."

President Allen awarded Tucker, Maya and Indira the highest honor a civilian can receive, the *Medal of Freedom*.

Winston Allen was so grateful to Maya that he offered her a role in his administration as the National Science Advisor.

It looks like the Cherokees are returning home to America.

CHAPTER 74

WHO WAS HENRI LI?

Henry Li was just who he claimed to be, nothing more and nothing less. He was a second generation Chinese American with ancestral ties to Taiwan. He was an accountant with a business degree from the University of Illinois-Champaign where he met Ingrid Michelsen. He worked for a large top-five accounting firm which was contracted by the United States Government to audit its various departments, divisions, bureaus, agencies, branches, authorities and government contractors. There was nothing remarkable in Henry Li's documented past that could possibly account for his accumulated wealth. Henry told no one, not even his wife, Dr. Ingrid Michelsen Li, his secret.

Henry Li was probably the most successful gambler of all time. He limited his gambling to the poker table. Everywhere Henry went, he could find a poker table; the higher the stakes, the better. He'd travel to casinos in Las Vegas, Macau, Monte Carlo, Atlantic City, San Manuel, Nassau, New Orleans, Bali and Charlestown, WV just to name a few. There were 1,623 casinos in North America and 1,160 casinos in Europe. He'd never have to stay too long at any one casino or guarded back room table and overdo it, nor did he ever have to win too much. He worked hard at not drawing attention to himself. He'd lose intentionally at times; he'd lose two small hands in a row and then win a big hand. Henry would open a bank account in every city in which he gambled. If he started to draw attention to himself, he'd leave and go to another city. He claimed just enough income to stave off Ingrid's curiosity and stay off the Internal Revenue Service's radar screen.

Ingrid never knew that Henry had retired from the accounting firm 12 years before his murder. Dr. Li learned after his death just how wealthy she was. She wondered the rest of her life how Henry made his money and what he was doing instead of auditing companies, around the globe.

But Henry's real secret was that he could read the thoughts of others. He and only he knew that he had this special gift. It was easy to win at poker when you could read the mind of your opponent. The 'gift,' as it were, skipped a generation in his family tree. His grandmother had the 'gift;' it cost his grandmother her life. She was stoned to death by neighbors and alleged Formosan friends as a witch when she was in her early thirties. Her death was the main reason his family migrated to the United States to become citizens. Henry was afraid to tell his parents, though he knew they suspected he had the gift, based on his conduct in his formative years. Conduct very similar to the conduct Star Li Cherokee exhibited at age five.

Henry was afraid to tell Ingrid before they were married about his special gift. He used his special gift when he met Ingrid at the University of Illinois. Though Henry was an inch shorter than Ingrid and not particularly handsome, Ingrid fell in love with him because he always seemed to be able to empathize with her when she needed comforting, and always seemed to know what pleased her. He figured that she would not want to marry someone who could read her mind. Once married, he found it advantageous to keep the secret to himself; there never seemed to be the right time to tell her. The skill did, however, come in very handy for him in their marriage. He never understood her thought process -- after all, she was female -- but he could at least read her thoughts.

Over a 28-year period, Henry had set up 209 separate bank accounts around the globe. He put all the money in certificates of deposit which rolled over automatically, if the bank didn't hear from him. He created trust funds for his wife and children in the event of his death. He also set up other beneficiaries from some of the bank accounts, which were his charities. One of his charities was to the University of Illinois for the U.S. Brain Project for research on brain-to-brain interface control that demonstrates that the brain can transmit thought from one person to another.

Not all of Henry's bank accounts had been disclosed. One of the charities that received funds after Henry's death was the "*Society for Environmental Justice.*"

CHAPTER 75

YELLOWSTONE VACATION (ZERO+526 DAYS)

YELLOWSTONE NATIONAL PARK, WYOMING – SEPTEMBER 25TH: A herd of buffalo were scattering, under the "whop, whop, whop" sound of Powers' rented Augusta AW119 Koala helicopter. Star was beaming with joy and excitement; her expressive eyes and happy disposition made the experience for Tucker, Maya, Ram and Powers all that much more pleasurable. "Look over there, Daddy; those are elk. And look, there are some coyotes. Uncle Powers, can we see a grizzly bear and an eagle?"

"We'll try, sweetheart," Powers answered. Powers was silently enjoying the majesty of one of the world's greatest national parks. The beauty was magnified with the sun reflecting shimmering light off lakes and riverbeds. Everything was green instead of gray; the ash had been washed off of the flowers, and colors of yellow and blue took on new meaning. Tucker's new influence (granted him as a result of a generous gift to the national park, and for research for about the prediction of volcanic eruptions using animals) allowed Powers to get a special permit to fly the helicopter over the park, anywhere they wanted to go.

Yellowstone was resilient; it hardly looked like it had suffered the year of deadly cold weather, high winds, and abrasive ash. The population of deer and black bears fell, but other species seemed to survive undeterred by the extreme weather. Powers said, "It is about time for Old Faithful to blow, so I'll guide this old girl in that direction. Star, did you know that Yellowstone has the world's largest collection of geysers?"

Star said, "Yes, I know."

Powers teasingly asked Star, "Did you know that Yellowstone has 1300 native species of vegetation including 1150 flowering species?"

"Of course I knew that, Uncle Powers. Did you know that Yellowstone has cougars and beavers and rattlesnakes and moose and raptors and…."

"OK, OK, I give up. You know more about Yellowstone than anybody else I know."

The Yellowstone Volcano is still active as evidenced by the 1,000 to 3,000 earthquakes per year, active ground deformation, and the 10,000 thermal features found in the park. Volcanism at Yellowstone is relatively recent, with calderas that were created during large eruptions that took place 2.1 million, 1.3 million, and 640,000 years ago. The calderas lie over a hotspot where light, hot, molten rock from the earth's mantle rises toward the surface. While the Yellowstone hotspot is now under the Yellowstone Plateau, it previously helped to create the eastern Snake River Plain (to the west of Yellowstone) through a series of huge volcanic eruptions. The hotspot appears to move across the terrain in the east-northeast direction, but in fact the hotspot is much deeper than the terrain, and remains stationary while the North American Plate moves west-southwest over it.

Over the past 18 million years or so, this hotspot has generated a succession of violent eruptions and less violent floods of basaltic lava. At least a dozen eruptions were so massive that they are classified as super-eruptions. Volcanic eruptions sometimes empty their cavities of magma so swiftly that they cause the overlying land to collapse into the emptied magma chambers, forming geographic depressions called calderas.

Camping near Mount Washburn, the Cherokee team listened to the sounds of the national park: Bighorn sheep, Osprey, red foxes, gray wolves, coyotes, moose, owls, antelopes, bobcats, bison, black bears and grizzly bears. The millions of stars that populate our galaxy appeared abnormally close in the moonless night.

Star asked, "Daddy is it true that animals can predict earthquakes and volcano eruptions?"

Tucker answered, "We believe that dogs may be able to hear the microfracturing of rocks a few milliseconds before a quake shock reaches the surface. So it **is** possible. Electromagnetic changes in the earth prior to an earthquake may also be sensed by birds and other animals."

Maya translated, "Dogs can hear things we humans cannot, including sounds made underground right before a volcanic eruption or an earthquake. Other animals and fish sense things we can't, so it is very possible that they sense earthquakes."

Tucker went on and said, "Biological studies on pigeons have determined that a hundred tiny nerve units exist between the tibia and fibula on a pigeon's leg. These sensors are connected to the nerve center, and are very sensitive to vibrations."

Suddenly, the frogs, katydids, and mammals quieted. Something happened that had never happened before. It was frightening, both by sound and by implication.

Ram was howling like a wolf.

Star, who could not only sense Ram's thoughts, but also his emotions, said: "Something really big is going to happen."

ACKNOWLEDGEMENT

My thanks go out to all the friends and family who made this book so much fun to write.

My special thanks go out to my friend of 45 years and editor, John **Powers** Mason.

JED O'Dea's

UNSUSTAINABLE

(A Tucker Cherokee Novel)

Available in the Spring of 2015

DESCRIPTION OF THE NOVEL

Pug Nash knew they would come eventually; it was inevitable. He could hear the platoon of ATVs three miles away announcing their arrival -- giving warning to the defenseless. Pug could hear the rifle and shotgun fire as his distant neighbors tried to resist the plunder. Survival in 2018 America had become a severe challenge. It's hard to believe but Day Zero was only 34 months ago.

Fortunately, Tucker and Maya have a plan to put the pieces back together.